PRAISE FOR PETER HANDKE AND *SLOW HOMECOMING*

"[Peter Handke] was and is, one of the most eminent narrative and dramatic writers of postwar Europe." —*The Boston Globe*

"In power and vision and range, Peter Handke is the most important new writer on the international scene since Beckett."
—Stanley Kaufmann, *Saturday Review*

"His prose is reminiscent of the writings of Henry James...a passion for understanding, for grasping the tortured complexities of contemporary life." —*The Philadelphia Inquirer*

"The three works comprising ***Slow Homecoming*** are closer to a true dialectic than Handke's work has ever before sought."
—*American Book Review*

"This is postmodernism in its most exciting and challenging form, a work of literature that makes the redefinition of reality and of fiction a possibility." —*Choice*

"Peter Handke must be acknowledged as one of the major voices in contemporary fiction." —*Partisan Review*

"One awaits with pleasure whatever Peter Handke turns to next....Since the 1960s, he has been a popularly acclaimed novelist, playwright and poet and a long-standing critical success. He now creates a more rarefied, demanding art coupled with a lucid yet mythic affirmation of life." —*The Boston Herald*

Also by Peter Handke

Kaspar and Other Plays

The Goalie's Anxiety at the Penalty Kick

Short Letter, Long Farewell

A Sorrow Beyond Dreams

The Ride Across Lake Constance and Other Plays

A Moment of True Feeling

The Left-Handed Woman

The Weight of the World

Across

Slow Homecoming

Peter Handke

Translated by Ralph Manheim

Collier Books
Macmillan Publishing Company
New York

Published by arrangement with Farrar, Straus and Giroux, Inc.

Collier Books
Macmillan Publishing Company
866 Third Avenue, New York, NY 10022
Collier Macmillan Canada, Inc.

This is a work of fiction. Names, characters, places, and incidents either are the products of the author's imagination or are used fictitiously. Any resemblance to actual events or persons, living or dead, is entirely coincidental.

Library of Congress Cataloging-in-Publication Data

Handke, Peter.
Slow homecoming / Peter Handke ; translated by Ralph Manheim. —
1st Collier Books ed.
p. cm.
Translation of: Langsame Heimkehr, Die Lehre der Sainte-Victoire,
and Kindergeschichte.
Contents: The long way around—The lesson of Monte Sainte-
Victoire—Child story.
ISBN 0-02-051530-8
I. Title.

PT2668.A5A25 1988
833'.914—dc19 87-31979
CIP

Cover illustration © 1988 by David Montiel
Cover design by Lee Wade
First Collier Books Edition 1988

10 9 8 7 6 5 4 3 2 1

Printed in the United States of America

Contents

The Long Way Around

Then, as I stumbled headlong down the path,

there was suddenly a form . . .

One /

The Primordial Forms

Sorger had outlived several of those who had become close to him; he had ceased to long for anything, but often felt a selfless love of existence and at times a need for salvation so palpable that it weighed on his eyelids. Capable of a tranquil harmony, a serene strength that could transfer itself to others, yet too easily wounded by the power of facts, he knew desolation, wanted responsibility, and was imbued with the search for forms, the desire to differentiate and describe them, and not only out of doors ("in the field"), where this often tormenting but sometimes gratifying and at its best triumphant activity was his profession.

At the end of the working day, in the light-gray gabled wooden house at the edge of the mainly Indian settlement in the Far North of the other continent, which for some months had been serving him and his colleague Lauffer as both laboratory and dwelling, he slipped the protective covers on the microscopes and binoculars he had been using alternately and, his face still distorted by the frequent changes from short view to long view and back, passed through the episodic space created by the sunset light and the hovering woolly-white seeds of the dwarf poplars, an after-work corridor, as it were, to "his" beach.

A clay platform so low that he could have jumped off. There began the immense realm of the glittering river, extending to the whole circle of the horizon, flooding the continental shelf from east to west and at the same time meandering northward and southward through the sparsely settled but to all intents and purposes uninhabited lowlands. Narrowed, because it was the dry season and the glaciers had stopped melting, behind first a broad bank of gravel and shale and then a muddy slope, the river at Sorger's feet sent long, light sea waves beating against the land.

Another thing that made the valley look like a body of standing water was that it reached out to the horizon on all sides but that, because of the river's meanderings, the lines of the horizon were formed not by streams flowing from east to west but by dry land, by the banks of that bend in the river surmounted by dwarf poplars and the tops of primeval conifers, which, though in reality sparse and stunted, seemed from a distance to form serried files.

True, this apparent lake, bounded on all sides by land that looked to be flat, flowed at a speed hard to estimate, silently and quite smoothly except for the bathtub-like lapping of the waves on the muddy beach—one might have said a foreign body, filling the entire plain, mirrored yellow by the sunset sky, perceptible at first glance only as wetness, dotted here and there with island specks and sandbanks, they too lying flat in the hazy evening air. Only the eddies that formed over unseen depressions in the sand-and-gravel riverbed, swiftly circling funnels in the otherwise metallic yellow surface, were not yellow but, because of their sharper angle to the sky, a remote daylight blue from within which, amid the almost silent flow, soft brooklike gurglings could be heard.

Sorger was buoyed by the thought that the months he had spent observing this wilderness, learning (approximately) its forms and their genesis, had made it his own private domain. Destructive as they may have been (and still were) in the objective world, the forces that went to make up this landscape, in becoming present to him along with the great flowing water, its eddies and rapids, without mental effort, through the perceptive process alone, were transformed by their own laws into a benign inner force, which calmed him and gave him strength. He believed in his science, because it helped him to feel whatever place he was in; far from putting him off, his consciousness of standing on a flat beach while the opposite shore, miles away and scarcely visible through the islands, was slightly steeper, and of being able to attribute this strange asymmetry to the rotation of the earth, gave him the feeling that the planet earth was a civilized, homelike, intelligible place, a feeling that made his mind playful and his body resilient.

This state of mind was also favored by the fleeting thought that while poplar seeds were drifting through the air, the pebbles on the riverbed were at the same time shifting unseen, rolling or slowly leaping over one another, enveloped in clouds of mud and propelled by waves deep below the surface which he could sense rather than infer. Wherever he was, Sorger tried to experience minute burlesque processes of this kind, which sometimes merely amused him but sometimes aroused him and filled his whole being.

For some years—since he had been spending most of his time alone—he had felt the need to sense the place where he was at the moment: to know distances, apprehend angles of inclination; to gain some idea of the composition and stratification of the soil he was standing on, at least down to a certain depth; to supply himself, by measurement and delimitation, with spaces which were hardly more than "forms on paper" but which, for a short while at least, enabled him to construct himself and make himself invulnerable.

Sorger needed nature, but not only in its "unspoiled" state; in big cities, for example, he was satisfied to gain awareness of scarcely perceptible asphalt-covered humps and hollows, gentle rises and falls in the pavement, of church floors or stone stairs, worn with the steps of the centuries; or, visiting an unknown high-rise building, to fancy himself passing vertically through all the floors from roof to basement, and, finally, to daydream its granite foundations—until, in the end, orientation and the breathing space (and hence self-confidence) indispensable to life engendered each other.

He had the ability (not constant, to be sure, but sporadic and accidental, though his profession made the accident possible and gave it some constancy) to call upon those parts of the world to which he had become accustomed in his work for help, or merely to conjure them up for the entertainment of himself and others, with all their specifications, their degrees of longitude and latitude, their light and wind conditions, their planetary conjunctions, as eternally peaceful images, belonging to everyone and no one, and betokening events still to be imagined.

In every new scene, which might at first sight seem surveyable in its uniformity or picturesque in its contrasts, but in either case intelligible, this moment of naïve familiarity was followed, often definitively, by a bewildered sense, akin to a loss of balance, of once again confronting a mere stage set, and a familiar one at that, further intensified by a sense of guilt at being, here too, "out of place." In the course of time, it had therefore become a passion with Sorger, while enduring this first feeling of emptiness, to win back these quickly squandered places by observing and taking notes. Unable, because he had long been nowhere at home, to recapture his self within his own four walls after such touristic humiliations by regions of the earth, he saw each new place as his only hope; if he did not (often reluctantly) commit himself to it through hard work, there would be no refuge for him in the scenes of his past—but then with luck, in times of exhaustion, all his localities joined together, the particular, freshly conquered one with those that had gone before, and formed a dome encompassing heaven and earth, a sanctuary, which was not only private but also open to others.

After his initial irritation with a nature too quick to promise itself and even quicker to withdraw, Sorger was obliged, on pain of losing himself, to immerse himself in it. He was obliged to take the environing world seriously in the least of its forms—a groove in the rock, a change of color in the mud, a windblown pile of sand at the foot of a plant—as seriously as only a child can do, in order to keep himself, who scarcely belonged anywhere, who was nowhere at home, together, for whom he had no idea; there were times when this cost him a furious effort at self-conquest.

For whom was he keeping himself together? Sorger knew that in devoting himself to his science he was to some extent practicing a religion. It was his work that enabled him, time and again, to enter into relationships, to choose and be chosen. By whom? No matter, as long as he was choosable.

Indeed, his study of the earth's forms, carried on without fanaticism but so intensely that little by little he awareness of his own form in the process, had saved his soul by differentiating him from the rmlessness and its dangerous moods and caprices.

And what of others? Thus far in his profession Sorger had done no work expressly useful to anyone, let alone benefiting a community; he had neither drilled for oil nor predicted an earthquake nor even contributed to a construction project by testing the solidity of the subsoil. But of one thing he was sure—without the effort he made to endure the strangeness of every region of the earth, to read the landscape with the available means and give an orderly account of his reading, he would not have been fit company for anyone.

He did not believe in his science as a kind of nature religion; on the contrary, his always "measured" practice of his profession (in the eyes of the chaotic and often charmingly erratic Lauffer, Sorger's work was always "made to measure") was at the same time an exercise in trusting the world, for the measured quality of his technical manipulations but also his personal, everyday movements resided in his constant attempt at meditation, which sometimes made him fumble majestically about in such places as bathrooms, kitchens, and tool sheds. Sorger's faith was directed at nothing; when successful, it merely enabled him to participate in "its object" (a stone with a hole in it, or perhaps only a shoe on the table, or a thread on the lens of his microscope) and endowed him, who at such times was able, despite his frequent anguish, to feel like a real scientist, with humor. And then, caught up in a gentle vibration, he would simply look at his world more closely.

At such times of selfless tenderness (in his fleeting moments of hope he thought himself a fool) Sorger was not godlike; he just knew, for a brief moment—but one that could be perpetuated with the help of forms—what was good and beautiful.

He longed, it is true, for a faith directed at something, though he could not conceive of a God; but in moments of distress he noticed that he positively thirsted—an automatic compulsion?—to *share* in the thought of God. (Sometimes he tried to be pious—he did not succeed; but then he was sure that "the gods" understood him.)

Did he envy the unflagging believers, the hosts of the already saved? In any event, he was touched by their freedom from moods, their easy transitions between gravity and good cheer, their enduring, benevolent, *good* extroversion; often enough he himself was simply *not good*, and to this he could not resign himself; too often he greeted some new object with loquacious enthusiasm and almost immediately thereafter turned away from it in silent revulsion—instead of responding to it once and for all with overarching humor.

Nevertheless, he could not hobnob with believers. He understood them, but he could not speak their language, because he had no language or because in his exceptional states of credulity he would have spoken a language foreign to them; in the "dark night of their faith," where there was no speaking in tongues, they could not have understood him.

On the other hand, for all his conviction, Sorger never ceased to regard the linguistic formulas of his science as a hoax; the rites in which it apprehended the landscape, its conventions of description and nomenclature, its conception of time and space, struck him as dubious. Having to use a language that had grown out of the history of mankind to describe the different movements and formations of the earth still made his head swim, and often he found it quite impossible to take account of time along with the places he had set out to investigate. He suspected the possibility of an entirely different schema for representing the correlation between time and geological formations, and saw himself smiling craftily, as the overturners of systems have always done (that had struck him in all their photographs), and he foisted his own little hoax on the world.

And so Sorger, his thoughts made playful by his afterwork elation, was able, while contemplating the yellow wilderness, to sense the desolation of a man who, without faith in the power of forms or rendered incapable of such faith by ignorance, might find himself, as in a nightmare, confronting this part of the world alone: his horror face to face with the Evil One at the irrevocable end of the world, unable to die of loneliness then and there—since there would no longer be a then and there—or even to be carried off by Satan—for even such names would have ceased to exist—but doomed to die of horror, for time, too, would have ceased to exist. The fluvial plain and the wide, flat sky over it suddenly looked to him like the two shells of an open bivalve, emanating the terrible, the poignantly voluptuous seduction of those who have died since the beginning of time.

Involuntarily, wrenched away from his play, Sorger—as though he had been his own double, as though exposed for all time to whirling emptiness on his outcropping of clay, marl, and possibly gold dust—turned toward the civilized hinterland, where the bushy light-colored tails of watchdogs could be seen wagging in the shrubbery, where tufts of grass growing on the earthen roofs of Indian huts glittered, and where the "eternally other"—his name at the moment for his colleague Lauffer—in mud-caked high boots and characteristic multi-pocketed jacket, a sparkling magnifying glass hanging from his neck (he had just come in from his fieldwork), was standing on the topmost wooden step outside the gabled house, his face and torso still in the sun, in the first perplexity of return to a place where he only happened to be living, for a time stiffly and awkwardly imitating Sorger's stance, like Sorger looking out over the great fluvial plain, smoking a cigarette—a strangely helpless figure, with the same pinched look on his face as the row of Indians lined up outside.

The familiarity between these two friends expressed itself not in chumminess but in a politeness that was almost diffident. Subject as they were to moods, the outburst of moodiness that might occasionally have done them good was not possible. Though they were obliged to share their workroom, it was only at first that they felt in each other's way; in the bedroom as well—the house consisted only of those two rooms—each had his place without need of planning. A certain neighborliness was taken for granted, yet it seemed accidental when they did anything together; each went about his own affairs and even in the house each had his own itineraries. They didn't really eat together; one might be eating a regular meal; the other would sit down with him, and the first would issue an invitation: "Won't you have a glass of wine with me?" If one wanted music, the other wouldn't leave the room; he would stay, showing no express interest and gradually perhaps begin to listen, or even ask to have a piece repeated.

Lauffer was a liar; Sorger, for all his impenetrable calm, was unstable to the point of indifference or even disloyalty. Both suspected, or tacitly recognized, what was bad in the other (sensing it perhaps more uncannily than the person against whom it was directed), both were shrewdly aware that they were capable at any time of behaving like scoundrels to someone else, but—so precious had their companionship become to them over the years—never to each other. Each with his friend thought of himself as kindly, never as wicked.

They were not "a couple," not even by contrast; but in the course of time, even when separated, they had become partners, a team, though not unconditional allies; each remained capable of friendship with the other's enemies.

True, Lauffer, the liar, had no enemies; his lying was noticed only by occasional women, who then, however, as though privy to a tragic secret, would ally themselves with him to the death, claiming him exclusively for themselves and excluding all others from their relationship.

Everyone liked him, though he made no effort to ingratiate himself; everyone called him by his first name even in his absence, and not only here on the American continent, where this was customary. True, his friends ran him down, but always in the tone of one deploring the shortcomings of one's hero; they would never have allowed an outsider to attack him. Despite his physical bounciness—when he forced himself to sit still in the presence of Sorger, who was often deep in thought, he gave the impression of a jumping jack on its good behavior—his massive bulk, which struck one as more jocosely fraternal than athletic, suggested a happy unity, a restlessly mobile center in which others were eager to participate; liar or not, there was something reliable about him: people were always relieved, or perhaps just glad to see him, even when he looked in only for a moment.

He didn't lie to please himself; lying was his response to the hopes of his well-wishers—everyone wished him well—who expected him to draw them into his center, hopes which of course he could not fulfill for long but could not bring himself to disappoint. In this situation he would lie shamelessly, obscenely. The fact is that, without meaning to, Lauffer collected misfits and for that reason found himself condemned to a blandness in which he did not recognize himself. He was not sexless and not without passion, but in secret—a hero to himself in an entirely different way than to those who called themselves his friends—he pursued the dream or delusion of greatness.

"I would like to be dangerous like you," he said, while sitting in the house with Sorger, at an evening meal which as usual had come about by chance.

The table stood by the screenless window, at the center of which, traversed by river and the evening sky, was a rectangle with long, dark stripes; above and below, a deepening black (cloud bank and dry land). Now and then, a mosquito would come in, reeling rather than flying. But the mosquitoes had stopped biting; they would just settle on the back of your hand and stay there.

The meal consisted of light-brown mushrooms gathered "in the field" (they had absorbed some of the dampness of the soil, and tasted rather like Chinese mushrooms); whitish chunks of salmon bought from the Indians; and the last oversized potatoes from the somewhat disorderly garden on the east, lee side of the house. They drank a wine bought at the Trading Post, as the settlement market called itself, so cold that its sweetness, in conjunction with the bitter mushrooms and the fish, was pleasant for a time.

This was one of the first days of autumn in a house whose absence of mystery, the practical anonymity of its furnishings and utensils, made for an easy, homelike feeling. It was only when looking out, even absently, into the open that one was likely to know the exalting yet terrifying sensation of flight into the Great North; and even without looking out, as you sat eating and drinking, a strange light might fall on the corners of one's eyes and play unceasingly on the objects roundabout, yet their intrinsic glow was manifested only by the incredible inner jolt you felt when it came to you that you were "far, far away," on another continent.

The black-and-white spotted cat that came with the house settled on the table after eating the leftover fish—the wooden walls were too thin to allow of a window seat—and looked out at the bushes on the riverbank, which were blowing furiously in the evening wind; now and then, its otherwise motionless head or paw would follow a contrary movement in the bushes.

The surface of the water was still yellow. The wind was blowing upstream, stirring up ripples that moved eastward as if the river were flowing in that direction; only at the edges of the picture was the real current visible in great, compact, night-black swirls, which looked as if someone had thrown a mess of tripe into the water. Far below in the west, now half in the shadow of the bank, a dark shape rose up from the surface of the water, rose and fell with a rhythmic, creaking sound that invaded the house and filled the entire countryside. The water level was falling, and this was one of the last days on which the Indians could operate their big wooden fish wheels, which, driven by the current, filled with salmon overnight.

Beyond the wheel, where the river pursued its northward meander, a jagged line of stunted virgin pines seemed to form the arc of a lagoon. Since the tops of the few taller trees towered above the long, flat horizon, one had the impression, when looking into the distance beyond the lagoon formed by the river islands, of seeing the spires of Venice against a cloudless sky. In this fully darkened city, the details of which could be seen only in the reflection of the light-colored river water, rifle shots would sometimes ring out, or a lost dog might bark. But perhaps these were mere echoes, carrying village sounds back to the village, where the dogs, for the most part kept in packs, barked until late into the night.

A boat, in which no one could be seen because the occupants were kneeling or crouching, glided from the darkness of the lagoon into what remained of the light, trailing an inky-blue wake. A rifle shot fired across the water, as though from ambush, grazed but barely ruffled the smooth surface, then ricocheted into an island thicket, flushing a few crows.

Early in the night, Sorger drove Lauffer's jeep along the rocky shore on his way to see the Indian woman, who never expected him but ministered to him, sometimes with good-natured irony, and sometimes even with a certain dignified satisfaction. Ahead of him in the potholes lay a row of no longer sparkling but still pale-bright puddles, which seemed to merge with the likewise pale-bright surface of the river. And this surface itself, broken here and there by sandbanks, was not self-contained but melted without perceptible dividing line into the luminous strip of sky which covered the whole distant horizon as though to symbolize the Arctic Circle. The thin black ribbon of cloud in it might equally well have been the farthermost islands in the fluvial plain, and the last stretches of bright sky framing the clouds might have been the westward-flowing river.

Sorger stopped; he wanted to capture this event in space and hold it fast. But already there was no more space before him, only a gently rising openness without foreground or background, not empty but ardently material. Alive to the pitch-black night sky above and behind him and to the deep-black earth beside and below him, thoroughly aroused, Sorger tried to prevent this natural phenomenon and the self-forgetfulness it engendered from passing, by frantically thinking the contradictory details out of the picture—until perspective, vanishing points, and a pitiful loneliness set in. For a moment he had felt the strength to propel his whole self into the bright horizon and there dissolve forever into the undifferentiated unity of sky and earth. Driving on, he sat stiff, dissociating his body from the mechanism of the car, and barely touched the top of the wheel, as if it had nothing to do with him.

Roads without names led past huts without numbers. Some of the windows were already covered with sheepskins for the winter. The elk antlers over the front steps looked enormous and very white in the beam of the headlights. In the dark space under the huts, which were raised on wooden blocks, moved the shadows of the miscellaneous objects stored there. The airstrip along the edge of the forest, a rocky field that narrowed in the headlight beam, lay deserted, edged on both sides by short-stemmed red marker lights. A stray dog raised gleaming eyes from a hole in the ground. In this lost outpost, which could not be reached by road—or by ship for that matter, but only by plane—there were nevertheless any number of roads that went a little way into the forest and broke off when they came to the swamps. At least one car went with every house, even for the shortest distances the inhabitants used their cars, zigzagging in and out of the bushes at top speed, hurling great blobs of mud from the roads, which never dried out, against the trees and the walls of the huts. In this country, which though flat derived each day a rough, bony, cutting quality from all its objects, plants, animals, and people, the Indian woman (as Sorger always called her in his thoughts, even when he was with her) took on for him an inviting, coolly-bright smoothness. "Smoothness" might have been his pet name for her.

In the season when there was virtually no dark night, they had met in the bar attached to the market and she had asked him to dance. At first, as she showed him the movements, her wide, unexpectedly delicate body (he didn't know where to put his hands) had troubled him and aroused him in a way he himself had not wanted; she, on the other hand, found everything about him normal. In any case she accepted him; her smoothness was alluring, her indulgence contagious.

She was determined to keep her relations with the outsider secret from the members of her tribe—actually, there were hardly any tribes left, only relics drinking beer and listening to cassette music in the huts, and in the woods behind them the great grave mounds of the old cemeteries. As a Health Department nurse, in sole charge of the settlement's supplies of medicine, she would otherwise have lost the confidence of her people; she would "get body odor," "frogs would jump out of her cheeks" and infect the village with mysterious diseases, and if that happened, they'd have to kill her "with stone scissors." Her husband, a nonswimmer like so many inhabitants of these latitudes, had been drowned while fishing in the river; time and again she dreamed of pulling a feathered mask out of the water.

Outside her house stood a totem pole, bright with color in the beam of the headlights: her two children's bicycle was leaning against it. Through the curtainless window he first saw her round forehead, which he interpreted as so intimate a greeting and welcome that without waiting for her signal he went right in, sure that the children were already asleep.

The one child, sexless in its deep slumber, had gently closed its mouth on the crook of the other sleeping child's elbow, and the large, half-darkened but not somber room seemed separate from the rest of the house, a place accessible only to them. The shadows of the waving bushes outside moved over the walls. And nevertheless—watching her, giving in, resolutely transforming himself into her fantastic machine (as she did into his), and, more than "making her happy," sharing in her durable pride—he did not regard himself as a deceiver, but saw the deception as an ineluctable phenomenon for which he was in no way responsible.

It was not only that with her he had to speak a foreign language (foreign also to her), in which he had another voice than his own. More fundamental than this particularity, which perhaps concerned them alone, was the discrepancy between inactive desire—here he knew himself and his partner to be in a state of perfection—and its physical accomplishment, which had to end one way or another, with the anticipation of a triumph that always failed to materialize. Each time it seemed to be the one thing that counted, and then it counted for so little. The anticipated union did not prevent desire, but reduced it to an abrupt, unstable instantaneity, and through its very weakness made for a guilty conscience, followed by a total lapse of conscience. In other words, he did not love her; he knew that he shouldn't have come to see her, and when he was with her his indecision made him act brusquely. How was it that he could not see himself embracing anyone, but always alone?

He would have liked to love her in his language and through his language, but instead he merely stared at her menacingly, until after the first surprise—and not just to please him—she felt afraid. He toyed with the thought of killing her; or at least of stealing or breaking something; after all, no one knew he was there. "I hate this century," he said finally, and she answered slowly, as though reading his future: "Yes, you are healthy and perhaps you are doomed."

She didn't know where he came from and laughed at the inconceivable notion that there might be another continent. Had the stripe in the sky at last disappeared? The generator hummed in its tin shelter behind the house, and in a placeless darkness, beyond all degrees of latitude and longitude, puddles of water trembled and whirled around in a circle. White yarrow blossoms curled in the frost; clumps of yellow camellias became aerial photographs of burning forests. From deep within Sorger, an alarm bell signaling disorientation passed through the dark silent lowlands, farther and farther northward—which way was north just then?—as far as the alluvial tundra, where it shattered a cone of ice that had formed a thousand years before but could not be recognized as ice under its sheathing of sand and gravel; and now a crater would form with a lake in it, as if there had been a small volcano up there, so close to the pole. The river behind the house flowed only on the surface; just below, seizing and quickly encapsulating the flowing branches and leaves, a smooth sheet of ice filled the riverbed from source to mouth, giving the water the appearance of glass. The foreheads of many people lay on the cool enamel edge of a washbasin, and that night these children in bed would not turn over again. Lauffer, standing, reading a letter—hadn't this been mail day?—holding the paper more with the pads of his palms than with his fingers, a slightly tilted basket of fruit on the sofa beside him, glanced now and then at the cat, which didn't let him out of its sight but finally dozed off. The wind roared over the empty beer cans in the bushes outside, and at the same time the primeval wind, which had gathered the soil on which the hut was now standing, set up an Aeolian roaring in his head. Sorger could literally taste the unreality compounded of so many simultaneous irreconcilables, which condensed around him and would soon blow him away; and again it would be his own fault. "I have to go home. I have to sleep." He struck his head with his fist: a prayer, of sorts, which actually worked. The hallucination passed; his spatial sense came back. "What do you see?" the Indian woman asked. He felt a liking for her in the corners of his eyes. He hugged her and meant it. She held him close, and when he looked up he noticed for the first time that the expressionlessness of her face, in which he foresaw a beautiful old age, was perfect sympathy.

While she was ministering to him, Sorger listened to a long story about someone who seduced a sleeping woman by giving her copper to smell. She saw him to the door and then, in a good humor, he drove home through the friendly Arctic night. His premature fatigue, which had burst upon him "like a deviation from the vertical," brought on in part by the effort of speaking a foreign language, had never been. The gabled wooden house glowed in the darkness. From a distance he transferred its color, shape, and material to himself in the form of energy (the river behind the embankment had become a soft plashing). Entering, he felt enterprising, filled with a passionate urge to investigate nature, though all he actually did in the deserted laboratory—Lauffer was already asleep in the other room—was to settle down with a glass of wine and, holding the cat in his lap, project a vision of order and clarity into the near-darkness without and within.

At length, letting himself go in his own language, he said to the cat: "Revered demonic animal, giant eye, eater of raw meat. Fear not. No one is stronger than we are, no one can harm us. On the other side of the window, hostile water is flowing, but we sit here in our element. We have been lucky up until now. I am not entirely weak, not entirely powerless. I am capable of freedom. I want success and I want adventure. I would like to teach the landscape to be rational and the heavens to mourn. Do you understand that? And I am restless."

They both looked out into the night, the cat far more attentively than the man, the orifice under its upraised tail turned toward him like a burning eye. A wind unusual for the region thundered outside, and inside made the wood of the silent house creak. Sorger sat motionless until he felt he was weighing his brain with his skull—scales designed to make what they weighed weightless. A nervous flutter circled his head as though wings were beating under his skin; and then came a total calm, in which everything could be said with the words: "Night—Window—Cat." The cold and the wind outside were a blessing to Sorger's lungs.

He lifted the cat by the forepaws, making it stand stretched on its hind legs, and put his ear to its mouth: "Now say something. Stop pretending, you sanctimonious quadruped, you parentless monster, you childless thief. Make an effort. Everyone knows you can talk."

He held the little round skull pressed to his ear and stroked the body more and more violently, until his hand was stroking the skeleton through the fur.

The distressed cat didn't move; it scarcely breathed; its eyes became round and glassy, and the man's image appeared in the slits. After a long while, it began to pant and finally, along with a puff of warm air, poured a brief plaint into Sorger's ear, expressive not of pain but of desperation followed by appeasement; that done, it patted him on the face with one paw, almost like a domestic pet.

"Absurd beast," said the tormentor, "satanic creature of the night, slavishly available metaphor."

The cat scratched him; then, when he let it go, used his knee as a jumping-off place and crawled under the carpet, forming a motionless bump.

At first Sorger had a sensation of coolness on his cheek; a little later the scratch began to bleed. Behind the fugitive animal the furniture was still creaking. On the table in front of Sorger the brown tip of a compass needle trembled, and in the adjoining room, tossing and turning in his bed as though unable to find his place, the other man was talking in his sleep. Or could he be singing? But what was there to celebrate? How easy it was to give oneself away. How ready one was to speak. How beautiful by contrast was the cat's reserve. Be silent, man. Dawn, age of silence.

Beside the compass lay a letter for him from Europe, which he had not yet opened. (To see what smoke arising from what country?) And how much else had he missed in just this one day? A sense of inexpiable guilt more played with him than took hold of him, but since it was only a vague intimation he could not repent or make reparation. "Never again," he said. This was the hour of sleep-heavy night resolutions: "That was the day when for the last time he . . ." He what? A heat so stifling that it almost stank weighed briefly on the room and on the man still sitting obstinately awake; it was the consciousness of insatiable privation and infinite incapacity. He had no right to his scientific instruments; no right to look at the river; and it was dishonest of him to let himself be embraced. Now Lauffer was really singing in his sleep. "Comical fellow man, ridiculous self, laughing witness." Something was wrong, always had been, with all of them; they were cheats without exception. The night became a solid body pressing against the windowpanes from outside; and now Sorger saw himself as someone really dangerous, because he wanted to lose everything and himself as well.

Of course he had long been acquainted with these no-man's-land states; they were dispelled by sleep or the next day's fresh air; besides, the cat came out from under the carpet and, while Sorger was getting ready for bed, ran across his path several times in token of affection. "As you see," he said to the cat, "I'm going to bed." And he added: "Rejoice, dear animal, that you have a home." In the storm the house flew through the darkness, and Sorger looked forward to the morning light. "If only I could live for a while with animals. They don't sweat, and they don't whine about their condition . . ."

But, along with the need for silence, wasn't there such a thing as joy in a spontaneous outcry, in the pure act of crying out? For not only did it demonstrate absence of guilt; it also restored the radiant innocence that one could live with forever and ever.

Sorger had no outcry to make, not in any language. In his half sleep it became clear to him that another day had passed in which he had postponed something that it would soon be impossible to postpone any longer. A decision was due, and that decision was in his power, or perhaps not—in any case, it was up to him to bring it about.

Breathing deeply—without moving, he saw himself striking a pose—he felt a longing for such a decision, an almost indignant expectancy and impatience; and the strange, for Sorger unprecedented, and at the moment of falling asleep not at all funny thing about this phenomenon was that in it he did not feel alone but for the first time in his life felt that he belonged to a people. In this moment, he not only represented the many but committed himself to their demand—the demand that united them and gave them life—for a decision.

For a moment he even saw the uniform window patterns of whole complexes of high-rise buildings as congealed expectation machines which had been let into those barren walls for this sole purpose and not to admit light or air. Unusually for him in his half sleep, he had before him no uninhabited landscapes but instead, very close to him, many passing faces, sorrowful, and not at all plebeian. Not a single one of them was known to him, but taken together they formed a living multitude, to which he belonged.

Was he prepared for a decision? He didn't know; and would never find out unless he took the leap.

But what decision? Now almost asleep, he saw but one answer: a silent picture of himself sitting in a small room in a tall building, a round-shouldered, hardworking public servant; and the composite window fronts beckoned to him from beyond a large body of water, which separated him from everything.

A strange desire came over him to exert himself to the

point of exhaustion; and he saw himself, in the event that he lacked the strength, disappearing into an arcade which led him on into a refuge, still closed at the moment. A great deal was at stake, but something very different from life and death.

Warmth spread through his whole body, and he found himself in the hollow of his limp open hand. Contented, he was aware of his male organ, but without excitement; at the same time he felt hunger and greed. The cat jumped up on the bed and lay down at his feet; "an animal in the house." The narrow cot was just right for him. In the next room Lauffer was laughing in his sleep; or was that he himself? The wind outside became a cloud. Doubled up in her bed, the Indian woman was forgetting him, forgetting everyone, even her children. (And now she, too, was right for him.)

During the day, in the "township" (as his chosen terrain, the square of wilderness that had become his "field of operations," was called), his work made him one with himself and the landscape, but at night, asleep on his iron cot, Sorger remained alive to his remoteness from Europe and his "forebears." What he perceived then was not the unthinkable distance between himself and another point but himself as a distant one (guilty of being far away). His sleep was disturbed by no image of this other point, only by a constant awareness of not sleeping in his own bed. Conscious in his sleep of being wrenched out of place, he never, though years had passed since his change of continents, enjoyed a quiet, homelike sleep; immediately on closing his eyes (a moment against which he invariably struggled), he began to gravitate, growing steadily heavier and more clodlike, toward a magnetic horizon. And what happened then?

A group of screeching, drunken Indians were standing around a fire on the riverbank. One reeled back and fell, still clutching a bottle, into the smooth swift current and sank; but instantly the dreamer jumped in after him. He didn't come up again, and no one paid attention to his disappearance.

Seen in bird's-eye view (from a low-flying helicopter, for instance), the river was so transparent at its surface that below it, as though framed in clear, still water, the brownish-yellow clouds of mud became a self-contained image of turbulent power pulsating upward from the riverbed, rolling westward, and filling the whole breadth of the stream.

Over these clouds, but just below the transparent surface, drifted, unrecognizable from the shore, dark tree trunks, for the most part birches, stripped and blackened by the current, occasionally veiled momentarily by a surge of mud. Clearly visible from the bank were singly drifting dwarf pines, weighed down at one end by their roots, so that the tops would intermittently rise above the surface and dive down again.

A few tree trunks, diverted to the shallower spots, anchored their roots in the bottom, so that only their spreading crowns could be seen.

No more cries; in the gray of dawn, the river arched, becoming a quiet bay in an otherwise turbulent ocean. Occasionally, breeze-blown ripples crept darkly in all directions.

A dead pink salmon had been washed up on the sandy shore, a faint color in the rigid recumbent darkness, over which, strictly separate, lay a pale sky with a colorless moon that seemed to have fallen over backward. The fish, which lay lopsidedly bloated on the sand made muddy by the dew, as though tossed at random into the cold early-morning landscape, seemed to form a companion piece to the bloated mounds enclosed by white wooden fences in the Indian cemetery on the far side of the huts, whose black and gray walls gave no sign of life except for the humming of generators; the abandoned fire on the riverbank was still smoking.

Many of the countless paths that traversed the settlement did not even connect the huts with one another but merely led around clumps of trees or into the woods, where they broke off or led into tunnels that might be fox earths. The village was surrounded by wilderness; and indeed the whole region, including the village, was largely wilderness. The area had never been cleared; fields and meadows were unknown, as were all other features of civilized landscape; apart from construction sites, the natural relief of the earth's surface had rarely been tampered with; even the wider roads followed the irregularities of the terrain, which seemed flat only when seen from the air (except for the landing strip, the only level space of any size was the short, wide gravel road, formed by alluvial deposits, which was off-limits to the civilian population and led to an army base in the swamps). And since most of the huts were raised on blocks, the original contours of the earth had been preserved even in the built-up areas, in the little hollows, ditches, and humps under the houses.

As though adapted to the rugged, primeval landscape, the houses scattered through the woods showed no systematic relation to one another; they were placed higgledy-piggledy, without regard for their neighbors, and many not only were far from the road but also faced the other way. An overall view of the colony was nowhere obtainable, though it was known to be the only settlement far and wide. Each dwelling seemed to appear out of the void, as though nothing came after it.

Only from a plane might one have unexpectedly discovered the design of an almost charming little town between river and virgin forest, a rectangular network of streets traversed by a diagonal avenue, a kind of Broadway—an ideal spot, civilized yet elemental, with here and there a brass doorknob sparkling in the morning light while at the same time mist arose from the measureless light-brown pine forest.

True, this friendly, fertile-looking valley—the bushy little conifers might have been grapevines—showed no sign of field or meadow (their absence seemed incredible at first sight), and the great overland road leading into the horizon was also absent. (Seen from the air, most of the huts, surrounded as they were by beaten-up cars and rusty electrical generators, were transmuted into vandalized garbage cans.)

Except for the white wooden church, the gabled house was the tallest structure in the region; it alone had an attic, which the present tenants occasionally used as a darkroom; the gable was useful as a landmark, because even within the village area it was only too easy to lose one's way among the swamps and thickets.

Sorger got up early, eager to be doing something. The sun had not yet risen, but the smooth pebbles on the shore road where he was standing were already glistening and a nearby sandbank, marked with swollen lines composed of leaves, bits of branches, and pine needles, showed how the water level had fallen overnight. There was a nip in the air, but he wasn't cold; all kinds of weather made him feel good, as long as he could be out in the air and active.

Even in his work, he preferred drawing to photography,

because it was only through drawing that he came to understand the landscape in all its forms; he was invariably surprised to see how many forms revealed themselves in what seemed at first sight to be a dull and monotonous vista. A place took on meaning for him only when he drew it line for line—as faithfully as possible, without the schematizations and omissions that had become customary in his science—and it was only then that he could claim with a clear conscience, if only to himself, to have been there.

As usual at that time of year, the river valley was deserted, yet on that morning, which might have arisen out of the depths of the earth, it seemed everywhere to have caught fresh fire from that short period at the turn of the century when, traveled by side-wheelers, parceled out by trading companies, swarming with gold diggers, it had made its mark on history: all that had passed irrevocably into plastic sieves from the phony Trading Post, into miniature dog sleds carved by Indian home workers, and inscriptions on tombstones, effaced more quickly than in other regions by the radical extremes of the weather. But in this moment it formed a conscious, eternal current in the timeless, unconscious river. In perceiving it, Sorger felt cheered and comforted and eager to accomplish something.

The firm, smooth paper of his drawing pad; for the alternation of thin and thicker lines, a drawing pencil sharpened to an asymmetrical cone; the beautiful first glow of a cigarette; a windless day, in which the smoke did not fly away but sank slowly to the ground.

The first colors in the landscape were objects in their own right: a gravel red, an oil-drum blue, an ash-leaf yellow, a birch-tree white. Little burst puffballs in the grass. Elsewhere a hairy poppy stem, whose flower was not red but a wonderful silken yellow. The locusts—bushes rather than trees—had dark thorns all over them. The flaming-red rowan berries, icier than snowballs inside; you can feel the sting in the palm of your hand. The brick-red willow bark, as though to bind a book with. The brown shaggy bearskin nailed to a shed.

The first movements were the clouds of mist just over the river, drifting eastward. Sand martins darted out of holes in the clay embankment and soon turned back. The black mongrels, rooting about in the shore rubbish, proved to be giant crows, which rose into the air with a whirring of wings, circled around the man, and flew away with raucous cries; one came back again, this time without a sound, and flew over the standing man, so low that its wingbeats sounded like a flapping fan belt.

Almost all the fish washed ashore during the night had been eaten; here and there the picked-out eyes had left their imprints in the soft sand. A stray dog ambling down the beach was silvery gray, its head white from the bluish eyes down: a real face. He dragged a dead sea gull back and forth over the sand, crunching it—that was the only sound far and wide—with his side teeth. The chained village dogs emerged from their underground kennels and ran as far as they could, whining and yapping with still-tamed violence.

Then came the usual sounds of morning traffic: not a single car driving over dry land, but several small planes rose above the bushes, and the hum of others could be heard from beyond the river. "You must know that no one ever abandoned himself to such an extent in this life that he might not have abandoned himself still more."

Whom was he to honor? Wasn't that what he needed—someone to honor? Didn't he want to be independent?

Where was the person for whom he could do something? Where was he at this very moment?

The beer cans, which in addition to being crushed flat had been ground into the road, seemed to demonstrate extreme violence and a despair, which he had never known but could now suspect, over an insurmountable privation and a stony absence, that had set every last dog in the village to howling with murderous fury.

His colleague Lauffer, already uniformed in his coat of many pockets and his high boots, was trotting back and forth in the background, playing basketball with himself with the help of a windblown net that had been fastened over the door of the house. Sorger started running, snatched the ball from his friend, and joined in the game.

Far away in the flatlands, the sun rose slowly, darkening the landscape with deep shadows: a darkness, or rather a gloom, which would persist all day, with barely shrinking and barely moving pits of shadow among the trees and bushes; and on the spot, from the moment when Sorger joined in the game, time transformed itself, as on an open stage, into a dimly sunny space, without particular events, without day and night, and without self-awareness, a space in which he was neither a doer nor an idler, neither an actor nor a witness.

He had just jostled his opponent, sniffed at the ball, breathed in the other's sweat and then his own, had once been grabbed around the waist and easily thrust aside by the powerful Lauffer. By then, only a few stray swallows, abandoned by their flock, white of belly, fatter and much smaller than elsewhere, were flying from their recesses on the shore to far beyond the middle of the river, from where they darted back as though from a secret boundary.

They would repeat this long-short two-stroke movement all day long and day after day, occasionally meeting a gleaming-white eagle flying along the river, and going a bit of the way with it.

This was a time of constant presence, constant whereverness, and constant habitat. The presence was an omnipresence, shared by the once-beloved dead, in which the most distant loves were sheltered and of good cheer in an accessible next-door; the whereverness was a foreign country, where no one forced you to run away home or to emulate the habits and customs of the natives; and the habitat was the home-and-workshop quality of the whole region, where it was possible to live in privacy, free from servitude to habitual inner partitions.

The autumn sun might be watery or hot, or it might shimmer only on a distant spot in the plain—in every case it was something more than the usual indifferent source of light behind one's back or before one's eyes. Leaves fell on dishes that lay on tables in the open, or blew down the river in colorful swarms; or they were not leaves at all but birds that flew back into the bushes from the grass, or stopped in midair and whirled about in a flock, or turned into land animals and scurried away in an entirely different direction; now they were frogs' heads peering through the layer of leaves on marshy black puddles, or hares scampering off into the lowlands and somersaulting to the sound of shots; or perhaps, after all, they had only been leaves (just as the dead birds falling from the trees had only been bits of bark broken off by the wind).

At the time these phenomena were something more than the eccentric delusions of someone who happened to confuse his details. They were unmistakable signs implicit in nature itself (just as they could transform each season into the annual cycle as a whole) and had the power, regardless of who the observer might be, to convert themselves into great and diversified happenings in space—delusions only at first glance, then welcome as metamorphoses in the deeper area of vision, where, in a way that is always unique, plants coalesce with animals and even with humans, and absence merges with presence. In fusing Sorger's individual history with the movement of the northern autumn, the landscape was in turn transformed by this human history into a temporal vault in which this self-forgetful man, without a destiny but also without sense of loss (freed altogether from fluctuations of feeling), was still present.

In this landscape there was one particular place (which Sorger sketched each day) where this promising history, in which nothing violent or abrupt ever happened, was clearly revealed to him. The place was not conspicuous as a scene or site; it took shape through the prolonged effort of sketching, which alone made it describable.

It was the middle ground of a quite commonplace segment of the landscape, chosen by Sorger because of an earthquake fault in the foreground and a fragmentary shelf of loess far behind it. Through no intention of his, this center, which disclosed no particular surface form, not so much as a small swampy depression, and which only a sense of having to fill up his page led him to sketch, gradually took on a decided individuality. It was a smooth bit of meadow, almost entirely bare of trees or underbrush, with a few huts and a straight path in the foreground demarcated on the far side by the sparse virgin forest, which, however, was so close that the sketcher could look into it, while the foreground with its many perceptible details suggested a gardenlike fringe, distinct from the wilderness in the background. Between these two zones, which were clearly set off from the landscape as a whole, lay the formless middle ground. Though on a plane with them, it gave the impression first of a meadow that had formed in the course of the weeks and finally of a human valley in a possible eternal peace.

The Indians who traversed this sunny autumnal scene passed every day, driving left to work or right on their way back home, while their children passed one by one on their way to school and at noon in homeward-bound groups. Here their lives unfolded without the usual incidents. In every instance, the person who entered the stage from one side complemented the one who had just left it on the other side; those who met on the road stood together for a while and then separated; they were only on their way to farms, always in the same village area, and the howling packs of dogs on the trucks were their household pets, which they were taking for an outing.

Otherwise than in the market, town hall, or bar, the people who kept passing through this middle ground presented the picture of an indestructible, lively, and often exuberant community; and Sorger knew that he could trust this picture, which had freed him from several obsessive beliefs. Up until then, the Indians had indeed been a hostile race and he an undesirable intruder on their land, which moreover belonged to his Western world only in the most superficial sense. Formerly, he had been able to think of a Great Indian Nation—but now that the "intruder" and the "alien" had at last been swept away, he was not afraid to think of them with sympathy or simply to take them for granted; and then it turned out that their anti-white slogans and curses had hardly been directed against him after all.

Throughout the past months, they had ignored Sorger.

They looked straight ahead when he passed, or jostled him slightly and possibly looked around, but more as one looks at an obstruction in one's path, wishing to know what sort of thing one has bumped into. But now, perceiving them as members of a village community, he saw that through this very fact he had become noticeable to them and that it had been in his power not to be ignored by them. At present, to be sure, they did not in passing turn their heads in his direction as he stood there with his instruments, deep in thought, and nevertheless, relieved of his old misconceptions, he was sure of their closeness to him; he now no longer disturbed them, and their unabashed merriment was in itself an attention, an expression of friendliness.

It seemed to Sorger that his first sight of Indian children at play had been in this spot, as though this had been his first experience of children in the Far North; and as though even the adults had become so friendly that whatever they did in his presence—even if it was merely to rush past in their cars—they seemed to be playing for his benefit. *He* overcame his inhibitions—and *they* began to play.

And in the evening he actually sat down in the bar among them, huddled in close-packed rows as in the half darkness of a movie house. He looked at no one in particular (always taking in several figures at once), nor did they look expressly at him; but their movements around him were always attentive, almost like dance steps. A threatening face might approach him, then would withdraw with a look of contentment, because the threat, but not the face, had been disregarded in Sorger's first answering glance. (If the drunk persisted in his threatening attitude, because he couldn't bear to meet anyone's eyes, an Indian woman, usually of a certain age, would draw him away to a long, sad dance of appeasement, from which he would not return.)

Sorger did not belong to the Indians as one belongs to a tribe, but he was one with them when he met them in the bar, in the village, or anywhere else in the district; he had not forgotten the color of their skin, but when with them he was no longer conscious of his own. Sometimes he could even see himself adopted by one of their clans and staying there for good; or rather, this autumn with its thoughts and perceptions had the effect of a natural daydream going beyond Sorger's personal world; as though for this man, who was contentedly present and no more, nature itself was a transpersonal history. He would live with his family in the village, which of course included church and school, and with his work he would even make himself useful to the community. Church, school, family, village, offered the possibility of an entirely new life, and to Sorger the smoke that arose each day from the huts in the middle ground was something new; of course he had seen such smoke before—but where? when? Freed from where and when, he was relieved at no longer having to think that the people here were lost souls in a godforsaken hole "where there was nothing." Actually, everything was there.

Now he met the Indian woman without secrecy; he even introduced her to Lauffer, though ordinarily he kept his dealings with women to himself: "This is my girlfriend"; and after that she came to the gabled house now and then with her children, or by herself in the evening to make a third at cards. Sorger actually longed to show himself with her, though he couldn't have said to whom. Formerly he had not felt concerned by the gaze of her strange eyes, with the black pupils barely visible in the dark irises; now he trusted her—and welcomed her gaze (which had not changed). While with her he was just absent enough to feel constantly at one with her, and he no longer had guilt feelings about her, only a feeling of pleasure, which now at last was just the kind of pleasure he wanted and no longer upset him. (It was as though he first experienced the weight of the world through her. One night they seemed to be lying on a high plateau, which was suddenly too small for them; they grew and grew until, incredulous with pleasure, they became the world to each other.)

Long ago Sorger had thought himself capable of happiness. This took the form of a brotherly light-headedness, which sometimes communicated itself to others. Since then he had ceased to demand states of happiness; in fact, he avoided them like the plague. Still, it had surprised him now and then to see how easily others could be happy with him; for a short time this had given him the certainty of being able to live an acceptable life even at cross-purposes with the times, but aroused guilt feelings because he made no attempt to make anything last. At present, however, he promised no future; he had ceased to be anything more than a stimulus; in his thoughts he saw the woman and himself nodding to each other and going their way; being together as they were now was to be united forever.

In taking his leave, he moved at ease in the foreign language, but made no pretense, by using slang or home-grown intonations, of being native to it. In speaking, he lost his awareness of his own voice; just as his being had merged with the autumn landscape, so his speech now seemed to blend with that of the people around him. Altogether, he found a new pleasure in foreign languages and made up his mind to learn several more. He said:

"In my native country, I couldn't even conceive of *belonging* to the country and its people. The words 'my country, my people' meant nothing to me. Can it be that the wilderness has helped me to form an idea of what a village can be? Why is it this strange land that has first given me the thought of permanence?"

And with Lauffer it was very much the same. Though he ordinarily yearned for his Europe—going to bed early and lying abed late like a child at boarding school, "so as to think about home"—the region had become his "geological garden," which he tilled with an almost peasant-like devotion.

He often got up before Sorger and with bottles, planks, and strips of metal fashioned devices with which to measure the wind and water erosion on the riverbank, the movements of slopes (underground "creep" or "flow"), and the frost in the ground.

Lauffer, the student of slopes, even forgot in the end to lace himself up in the stiff professional garb that gave him, it is true, the look of a scientist, albeit a strangely uninspired one, and converted himself, with a checked flannel shirt, wide suspenders, and light linen trousers baggy at the top but tapering toward the ankles, into the rather bulky sort of figure one was likely to meet in this region.

What he built was chiefly "sand traps" of different kinds, horizontal with juxtaposed compartments (with which to measure the horizontal movement of the sand), and vertical, on several levels, with which to measure the lifting power of the wind. He also made use of a "sand bottle," which he buried in the ground, so that nothing protruded but a sand-catching device attached to the neck, with the opening turned toward the ground wind. To avoid the admixture of secondary debris, which would have masked the true movement of the slope, the conscientious Lauffer attached long plank gutters to the rubble boxes he placed at the foot of the slopes. And in order to register the "heel clicking," as he called it, of the stones in the subsoil of the slope, he sank strips of lead vertically into holes in the ground, which he had made with a drill the exact size of the strips, and then measured the movement of rubble by carefully uncovering the strips and observing their inclination. Having planted the area with these devices, he stalked about like a trapper, waiting for results.

But his special interest was the ground under the raised huts, where the miniature geological formations, sheltered from the effects of precipitation, differed from the originally related but subsequently ruined forms in the outside world.

This little discovery had greatly excited him: here civilization, instead of destroying natural forms as usual, had preserved them almost entirely from the action of time. Conversely, in a South American desert where there had been neither wind nor rain nor dew for more than a century, human footprints and the marks of horses' hoofs dating from a time long past had remained untouched by nature. (The rocks in that desert had weathered to so dark a color that the heat radiating from them served as a barrier against the wind.) Lauffer was planning to write a paper comparing the two phenomena: "It won't be a study," he said. "More like a description of pictures."

Sorger said: "Sometimes when I try to form an idea of the age and genesis of different forms in the same landscape and their relation to one another, the incredible diversity of this one broad canvas starts me daydreaming. I'm not a philosopher, but at such times I know that it's natural for me to philosophize."

Lauffer: "I'm sure your thoughts in the matter are not what the professors would ask for, and there would be no place for us in a discussion among professional philosophers. I for my part can boast only momentary bursts of philosophical imagination, and these exclusively for my own benefit. My science gives me daydreams that no one else could equal even in his sleep."

Sorger: "Then you should have things to tell me."

Lauffer: "About the landscape?"

Sorger: "About the landscape and about yourself."

Accumulation of passion; enjoyment of order (of a rectangular table, for instance); the joy of just living somewhere; rediscovered pleasure in study; enjoyment of my body, its needs, even its mere activities. Nothing more to desire; no harm in that. Nothing supernatural about fulfillment. Not thought out of existence, but stripped of individual meaning. A feeling of constant warmth in my head: no personal or purposive or predigested thoughts, breathless ("Help!") and then breathing deeply ("Thanks to whom?"). No thinking that is not a "thinking with." Thinking the earth with the earth as a thinking world without end. The earth whose circling begins with my circulation, with me, the finite object of thought, the only remaining *object of thought.* No more blood, no more heartbeat, no more human time: only a universal transparence, pulsating mightily and trembling with my pulse. No more century, only this season. From lying to standing; from standing to jumping or running. The joy of talking and arguing. Loath to play, but glad to watch others play. Strong wind, but not a leaf falling from the birches. Moment of stillness; then a light breeze and the leaves fall to the ground in swarms. On a dead arm of the river, a serried flock of gulls, drifting as slowly as a cloud. White crow droppings on dead fish stuck with red willow twigs. Empty cartridge cases in the gravel, shots elsewhere. In the house a shirt is hanging on a chair; the low-lying sun shines through the topmost buttonhole. The room cowers in the shadow of a passing bird (or airplane). "Greetings, ye smiling dead": but only my own memory smiles, behind my forehead, too weak to bring back the dead, which turn up for a moment in the form of lopsided sacks. River. House. (Outcries.) Just back from work, my friend is standing outside, in the open window frame. Leaves circling in the puddles. Blades of grass—they, too, look like fallen leaves.

The day preceding Sorger's departure from the northern lowlands was a holiday, the anniversary of the discovery of the continent. It was almost mid-October. In the morning the water clicked against the narrow frieze of ice growing out of the riverbank; bristling snow crystals lay on the ice; the many little lumps of snow on the surface of the water were drifting gulls.

Beside an abandoned, tumbledown hut there was a birch tree; the basketball net fastened to it had been blown over its iron frame by the strong wind. In the fine-grooved river landscape, dark wind spots moved like wandering underwater sandbanks. Later on, spots of shadow on white tree trunks would remind Sorger of the cat, which, with its head buried in its fur, lay on the table by the window, as at peace with the world as only a house cat can be.

Lauffer was still asleep, his head buried like the cat's; he had got up in the middle of the night and wandered about the living room. Questioned on his return, he had only mumbled with thick, heavy lips (which reminded Sorger, who was sitting up in bed, of his brother) and no tongue, shutting his eyes for a moment (and not just flicking his lashes) at every syllable, as he sometimes did when telling a lie. Only then did it dawn on Sorger that his friend had been sleepwalking.

Now it looked as if he would sleep a long while; and meanwhile, the wind piled up sand in his sand traps. Gazing at him and the cat at the window, Sorger recovered his (so lightly forgotten) feeling for the passage of time, and realized that it had been absent from his weightless existence of the last few days, which seemed to have passed from him "after his time." In all the images which had played without violence on a middle ground without birth or death, he had lacked not the feeling of himself but awareness of himself as the feeling of a form. And this he acquired now, for at the sight of his friend lying doubled up in bed he became aware of his own beholding, saw it in the oval of his own mortal eyes, which had just begun to capture the essence of the pictorial—consciousness was the feeling of this form and the feeling of form was gentleness. No, he had no desire to cease to be.

Sorger had gone outside with the cat, which was following him and seemed that day "to know a thing or two." On the beach, sticks of driftwood had been set down, or perhaps been accidentally washed ashore, in a circle. It occurred to him that the Indians might have made these circles to demarcate themselves from this holiday and what it commemorated, and at that point the whole settlement struck him as a secret magic circle in which he, now initiated, was making his last rounds.

And true enough, totemic signs had been painted here and there along the military road. The tire marks in the mud might also have been signs in a secret Indian picture script; and the wide-spreading elk antlers at the top of the wooden privies may have been there to mock the foreign intruders. "*Yes*, we are open"—on a national holiday this conventional formula on the door of the market had a strangely unconventional meaning. A passing police car (never before had Sorger seen a police car in the area) paraded the closed, anonymous faces of an occupying power, at which the natives merely encouraged their dogs to bark. "Rounds and maunderings," said Sorger to the cat, who was following him at a distance, stopping now and then.

The children were in the schoolhouse; he saw them sitting behind tinted glass in the long, low building, but he couldn't make out their faces, only rows of round, deep-black head tops, which were suddenly very dear to him. Someone played an American Christmas carol on a flute, not practicing, but evidently bungling it on purpose. A child came to the window and popped his bubble gum as Sorger looked up at him. Turning into a town hall, he leafed, as he had often done, through the warrant book chained to the wall. Many of those wanted were used to living in the open and were tattooed with the words: "Born to lose."

He turned to the cemetery. Almost all these people had died young. The ground was bumpy with fallen pinecones and spotted with clumps of white mushrooms. He stepped into the wooden church to rest. Leaves had blown between the chairs and even over the lending-library volumes spread out on the table; a book of music lay open on the harmonium; clouds of breakfast bacon blew in from the adjoining room, where the pastor lived. At the next bend in Sorger's path he caught sight of Indians' clothes, all dark, hung up to dry. Behind the windows of the huts, he saw the silhouettes of the inhabitants, who were so small that even standing they could be seen only from the neck up. And so, in going away, he managed to take leave of them.

The wind was so strong that it unbuttoned his coat as he walked, but warm, interspersed with icy gusts that tasted like snow in his mouth. The cat stopped now and then and the movement of its head followed the shadows inside the houses; when Sorger picked it up, it arched its back and blew cold air in his face; it disliked being carried when out of doors.

Followed by the animal, he returned to the riverbank, completing his circuit (at the end, his brisk walk had turned to a run). He thought: Today for the first time I've seen the yards around the houses and discovered that the village has a circular road around it.

The water level had fallen so far of late that a number of small ponds had formed between sandbanks, and the water whirled about in them as though churned up by a captive fish: "Here, too, in a circle." Though there was no one to be seen on the river, echoes of human voices came to him from all sides (along with the cry of a lone sand martin and the empty scraping of unmanned boats against the gravel bank). And Sorger saw the village population, a Great Water Family, gathered, as it were, head to head at the bend of the river. This whole river valley from source to mouth—"nowhere else but here" was a river valley worth mentioning; this, indeed, was "the only place worth mentioning in the whole world"—and that was the message of the lines which the sinking water seemed to have written in the sand (the opposite shore was already "beyond the last frontier").

The sounds that echoed from the river were Indian sounds, yet it seemed to Sorger (though he did not understand a single word) that he was listening to his own language, indeed, to the dialect of the region where his forebears had been at home. He crouched down and looked into the eyes of the cat, which shrank back from him; and when he tried to caress it, it seemed to find this so repellent, here away from the house, that it fled with movements rather like those of a fleeing dog.

The dried shore mud at his feet had broken up into a far-flung network of almost regular polygons (for the most part six-sided). As he examined the cracks, they began little by little to work on him, but instead of fragmenting him like the ground, they joined all his cells (a void that he hadn't noticed until then) into a harmonious whole. Something that rose from the split surface of the earth struck his body and made it warm and heavy. Standing there motionless, looking out over the pattern, he saw himself as a receiver, not of news or a message, but of a twofold force received on the two levels of his head. On his forehead, he felt the bone disappearing, simply because he had no other thought than to expose this obstacle to the air; and the surface of his face from the eyes down seemed once again to acquire the characteristics of a face; human eyes and a human mouth, each for itself but not separated by consciousness; and he actually felt that his lowered lids had become receiving screens. His head bent lower and lower, yet the meaning was not despair but determination: "The decision rests with me." Raising his eyes, he was prepared for anything; with every look, even into the void, he would have met other looks; indeed, he would have created them.

The murmuring of the stream—and once again the bushes were murmuring as gently as on the summer day when he arrived and gained his first intimation of the river landscape.

The man who rose from the ground was not ecstatic, only appeased. He no longer expected illuminations, only measure and duration. "My face an unfinished sketch—when will it be complete?" He could say that he enjoyed life, accepted death, and loved the world; and now he saw that, correspondingly, the river flowed more slowly, the clumps of grass shimmered, and the sun-warmed gasoline drums hummed. Beside him he saw a single yellow willow leaf on a flaming-red branch and knew that after his death, after the death of all mankind, he would appear in the depths of this countryside and give form to all the things on which his gaze now rested. The thought gave him a blissful feeling that raised him above the treetops; only his face remained behind, now a mask "representing happiness." (And then there was even a kind of hope—disguised as a feeling that he knew something.)

Seizing the moment, Sorger, "the hero," dropped the stone that he had meant to put in his pocket as a memento, and ran through the grassy meadow to the gabled house. The spotted cat, which was sitting out in front, had forgotten him again. Why had Lauffer once said that he would "probably live here for quite a while but go back to Europe to die"?

As Sorger stepped into the house, Lauffer greeted him with an almost mischievous look of superiority—meaning that he was staying in the place his friend was leaving. He was wearing white woolen socks and a bunched-up shirt. A checked handkerchief and a pair of gloves were dangling from his back pocket—he might have been mistaken for a native. All Sorger's ideas dispersed, he would somehow have to take his leave, and that dismayed him. If some people could go away while others were sleeping, why wouldn't it be possible to go away without consciousness, in one's sleep? Then suddenly *this* thought: Tonight we shall celebrate my departure, and in the gray of dawn, while you are still lying in bed, I shall take the mail plane.

It was decided that they would work together that day; or rather, one formally invited the other to participate in his activity, and in the end they agreed to take aerial photographs together.

The rented single-engine plane flew so low over the river valley that even the outlines of the dark little ice lentils under the surface vegetation were visible. Though Sorger had often observed the region from the air, it took on a special form for him now that he was about to leave it. He saw the essentially shapeless plain as a body with many limbs and a unique, unmistakable face that was now turned toward him. This face seemed rich, eerie, and surprising—rich not only because its forms were so varied but also because they seemed inexhaustible; eerie because innumerable forms, which always reminded him strangely of (or foreshadowed) a human world and seemed to cry out for names, were in large part nameless; and surprising because every time he looked at it, there was the rolling stream; every pre-vision was a mistake; the wideness of the river was always a new event, even if one had looked away for barely an instant; it was truly unthinkable.

What made Sorger, who soon forgot about photography, regard the river as a feature in a face was the palpable gratitude and even admiration he felt toward the territory that had been his place of work for the last few months. Horseshoe lakes, saucepan springs, trough-shaped valleys, lava cakes, or glacier milk from glacier gardens—looking down on "his" landscape, he understood these conventional terms, which had often struck him as unreasonably childish. If he saw a face here, why shouldn't other observers, in other parts of the world, see dream edifices with columns, gates, stairways, pulpits, and steeples, furnished with bowls, basins, ladles, sacrificial vessels, situated—why not?—in a trumpet-shaped valley and edged about with flocks of hills; and at the moment he felt like adding friendly epithets to the scientific names of all these formations, for the few names on the map were derived either from the region's brief history as a gold miner's mecca (Phantom Gulch, Hard Luck Lake, Chilblains Hill, Half-Dollar Creek, Fourflusher's Island) or they were mere numbers (Six-Mile Lake, Nine-Mile Lake, Eighty-Mile Swamp). The few Indian names had an archetypal ring: The Great Crazy Mountains to the north of the Little Crazy Mountains, or the Great Unknown Brook that ran through Little Windy Gulch and ended in a nameless swamp.

Although the river was forbiddingly cold even in summer, Sorger suddenly had an image of himself happily bathing in it, swimming and diving under. Hadn't rivers been embodiments of the gods in olden times? "Beautiful Water," he said, and realized that he had given the river a name. (Down below him, the truncated meander arms danced like garlands.)

He would never have expected to love this landscape, or landscape in general—and along with his surprising affection for the river he felt his own story, felt that it was not ended, as his nightmares and even opinions might have led him to suppose, but was going on as patiently as the flowing water. As he gazed at the richness of this landscape, the realization that he himself was immeasurably rich awakened him like a cannon shot, and urged him to give of his riches now and forever, for if he didn't, he would suffocate.

His next thought was that he would now be able to

handle his long-planned dissertation "On Spatial Configurations," and he said to Lauffer, who had explained his aerial photography camera to the pilot and to whom the pilot was explaining his flight instruments: "I'm going to treat you to a telephone call to Europe when we land."

The public telephone was in a windowless log cabin built in one corner of a sheet-metal hangar on the side of the airfield. As though meant to be lived in, the cabin was furnished with a table, a reading lamp, a bed covered with wolf hides, a shelf of books, and a small cast-iron stove (it took a long time to put a call through). The telephone, which had a distinctly public look, hung on one of the two sheet-metal walls formed by the hangar; the key to the cabin could be obtained in the market at the other end of the village.

In the early days Sorger had often driven the jeep here, in part because he enjoyed sitting at the table in the dark cabin, waiting. Just before the line was at last opened to him and he could hear the bell ringing far across the seas, a satellite crackling set in and with it an image of oceanic distances. As he was preparing his mind for the conversation, this brief sound threw him into a state of indescribable excitement in which he literally "called" the person "at the other end of the wire." After that, even in the middle of the conversation, he was often enough merely bewildered; clearly as it might come over, the other voice seemed to recede farther and farther as it spoke, and to make matters worse, there were never any background noises (music, dogs barking, or even a plain voice); at his end of the telephone cable Sorger felt excluded, his own voice echoed in his ear; and his dizziness as he hung up had all the earmarks of unreality.

Consequently Sorger, who was nevertheless attracted

more and more by the strange room, had gradually got into the habit of taking Lauffer to the phone and of drinking wine and playing chess with him while waiting. It had even become customary for Sorger to invite his friend to a phone call, whereupon Lauffer would invite him to come along and listen.

In Europe it had long been day, while here they sat in the little cabin, in the hangar, in the far-flung night. The only sound was an occasional clicking inside the phone, which, however, was meant for someone else in another "township," another numbered square of wilderness.

When the call came through, Lauffer became absorbed in asking questions, answering, or reporting events; Sorger didn't listen to his words but just saw him wedged into the corner, clutching the phone, all speaker or all listener; at such times his friend cast off his almost bashful one-man-to-another attitude and gave him a hint of who he was.

This last night in Eight-Mile Village (it was eight miles north of the Arctic Circle) was to prove adventurous for Sorger, though nothing in particular happened. Thoughts rose up which had long been turning over in the back of his mind but now became more distinct. They concerned a duty—not a neglected duty, but one that had gradually fallen due; and because this duty would call for actions that he was still unable to imagine, it seemed to him, though without precise images, that this was the first night of an adventure.

Sorger, who sometimes felt drawn to cooking, made dinner for himself, his friend, and the Indian woman. Afterwards the three of them sat around the table playing cards with a new, fresh-smelling deck that the woman had brought as a farewell present. The figures on the cards were ravens, eagles, wolves, and foxes; the joker had an Indian face in the middle, and all those animals formed a circle around it.

In the gabled house there was a chandelier with long, thin glass pendants, in the light of which each one examined his bright, tranquil hand of cards. The doors to all the rooms were open, including the one leading to the attic darkroom, and the lights were on all over the house. The cat was sitting glassy-eyed on Sorger's packed suitcase, twitching its ears and from time to time moving its tail from side to side; it displayed its claws, as if they were fingernails, drew in its forepaws, and finally fell asleep.

Lauffer's chin shone. He had on a white silk shirt and a black velvet vest with gilt buttons; elastic armbands gathered in the wide sleeves; and for the first time since his arrival he was wearing the low shoes he had brought from Europe, which could occasionally be heard creaking under the table—up until then they had been occupied only by shoe trees. He had snipped the hairs in his nostrils and was sitting up straight, never throwing cards but always setting them down gently. He took an innocent pleasure in winning, and lost with grim dignity. He seemed perfect, with his inner composure and outward splendor.

Though they were sitting at a table without beginning or end, their circle seemed to start with the Indian woman. She was not to the left or right of the men; no, they were at her sides; the initiative was with her. Her movements in playing resembled those with which she distributed medicines when at work; a deft, nonchalant, continuous, many-handed giving (while the gathering-in of what was coming to her was always done in guise of thanks). The way she had made up and decked herself out (a jade amulet hanging from her neck), she was no longer an Indian but a dark, dangerous machine in radiant human form; as soon as she lowered her human eyes to a card, the eye of the machine stared from the black-rimmed vault of her eyelid and held the room in its gaze.

"Yes" (with this one word Sorger finally accepted as an obligation what for so long he had only mused about). At times Lauffer had really been his friend, and recently he had been one with the woman in their true, screaming, and clutching bodies—but what presumption in him, the "Stranger" (the name of an emetic fungus), to importune these two with the claims of a "friend" or "lover."

Sorger did not foresee that these two would come together, he saw their union before him in the present: the perfect couple, the consummate student of earth forms and the divine beast.

No one asked why he was laughing—they knew. And the next moment placed Sorger, who mechanically went on playing, in the midst of a prehistoric event that was just taking place. In the river there was a narrow, gently sloping island with a small, rounded hollow in the middle, where the conifers, which were sparse and stunted everywhere else, grew dark and dense. This hollow had probably resulted from an underground cavern, into which Sorger—while his fellow players, who at that very moment were on a level with his eyes, rose to the upper edge of his field of vision—sank all at once, as slowly as in a dream. Already moss was growing in the pit and dark bears rose up between the trees.

As though in triumph, Sorger went out into the open. He moved in the glow of the windows; outside, there was no other light, not even the dot of a star. At first he saw the two of them sitting at the table; then the bushes merged with the receding bright rectangle, as though the panes had been smeared with dirt. "Please forget me." He saw so little ahead of him—now and then, a lighter-colored stone silhouette—that he had to feel his way with his feet and elbows. Not even a splashing; only a soft scraping from time to time.

Then nothing more stood out from the darkness; at last, no more images. A short while before, all distinct surfaces, regardless of color (wasn't there such a thing as a wedding color?), had reminded him of dead people, as though he were staring at those who had died there. Then he saw the river flowing in the darkness: thick anthracite against thinner black; and these forms, as a painter he admired had said, were now his "performers"; able to "perform" in his place because they were unabashed, free of his embarrassment.

Once all recognized techniques had been applied to the description of a phenomenon, Sorger's science called for one additional, ultimate technique, which he called "comprehensive vision"; here, in the face of the black-on-black Arctic night, such comprehensive vision was achieved, though it had not been planned and the requisite composure was lacking; a different sort of calm took hold of him (he literally experienced center and depth) and at the same time reached out beyond him; it warmed the palms of his hands (and his gently spreading fingers), arched the balls of his feet, made him conscious of his teeth, and transformed the whole of him into a body which became a radically extroverted organ of all the senses. Seeing himself in strips of darkness, he was overpowered by the calm of a savage—which could be expressed only in the one word "beautiful."

Not merely turning his head, but nimbly twisting his shoulders and hips on their axis, he recognized in the darkness that his life would inevitably become dangerous. He did not see the dangers; he had an intimation of them; he could not go looking for them, they were necessity itself; he had an intimation of necessary solitude and continued remoteness; and all these intimations crowding in on him, but forming no clear prophecy, added up to a feeling of adventure, as if he had just gone away from all his dear ones with no possibility of return; and, his head whirling with the intoxication of being forever alone, he rejoiced out loud: "No one knows where I am. No one knows where I am!" (For a moment the moon appeared, and he hissed at it.)

And then he heard a whimpering beside him in the darkness, as of an abandoned child. Or was it the breathing of some large animal?

But it was only a human, standing beyond reach but fairly near him, clearing his throat to show no harm was intended. And between these two, who could not see each other, the following words were said: "Hi, stranger. How are you feeling this evening?" Sorger: "Fine, thank you. How are you?" The speaker: "Short autumn. Run out of fuel." Sorger: "Isn't there a woodpile down by the river?" The speaker: "Good river. Fine summer. Long winter. Could you spare a quarter, mister?" (A hand, warm like Sorger's own, took the coin.) The speaker: "God bless you, man. Green northern lights, yellow around the edges. Where you from?" Sorger: "Europe." The speaker: "I'm going to tell you something. Never look at the snow too long. It can make you blind. That's what happened to me. Want me to tell you something else?" Sorger: "No, thank you." "You're welcome, friend. Don't eat too much fish. Enjoy the rest of your stay here. Take care. Have a good time. Pleasant trip. Touch home soon."

Sorger heard the speaker—whether Indian or white, man or woman, he couldn't be sure—moving off in the darkness, and sure of the way, sure of his direction and his body, he ran back to the village and the gabled house. The other two were standing at the window but didn't turn their heads in his direction, as though they hadn't even noticed his absence, or as if he had already been so forgotten that he would have to breathe at them. Over the Indian woman's shoulder, two glassy fox eyes stared at him.

No more talk; for a last time the smooth woman drew him to her with both her hands, pushed him away with a little laugh, and grazed him with a look of astonishment in which her whole face seemed to expand, though no part of it moved; but Sorger had thrown his arms around his friend, who had taken his place beside her in the goodbye line; and in the end gone dutifully ("the mail plane and all that") to bed in the next room, which was suddenly (but not for very long) freezing cold.

In his sleep, Sorger kept waiting for someone who didn't come. Once he woke up and saw the cat crouching in the corner of the room. "Monumental little beast." Quietly addressing the cat, he coaxed it to him. It came and laid its head on his knees. The cat wanted to live: and Sorger wanted to be forgotten by his best friends and perish. Unthinkingly he addressed the cat as "child," loved it (his arms grew strong with love), and named his loved one with its color: "Black-and-white."

In a dream, Sorger's brain became a map of the world, and when he woke up, he was a mound of earth with a lot of stones in it. In the gray of dawn, Lauffer was lying in the supposedly empty room, a malignant grimace with closed eyes. Hauling his suitcase, Sorger passed the absently staring cat, which now gave no sign of knowing him. He left many possessions in the house. "Let's get out of here!"

At sunrise in the mail plane (he was sitting in back with some Indians who had already dozed off) Sorger saw the yellow foliage of a lone birch smiling out of the endless virgin pine forest, thought of the Indian woman ("There's a sweet woman down there"), and sat up straight with directionless curiosity, which soon changed to a feeling of hunger, not for anything tangible, but for whatever might be coming. Without images, he anticipated "the future." In the midst of his imageless fantasy, he saw the pilot turn around and read from his lips the words: "We have to turn back."

The reason for turning back was the first snowstorm of the winter on the high plateau beyond the southern mountain ranges, where the larger settlement (formerly a gold-mining center), where one could change to a jet, was situated. Even as the pilot was looping back, the landscape changed its face. A round swampy lake became a hypnotic stare; meandering little rivers took on so dense a covering of aquatic plants that a sparkling of water could be seen only here and there, and the long gullies on the hillsides, long, straight stripes etched into the rubble by the spring thaw, curved in all directions. The plane would not be able to leave again until the following morning.

After landing, Sorger stood motionless at the edge of the little airstrip. There he and his suitcase loomed as in a fun-house mirror, with short fat legs and a great long neck. He hadn't been gone very long, just time enough for a short plane ride, but the whole village seemed to have turned into "premises" closed to the public. Sitting down on his suitcase, he turned "village" and laughed at himself, Sorger. Never had he come home to such unreality. How was he to avoid being seen? He stood up, started walking, and, shrugging his shoulders, changed direction. Play was no longer possible: the phony colors of the empty housefronts, the disenchanted water of the phony river—and through this utterly threadbare world, with an affectation of hail-fellow-well-met-ness, zigzagged not a face but the grin of a simpleminded dupe.

Not knowing where to go, he became dangerous—not as an aggressor, but as a potential victim.

A man of no particular age was walking ahead of the irresolute Sorger on the narrow path; moving as slowly as Sorger, he was not deep in thought, but neither was he looking at anything, and as a result the slowness of his walk gradually took on an air of viciousness. He didn't look around, but from time to time showed a bit of eyeless profile, as dogs sometimes do in running past. At length he stepped to one side, pulled a tire chain out of his pocket, and, clutching the heavy thing in his fist, came straight at "me!"

Just as he had no age, the man seemed to belong to no race. Bright eyes without a center. Whenever his knees threatened to crumple, he twisted his lips, but did not smile. When he ("actually") hauled off with the chain, neither of the two had a face left; in that moment the whole world contracted and became tragicomically faceless.

"Dear brother." The drunk brought the chain down on the suitcase, which burst open, and fell on top of it, dead to the world.

Sorger pushed the inert body away and, taking his belongings under his arm, went straight to the gabled house, which greeted him with its earthly beauty. By then he was so furious and hated everybody so intensely that all his movements had become angular. The door was locked, and he sat down on the wooden steps in front of it. A falling leaf touched the back of his head like a paw, but the cat was inside the house, strolling about the deserted rooms, now and then making a play movement, wholly absorbed in its own reflexes, which helped it to pass the time, whereas the man on the steps outside was humiliated by his forced idleness. The boot scraper at his feet—which reminded him of the floor-boards in a bathhouse—and the basketball lying beside it seemed to add insult to injury.

The assault had humiliated rather than hurt him; more than violence, it had been an expression of contempt for his person and belongings, as though a voice had shouted: "You and your photographs! You and your drawings! You and your scientific papers!" Only then did Sorger hit back—with his fist in the air. There was no more Far North, only the weather, which was cold and gray, as it had always been for an idler who, in the space under the huts, saw not Lauffer's "small static earth forms" but only rusting junk; while in the meantime his work, whose secret, he had thought, was known to him alone, was being done by some anybody, effortlessly, with one among many simultaneous manipulations. For a moment, when that creature lifted his chain to strike, Sorger had been dead; now he was alive again, but the formlessness was still there; the next moment of formlessness was already pulsating in the immensity of time; as in dire pain, he felt at once minute and limitless, an intolerably heavy dot and an intolerably weightless immensity. Once again the Indian woman was the "other race," and whatever might happen in the interim, she was sure in the end to plan his destruction. "And you, Lauffer, if you lie to other people"—said Sorger, grown abusive in his formlessness—"it's because their company, whoever they may be, makes you miserable—but on the other hand you don't want them to know it, because you're an amiable, kindhearted, compassionate sort, yet basically morose."

At this point the angry orator, becoming aware of himself as a formless creature with, somewhere, too small a breathing hole, looked up and saw the surface of the water, as though it were gazing at him. This level ground was much too quiet; Sorger expected an eruption; he felt the need to see a mountain coming into being that minute, or at the very least a boulder breaking off from a cliff. He jumped up and kicked the ball against the wall of the house, so violently that, in rebounding, it whistled in his ear; then he went on playing without catching his breath until the pebbles before his eyes sparkled like flowers and he felt creepy, playing by himself.

When he stopped, he saw the rows of low clouds behind him over the water. They were pale-bright and motionless, not flat underneath as usual, but rounded. A gust of wind blew from deep within the landscape, and suddenly great snowflakes were falling, whirling darkly on the horizon like a swarm of locusts, not from all the clouds at once, but from one after another at short intervals, breaking loose from the clouds and rushing downward like a series of avalanches, until at length a brief but powerful squall descended with a dry crackling sound on the house and the man standing in front of it, while not a single flake was falling on the great fluvial plain.

Just then, under the uniformly gray sky, a dense, windless, slow snowfall set in which tickled the lips and turned the surroundings of the house into a fairyland. Radiant joy! Delicious sweat! Unable to breathe only a moment before, Sorger ran into the recaptured air; a bundle of life, he ran several times around the house, shouting as in eternal childhood. Soon his dear colleague (visible at a distance in the flat tundra) turned up and was not a little surprised. So the hours passed in a new, sad, and formally perfect friendliness, until the next day, when Valentin Sorger, equipped with a different suitcase, flew from that nameless neck of the woods, where already the wintry dusk was taking over (but in which two pairs of eyes belonging to Lauffer and the Indian woman were clearly discernible), into the world of names. In the university town on the west coast of the continent where he had once spent a few years, there was a wide street, lined for the most part with gas stations and shopping centers, named Northern Lights Boulevard.

Two /

Space Prohibited

Sorger's house was situated, along with similar small houses, in a pine forest in a flat section of the Pacific Coast. Between the sea and the houses there was no road, only bushes and low, grassy dunes. The roads through the forest ran at right angles to the ocean and ended at the dunes; from there, all the houses appeared to be deep in the woods, each with its own driveway, which circled around the trees in complicated loops. The soil was sandy, covered with prairie-high light-yellow beach grass, interspersed with small pine trees. Some of the dunes, displaced by the wind, had moved so far into the forest that here and there they formed light-colored embankments, colonized with new grass, above which only parts of the parched trees, still rooted in the old ground, could be seen; but in the course of time this vegetation had halted the movement of the dunes, and since they were the only hills in the area, they had become playgrounds for children, as had the strange dense prairie, which, because of the trees with which it was interspersed, could not very well be mowed. Nearly all the houses were within sight of others, and yet, because of the woods around them, they gave the impression of hermitages; though trimmed with bright-colored stucco, they were all, because of the constant threat of earthquakes, built of wood, as a tap of the knuckles sufficed to show. Some ten years earlier a tremor had sent a small hill on the coast nearby sliding into the sea along with the stucco villas on top of it, and since then the colony, its stairways and terraces and great, overgrown clefts, had become an uninhabited Earthquake Park.

In the airplane the sky had long remained wide. Warmed by an afterglow of friendship for those who had stayed behind, Sorger saw himself with them as though imprinted in the triangle of the Arctic pediment. Immediately after takeoff, he had started saying to himself: "Last summer and fall I was in the Far North." The West Coast was in a different time zone (two hours later), and night had fallen when he arrived. He had just seen the dark mud rolling in the river he had left, there had been many people on the way, not companions on a long flight, just people picked up and put down by one plane after another. In landing, as the plane circled from the level of a snow-covered mountain range over a hilly countryside descending in distinct stages to the wide coastal plain shimmering with canals, he had glimpsed the sun setting in the ocean mist. Then he was walking over the plastic floor of the air-terminal building, past the backs of little television sets, each of which formed a unit with an egg-shaped chair and a temporarily egg-shaped viewer; and though he had lived here a long time, it was on his return to the Lower Forty-eight (as the Northern settlers called the rest of the United States) that he first noticed the imprint of government on this continent that seemed to govern itself, and though there wasn't a soldier in sight, the glaringly lighted air terminal looked to him like a military installation.

In spite of himself, he looked around twice. Though

no one could possibly have known of his arrival, he looked for a "familiar face" among those waiting at the exit. And then he looked for the man with the too-short trousers and the stiff, white-leather shoes who had boarded the mail plane with him that morning and at each stopping place had taken the same plane as himself. They had not spoken, but had exchanged looks of silent amusement, and Sorger savored the thought that from then to the end of their days, always by chance, never exchanging a word, they would go the same ways. In approaching the exit, he purposely slowed down in the hope that this man (whoever he might be) would see him and catch up with him.

He stopped the taxi before the housing development and walked the last bit of the way, sometimes in the glow of the house lights, which shone through the trees on the otherwise dark road. The houses in the woods seemed peaceful, yet festive because of all the lights. He trod the unaccustomed asphalt, at one with his image of himself as a figure resplendent with anonymity among the hosts of world travelers, devoid of origin like himself, hurrying this way and that between the arrival and departure gates. And because for him, coming from a different time zone, it was not yet night (and also because his few hours of flight had been largely in bright light above the clouds), he felt the daylight on his eyes and blinked his way through the darkness as though it were artificial.

He picked up his mail at the neighbors', deposited beside the bed the toy sleds he had brought for the children, and, barked at by a dog or two outside, glancing briefly at the sky, amazed that the shape of the waxing moon should be identical here to what it was a few hours before (in the gray of dawn) over another, so distant part of the world, he retired to his quarters, which were also his place of work.

There were many letters, containing a good deal of news; most were friendly, some neutral, without threat or hostility. Some saw landscapes in their thoughts of him and wished he were not "so far away."

All the curtains in the house were drawn. He sat there in his coat, which was still buttoned. Rock fragments were piled up in a spacious glass case, as though they had slid straight out of nature and stopped behind the glass panes. A bluish fluorescent tube at the top of the cabinet illumined the stones and hummed softly (the only sound in the room). The seat of the chair was still indented where someone had been sitting months before. In the dark adjoining room, the door of which was open, he glimpsed the silhouette of a hydrant-like bedpost; there, for a moment, sat the cat with its pointed ears.

The glass table was lit from underneath. On it, letters along with the empty envelopes had been tossed in a loose transparent heap; a few stood up like parts of a card house, confronting the addressee (who was no longer serenely musing, but just sitting there in silence) with their shiny folds and the frayed borders of their envelopes. They had seemed to be palpable objects, but there was nothing else near him that he could name; otherwise, there were only curtains, not falling gently, but stiffly stemmed against him.

Hadn't a steady blowing stopped suddenly when he opened the door, or perhaps when he turned in from the road? In less than a moment, a breathing quietness had turned to rigidity. Sitting upright, someone had tipped over, but had not fallen to the floor as usual in such cases. Now this someone was sitting motionless, pierced through by the plane of the tipped one.

Mere warmth without blood, Sorger on that night of his return to the Western world saw himself dreamless, born into a planet without atmosphere (karst and grotesque emptiness), heavy as lead, but not falling; not alone in the world, but alone without a world; and within him—timeless—the stars and nebulae were eyes that did not look at him. He was forsaken not only by speech but by the power to make the least sound; and just as he lay inwardly silent, so he remained outwardly mute. Not a sound; not even a cracking of joints. Only in his imagination was he able to turn toward a rocky wall and, converted into a stone image, nestle in the stones. In reality, his flesh was trembling with weakness.

"To be swept away by a whirlwind—into what native land?" In the image that followed, Sorger saw the reason for his rigidity; sitting in the "night of the century," far back in the low, empty "lobbies of continents," he at least was mourning for himself and his fellow men and this accursed century—and yet he was forbidden to mourn, because he "himself was to blame." In truth, he was not even a "victim" and therefore could not join in the Great Lament with other victims of this century and find his voice again in the ecstasy of common suffering. Maybe the "unknown seated one" was weak, but he was descended from murderers, he regarded himself as a murderer, and the mass murderers of his century as ancestors.

Besieged as he was by closed curtains, threatened by the pile of letters as by an enemy coat of arms, Sorger in that moment realized that without lifting a finger he embodied every one of the forefathers who had been foisted upon him; the rigidity of his paralysis repeated the rigidity of those violent monsters; and not only did he resemble them outwardly; he was inwardly one with them, more so than they had probably been with one another. Without a destiny, without human ties, without the right to suffer or the strength to live (those letters signified nothing but disorder), he was merely faithful—the faithful replica of death-cult masters. He smelled war; right there in his hut, it encircled him.

But seeing to the bottom restored his speech, and then he was able to hate himself for having been possessed by dead monsters, as though they were his kinsmen. In his hatred, he breathed more deeply—breathed himself free from the suction of the tomb. "I no longer have a father." He shut his eyes and behind his lids saw the bright afterimage of the river. His speech was "play" and in it he regained his mobility; he took his clothes off and washed; under the water he sang a wicked song, which ended well above the water; then he opened all the curtains.

Speech, the peacemaker: it had the effect of ideal humor, reconciling the beholder with the things of the outside world. The wind whirled through the trees; in among leaves and scraps of paper, a whole newspaper spun about, opening and closing in its flight; folded, it rushed at the window in the darkness, but turned aside just in time and slowly opened ("for me"), as once more it fluttered away. Behind it the grass swayed like wheat, and from the ocean came noises of a distant playground. For a moment Sorger was able to think of his child in Europe. He opened the front door and swore never to close a door again.

At length he lay down to sleep (until then the bed had been an unattainable distant object), and with the yellow of the sulfur-containing minerals in the specimen case the brightness behind his eyes vanished. The last thing that occurred to him was that he was lying with his head to the north (in the gabled house it had pointed south).

True, something was lacking, but the clear fact of inexpiability had paled to a vague nostalgia; and he did not forget that he had been branded with inexorable rigidity, his true condition, beside which all others (speaking, moving) reduced themselves to unreal fuss-and-bother.

In the sandy ground below him, a crag detached from the coastal cliff by the waves of prehistory formed a kind of bulwark against the ocean. Turned on its axis during the night, the house slowly settled on this reef (Land's End) like a wooden ark.

The neighbors had invited Sorger to breakfast at their house. From there, he gazed at last night's trap, which in the morning light looked to him like the cottage of a retired old farmer.

A dangling pine branch half covered the housefront, and in the tall grass that had grown outside the door in his absence a dog with the face of a human eccentric stood as though legless, watching the sea gulls gliding between the trees. Sitting with the neighbor family in a semicircular sun-bright extension of the living room, Sorger knew that for the present nothing could shake him; he was prepared for anything, capable of everything he wanted to be capable of. Without effort his eyes, which in the wilds had grown accustomed to long distances, adjusted themselves to the family circle on either side of him. Back at last, he participated in his neighbors' life with the authority of a man who knows the earth, who is still somewhat tired from what he has been through, and whose tiredness makes him seem alive.

He was not, as usual in company, divided among unstable, disparate images; today his imagination was one, encompassing himself and those with him. All attention, the (rather abstemious) Sorger actually grew strong in enjoyment; his pleasure in eating (and in things in general) moved him with an aimless desire for conquest; all the rest of his long life would be devoted to enjoyment. Meanwhile, he had a delightful feeling of his own face, especially his eyes and mouth, and the bank notes, which crackled from time to time in his trouser pocket, gave him another, related feeling.

"Our neighbor is looking well today," said the lady of the house, who sat there with her hands in her lap, inspecting him. In reply to which her husband said: "Like a happy man with a destiny." The children looked at him, frowned, and ran outside to play hide-and-seek with the dogs in the tall grass.

True enough, on the morning after his night of rigidity, Sorger was less anonymous-looking than usual; ordinarily, in a group of bus drivers, electricians, or house painters, he could be mistaken for one of them. His body seemed to have broadened, his face was serene, more so each time you looked at it, as only the face of a leading man can be (his feeling about the preceding night was that he had played a part successfully); his eyes stood deeper in their sockets, and sparkled with omniscience: a man worth looking at. "Yes," he said, "today my power emanates from me."

Like Sorger, the family hailed from Central Europe, and like Sorger they had been living for years on the west coast of the other continent; in his eyes the man and woman were a true couple, whose love had thus far struck him as credible. The children, on the other hand, seemed fortuitous, witnesses to the marriage rather than bona-fide members of the family; often they just stood there looking on in amazement as the grownups played.

Sorger's first impression had been: "A pair of innocents." Yes, innocent they were, but that turned out to be their brand of kindness: in the course of time, it transferred itself to the less innocent Sorger, who in their company managed to feel guileless. When he came to know them, he felt sure they must have started out as two afflicted halves falling into each other's arms. They sometimes seemed backward and even ugly in their backwardness. Still, they occupied his imagination, they were indeed the content that made it possible—hardly anyone else prompted Sorger to such tranquil imaginings (instead of imprisoning him in conventional fantasies). All in all, one could think only good of them as a subject for the imagination.

The husband came of a wealthy family but never learned to show it (even in counter-gestures). He was willing, but inept. He was willing and inept in many things, but then unexpectedly he would "enchant" one, if only with a glance or a word. His wife was a "villager"; at first sight she seemed a type from the "cottagy" zones that have sprung up around old-time villages, where people banished forever behind windowpanes have nothing else to do but cast unforgiving glances at the idle tourists who pass by. But it soon became impossible to see her in this light; only in her moments of stubbornness was she "petty" or "malignant"—and she grew stubborn whenever someone concealed his true nature from her. Sorger often saw her "at the window," but her look was always one of friendly sympathy; she felt a patient love for all human frailty, but quickly turned away from anyone in whom she found no weakness. Her way of looking at people (so Sorger found out over the years) was not angry but disillusioned and offended. Once again a man who had seen himself as the lord of creation had rebuffed her. Though she found fault with her husband, she looked upon him and him alone with unflagging compassion, and sometimes Sorger saw this same look (more polite to be sure, and not quite so candid, but for that reason all the more effective) directed toward himself.

Unassuming, awkward and slow in everything she did—others would be frantically waiting for her, while she was still absorbed in something they had begun together—she was nevertheless the exemplary one of the two, and it was only through her that the husband could be recognized as a person in his own right. This (to his own chagrin) mediocre, often impersonal man had once been discovered by her who was more, and even now it was only her presence that gave him a character of his own. His wife did not flatter him, but, herself a proud woman, she could admire him so completely that he forgot his inner contradictions and, deeply moved, believed her as a man believes "one of his own people." She was also moved by him, but for the sole reason that the two of them had once been pronounced man and wife. To her, who seemed free from servitude to all current opinions, marriage remained a sacrament, in which "the dispersed senses" were gathered together and made one, in which sympathy for others was greatly enhanced and made into an inexhaustible source of life. But what made her exemplary to Sorger's mind was that, for her, "others" were not confined to her husband (though he remained the man of her life), but included everyone, even a stranger. For her, marriage had become a form which preserved her childlike openness and expanded it into a sense of unconstrained fellowship, very different from a mere adult's sense of duty. (Sorger often saw her inactive; she liked to be waited on, and the children called her "lazybones.")

There was nothing oppressive about this couple. They

showed no sign of worrying about each other. It was simply unthinkable that they would ever die. Altogether, were they anything more to Sorger than convenient next-door neighbors? (The husband sometimes took him to town with him, and the wife had often quietly attended to little household chores that he was just about to undertake.) Their relationship had grown with living together and had developed without abrupt mutations. There had never been any confidences; for instance, one had never told the other what he had thought of him at the beginning of their acquaintance. Sorger didn't even know exactly what the husband did for a living—only that he had an "office" in town. They were simply "the neighbors," and yet at heart Sorger counted them as friends; like letters, his thoughts of them often ended with good wishes, and he would not have wanted them to go out of his life.

Thus far, Sorger had written a few papers, for the most part general descriptions of a limited territory or comparative studies of similar phenomena in different parts of the world. In his projected essay "On Spatial Configurations" he would have to abandon the conventions of his science, which at the most might occasionally help him to structure his imagination.

He had long been preoccupied by the fact that in every landscape consciousness gradually creates its own configurations, even when there seem to be no delimiting features as far as the eye can see. A person who lives for some time in a region seems to find a variety of distinct configurations in what on his arrival had looked like an endless plain surface. But even in a hilly or mountainous region the articulations of which were evident at first sight, quite different configurations arose (in Sorger's experience) from those discernible in the obvious monumental features.

His point of departure was that in any countryside whatever, if only the mind has time to form ties with it, characteristic forms reveal themselves; and, above all, that these forms are created not by the immediately evident, dominant features of the landscape but by inconspicuous elements which no scientific insight can lay bare (and which can be discovered only in the course of time lived day after day in these surroundings, perhaps only through repeated stumbling over the same piece of ground, through the involuntary change of gait caused by a spongy—once swampy—bit of meadow, the change of acoustic horizon in a gully, or the suddenly modified view from the vestiges, however tiny, of a morainic mound in a wheat field).

Another thing that stimulated Sorger's scientific curiosity was that most of these localities were not the mere fantasies of an individual, but bore traditional names. Rediscovered by an individual, they proved to have long been known to the local community, to figure in land registers and geological surveys with names that were often centuries old. The question then arose: which of these unimpressive forms could achieve autonomy (as such and such "meadow" or "hill" or "glen") and take its place in the daily life of a remote settlement, or of a big city, for that matter? What colors conspired, what substances—what special features? Here Sorger could still use the approved methods, but all the rest (his motivation as well as his dream of confining himself to the pure, unexplained description of these forms) was, in a manner of speaking, the geography of childhood.

And, indeed, that had been Sorger's original idea: to

describe the shapes of fields in (his) childhood; to draw plans of very different "points of interest"; to prepare cross and longitudinal sections of all these seemingly impenetrable configurations of childhood, which in retrospect added up to the feeling of being at home—not only for children but for himself as well. He wished, in the year of freedom that was to begin for him in a few weeks, to explore such spots all over Europe, especially in regions where he himself had known them. He knew, of course, that such "play" (or whatever it might be) could be of no use, but he often dreamed of it, anticipated it with joy or trepidation, as though everything depended on it. And when it was with joy, he was conscious of a new daring, he felt almost invulnerable. He would be making a leap, possibly to nowhere, but at least away from something.

He had never thought of himself as a scientist, but at the most (occasionally) as a conscientious describer of landscapes. As such, to be sure, he sometimes felt as excited as if he had invented the landscape—and as an inventor he knew that he could not possibly be wicked or selflessly good but was, in his work, an ideal human being. But then it might occur to him that perhaps he was doing good after all, not by giving something to others but by not betraying them. And this non-betrayal was not a failure to do something; it was a strenuous activity. At times he felt that his study of landscape was a science of peace.

"To bring peace to life." On the very day of his return, he had set out with a camp chair under his arm. Beneath the afternoon sun, he walked along the shore to the bay where Earthquake Park was situated. (His walk brought it home to him that the city was on the sea.) There he sat down on a hillock to sketch a profile of the terrain.

This park had not been landscaped. It was just a piece of land that had been torn loose by the earthquake and subsequently labeled "park." At first sight, there was nothing very striking about it. A broad expanse sloping gently toward the ocean, covered sparsely with bushes rather than the pine woods usual in the region; no vestiges of houses or cars jutting out of the clay soil, which had become quite firm again, forming a humped terrain, bare except for the bushes, and crisscrossed with paths made by hikers. The old fissures had formed small valleys or gullies, which zigzagged between the humps. Sorger had the impression that the walkers he saw there emerged from the alleys of a strange clay city and quickly vanished into other hidden byways; but for a long while their voices remained audible behind the walls, a phenomenon otherwise known to him only from Europe.

Sketching made him feel warm, and the water of the bay in the background came closer. Nothing distracted his attention, and he had plenty of time. His "subject" began to answer his gaze. Himself expressionless, he waited in the landscape for a "figure" to emerge. "Only in immersion do I see what the world is."

He was sketching a tract of land which the tremor had turned upside down, raising an underground stratum to the surface; the thin root ends of the trees that had once grown there could still be seen among the new grass (a mixture of old and new sometimes brought about by avalanches). It was a small tract, yet in it different strata could clearly be seen to disperse in all directions—and in ever minute change of direction Sorger, as he sketched, could sense the overpowering force of the tremor.

He was on the track of something and his lines, at

first almost fussily close together, began to diverge; they were aiming at something beyond physical reality. With excitement, he observed how the formless mound of clay transformed itself into a grimace; and then he knew he had seen that grimace before—at the Indian woman's house, on the dance mask that was supposed to represent an earthquake.

The forehead of the mask was edged with bright-colored feathers, and these he now found again in the fringe of grass. Wooden pegs took the place of eyes; these were the roots; the nostrils were thinner wooden pegs. However, it was not directly in nature that Sorger saw the mask but in his sketch of nature; and he did not actually rediscover this particular mask; rather, he gained a sudden understanding of masks in general. This led to the idea of a series of dance steps, and in a single moment Sorger experienced the earthquake and the human earthquake dance.

"There is a possible connection," he wrote under his sketch. "Every moment of my life is connected with every other—without intermediate links. The connection is there; I need only imagine in full freedom."

The setting sun revealed two women in one of the passages between hills. The light fell on their hips, and they were so splendid and so full of life that Sorger, fired with enthusiasm, cried out: "Are you movie stars?" To which they replied: "Are you a soldier?" And from the "valley" that had seemed so far below him they immediately took a few steps up to where he was standing.

Sorger knew that if he seriously wanted these women he could have them. Here everything was possible: the first casual contact, as he was just standing there, passed through cloth and leather; and instantly the three of them were one. He was not a "seducer," simply someone who was ready for these women who had been waiting for someone like himself.

Still sketching, Sorger tried to defend himself against his sudden power, but the women interrupted him: "Let yourself go." How beautifully irresponsible these adventuresses were. And their beauty was in the right. Or did he know of any other law?

They were even capable of being serious, and with them he experienced the triumph of perfect presence of mind. "The sun went down and all roads were bathed in shadow." He didn't ask them to go with him; they followed him.

Not only was their irresponsibility right; it was magnificent. The coldness of their fingernails. The clarity of their entrails. In the warm night he saw himself stretched from continent to continent and these women ministering to him as they would not do again for a long, long time.

After his apparitions left him, he sat in the dark, gazing at the house next door. "No, you were real," he protested, drank the wine that was left in the three glasses, and wished for rain, which, lo and behold, began to splatter down among the pines.

The lighted window of the children's room formed a yellow tent in which stood a black rocking horse. Sorger went out into the tall grass and tried to get wet; but his body was so hot that the drops dried instantly. The horizon was an inky strip over the ocean: in it the closed eyelids of the strange women still trembled, and the empty rooms were now filled with their cries.

The center of the city was situated on an arm of the sea that cut deep into the land (the low apartment houses and the colonized woods on the ocean front were only excrescences); consequently, the city as such was a kind of urban satellite, impossible to localize and independent of the earth, which had become an unattainably remote past. Long, long ago something had happened there—loving encounters in lucky times, outbreaks of war when the luck was bad—which in this part of the world had ceased to stir the imagination. (The concrete world-war fortifications on the rocky part of the coast had become incomprehensible testimony to a common prehistory.) The planet seemed to have become a machine sheltered from all complications; there was still a distinction of sorts between "lucky" and "unlucky"; luck was interpreted as no more than an absence of consequences, while "bad luck" consisted in being done away with for no reason at all; both were impersonal processes, and individual destinies had simply gone out of existence.

The worst of it was that there no longer seemed to be anything for people to do. The city was inconspicuously automated, as though for all time; only here and there was there room for a few improvements. In this perfected city, day and night seemed to turn each other on and off, without the dawn and dusk of the old uncertain times; and from inside the machine (instead of the sorrowful voice of a "people") came an all-purpose answer that helped one to go on.

Toward evening the mist, usually coming from the sea, took hold of the city and the back country. It evaporated in the next day's sun, which burst like a chariot through the whirls of mist, and grew larger and larger. In an instant the day grew hot and glaring, the houses white, and the sky blue. No autumn colors on the thick leaves, which fell quickly and almost vertically from the trees, and in this "sun of reprieve"—that was Sorger's feeling about it—he moved this way and that, never without his burden (after all, he could revoke his reprieve at the next corner), and never afraid (for he was not confronting a superior outside power), but—suddenly aghast at himself—always resolutely irresponsible.

He was not idle, and yet he would never have claimed to be working; what was lacking was the daily exertion it would have cost this ordinarily sluggish man to transform himself into someone else; as long as he was doing something, he was agile, as though engaged in one job among others, or in a pastime.

In this sort of solitary occupation, he needed no one (his neighbors had ceased to be anything more than distant sounds in the woods), and (just as he wished) no one needed him. Though he knew the city well, every time he set out to go somewhere it ended in a detour, as though he had gone astray; he would "stray" into a church, to the ocean, to a nightclub. True, he never lost his sense of direction, but it made him wander instead of keeping him awake as usual. Wherever he ended up, he had got there without a decision; it was only afterwards that he thought to himself: Oh well, now I'm here.

The two cardinal points which had always meant something to Sorger were north and west. But at present the words West Coast seemed to apply not to the whole length of the continent but only to a small zone distinct from everything else, not to a vast expanse but, like the term West End, to a mere part of a city. Here too, to be sure, Sorger found the polygons of dried mud known to him from the northern bank of the river (in the networks of asphalt cracked by earthquakes or in the sun-resistant coating of certain shop windows, which in peeling seemed to form deliberate patterns); but their similarities struck him as fortuitous, derisive. This world was not "old" like the river landscape of the Far North (which went on aging visibly, and the viewer with it), but remained unsuspectingly young, thrusting Sorger back into a time when, as he now recognized, he had been no better than an obstinately frivolous consumer. "Who is the king of this town?" he heard himself asking.

Often in the Far North, and particularly in the wilds, it had pleased him, in contemplating the vastness of the country, to know that he was in a nation. But this city on the coast remained a place apart. There was no particular character in its look, no unity in its confusion. Once upon a time, even the traffic noises had spoken to the inhabitants, saying: "See what we can do together"—that at least is what the trains rattling along the coast had once seemed to say—whereas now, even if the city seemed to offer itself in the sunshine, there was no other sound than the tooting of foghorns in the still-opaque bend of the bay. Of course there were houses and cars, resplendent as only luxury items can be, but there was nothing to carry the gaze farther, over land or sea, to similar people in a larger world. In the North, the distances to other points on the earth's surface had been fairy-tale numbers (in the tiniest settlement, signposts with bundles of arrows pointing in all directions indicated the distance in miles to all the world capitals), but Sorger had never felt as remote from all connection with anything as he did here. Thinking back later, he had difficulty visualizing an airplane rising above the houses or landing, but he could always see the colored paper tails of kites twisting and turning beyond the rooftops.

And yet, in passing, he often felt that someone was waiting for his sympathetic glance. When he turned away, he seemed to turn a second time as though to see into a distance which often enough was not there at all, his true purpose being to prevent people from noticing him; at other times, he would sit alone, grave and attentive, in a dark striptease joint, wishlessly daydreaming—"the man with the wineglass"—to the rhythmic movements of naked bodies. Or he would sit with other unknowns in a porno movie—"the man with the folded arms"—and recognize himself as one of the performers on the screen. He withheld all personal communication, not by lying, but by corroborating—always with a secret feeling of triumph—the many misstatements he heard people make. He kept appointments with strangers, determined to forget their faces before he had finished looking at them, and he, too, in leaving, was often asked: "What was the name again?"

Rediscovering the "thundering interior of the jukebox," Sorger converted himself into a player. Thus he became many-sided and discovered that he could be different—entirely different—anything and everything. Later, it seemed to him that all through these weeks he had understood no one but that with a gambler's instinct he had foreseen every reaction. He no longer experienced the momentary shifts between strength and weakness that ordinarily gave him a feeling of endurance; he just roamed unsteadily, accompanied by a clinking of coins, through this city, where autumn leaves figured as permanent decorations in shop displays. He was glad to have stopped passing himself off as a scientist, glad that, though he worked every day at his science, it had lost its professional character; that at last he was going through the motions of his life, as he wished, with the uncommunicative, somnambulistic gravity of a layman; averted from all, sharing his time with no one, he sometimes felt surrounded by a magical beauty.

Detached from the nation and indifferent to the self-confident world religions, the West Coast city was a festival of sects, a ballet of cryptic symbols. Here no one seemed related to anyone—but persons who chanced to be like-minded for a short time would get together and hastily hide in meeting halls. Thus one evening Sorger found himself moving down the street in a long line. Then he was standing in a spacious, darkened auditorium surrounded by "the masses," who like him were waiting for the singer, who had been a hero of their youth.

He had no great desire to go there; rather, he was fulfilling a self-evident, rather burdensome duty. Not for years had he been able to let someone else think, feel, and act for him. Now he required the guidance of forms which, unlike the final measures of songs, gave him the idea of a perpetual new beginning, something on the order of the first age-old, poetically appealing rather than coldly demonstrative literature of his science, or the formal investigations of painters, in which he could lose himself as in the music of this singer, but at the same time find himself again, strengthened by his own resources.

The singer was a short, broad-shouldered man; he seemed excessively strong and totally absent. He came out on the stage, stared at the light, and immediately began to sing. At the very first measure, the entire auditorium imitated the twining cord of the microphone, which the singer held in his hand. His voice was powerful but never loud. It didn't come from inside his chest but existed independently of him, firm yet impossible to localize. What that voice produced was not song but rather the sounds made by someone who after long, intolerable brooding suddenly lets loose. Only as a whole did each of his numbers have a tone; its elements were quick, strident, bitter, menacing, sometimes stuttering and repetitive cries of pain (never, in any case, of relief).

He never smiled. Once, with his heavy body, he jumped high into the air. Staring vacantly, he was able, with a voice which he took from outside and drove deep into himself, to tell about the people he had inside him—what he wanted most of all was to have nothing in common with anyone. He didn't sing with feeling but searched frantically for a feeling which was as puzzling to him as to anyone else.

For a long while, partly because he was accompanied only by rhythm instruments, he seemed lifeless, damned by his own machinery; but little by little the steady mechanical beat gave his voice the vibrant undertone with which, toward the end of his performance, though inwardly raging, storing up his almost vindictive disdain of the world, he broke through to a hymn that embraced his entire audience. Along with everyone else, Sorger learned what a "hymn" can be and saw this ungainly man, who resembled no one else, as a reluctant freedom singer. In earlier years he had revered him, though strictly speaking he had no right to; but now, as no more than an interested listener, he felt upraised to the singer's level. Going out into the crowded but quiet street, he wondered why he had forgotten almost all the heroes of his youth, and was glad that, body to body in the slowly moving crowd, he could still hear the singer's voice in its sounds, even in the scraping of his own shoes on the pavement.

In the end, something changed after all: the city split into two parts, both of which became steadily stranger (and Sorger with them).

Beyond the flat, narrow coastal strip and the pine woods where Sorger's house was situated, the land rose gently to a densely populated, woodless hill and then sank to the level of the narrow bay that delimited the university campus. The road leading there crossed the hill in a barely perceptible trough, which daily use had transformed into a "pass." The campus was not far from the Pacific (Sorger often walked there), and yet in time he came to feel that in crossing the little pass he was moving in and out of a mysterious gateway that held some vague meaning for him. On reaching this "summit," he would involuntarily stop still or at least cast a brief glance over his shoulder. Though lined with the usual bungalows, identical on both slopes, this pass was to Sorger an important place where a "decision" would be made (though the only striking thing about it was the fog bank which in late afternoon rolled over it like a slow-moving avalanche and descended to the center of the city).

Sometimes, when Sorger thought about the city, he saw the pass rising from it, unreal, uninhabited, and even without vegetation, sunk in the somber-gray granite of a stony mountain range; and toward the end of his stay his own person became just as unreal to him. Talking to no one, he had finally stopped talking to himself. For a time, long and short breaths had conveyed secret code messages, and he was almost relieved at the thought that he could manage without speech; it gave him a sense of perfection. Then he sensed a danger in his inner muteness—as though he were an inert object whose sound had died away forever—and he longed to have back the suffering of speech. Unreality meant that anything could happen, but he was no longer able to do anything about it. Wasn't he resisting an overwhelming power? Sorger feared the decision, because he would have no part in it. He had lost his image of himself (which ordinarily enabled him to take action); and there was no one—though he often looked around for the women from Earthquake Park—to set limits for him by touching him. He consistently did his work (preliminary notes for his projected paper), without side glances at anything else, without stopping, in a state of frenzied concentration. And the city moved away from him, as though, little by little, all the windows had been closed to him. Yet "being forgotten" had once been a pleasant thought, and "arranging to be forgotten," an art.

Far from creation, unapproachable in his pride, always running off without saying goodbye, he awaited his "punishment"; and meanwhile one of the singer's hymns ran through his head. "The day of my greatness is at hand."

The days were still warm. Like most such rooms, his workroom on the campus could also serve as living quarters. He sometimes spent the night in the lab and slept on a cot. (His house was up for sale, people were already going in and out.) Next to the microscope there was a shaving brush, and next to that a coffee maker. The lab was situated in an unusually long, one-story glass building, which in the architect's intention may have suggested a great skyscraper lying flat on a lawn. Sorger's window looked out on the aluminum wall of a shed where research animals were kept (for another science), and right behind it lay the rippling, almost always calm water of the bay.

The institute was divided lengthwise by a corridor; across from Sorger were the lecture halls, connected by double doors, which were always open when the halls were not in use, so that the eye could look from end to end of the long row of halls. To one side of Sorger was the windowless triple-locked room with filtered air where softly humming machines measured the age of rocks; to the other side, on heavy marble tables that would remain in place despite the most violent tremors, stood the seismographs, whose metal rollers ordinarily revolved slowly and quietly but could suddenly start racing with a shrill whistling sound. (One machine received sound waves from inside the earth, which produced a distant throbbing and intermittently, within the throbbing, a high, almost singing note.)

Here, too, Sorger had "his domain"; that was outside in the direction of the bay, the lawn between the aluminum shed and the lab, which (like some railway compartments) had a separate door leading into the open. Beyond it there were eucalyptus trees and, protected by a fence, a special variety of fern, one of the oldest species in existence. There was a table on the grass and beside it an iron chair.

When he had finished working, Sorger, as he often did, stayed a while doing nothing. The door to the corridor was open, and a dog ran past. Sorger called him, but the animal didn't even raise his head. Then, announced by the jangling of keys, came the campus policeman. He, too, ignored the man in the lab.

There was a typewriter on the table outside; a blank sheet of paper was in it. The sun shone through the paper, and it fluttered slightly; beside the typewriter lay an orange. Suddenly the sun had become an evening sun; orange and paper turned reddish. A stiff eucalyptus leaf clung for a moment to the back of the chair, then fell to the ground. A croaking was heard from the animal shed. Down below, crests of foam passed along the stone wall bordering the bay, not single waves, but a great flock, driven by the wind (or by a small earthquake far away) into the arm of the sea. The surface of the water remained smooth as far as the eye could see, but Sorger saw it at a slant, and thus tilted, it plunged headlong into the bay. Then the air in the foreground clouded and the fog descended in thicker and thicker layers on the crowns of the trees.

The large campus, which Sorger now left, sloped so gently in the direction of the water that the incline was discernible only in the tapering substructure of the buildings. It was a quiet neighborhood, but always seemed lively, even without the purring of the electrical buses and the sound of steps, which seemed to start up all through the day as though coming from all directions, and to die down again; and in the midst of which a male or female cough might be heard as distinctly as nowhere else in the city. The whole campus was covered with fog, not white but hazy, and of uneven density, so that here and there the sun formed almost motionless circles of light in which the grass sparkled and whatever moved through it took on color for a moment. On one of the tables an empty beer can rolled slowly forward and backward in the fall wind that was still pressing down in the fog, keeping time with the sustained but tinnily distorted strokes of the campus clock, which offered an electronic imitation of chimes. Just then a large plane with a gleaming metallic belly flew low and almost soundless over the trees.

A straight road led along the bay from the campus to the city. As far as the eye could see, cars and pedestrians were moving in the last rays of the sun, while already the upper stories of the high-rise buildings above them were bathed in gray mist.

Looking back, one should have seen the crenelated

university tower above the campus, which in the distance looked like a virgin forest; instead, there was only a great cloudy bubble, which had shot up from the ground and congealed—a dome of mist, gleaming metallically in the evening sun and, demarcated at its edges from the magnetic sky blue of the surrounding country, engulfing the whole campus.

It was already dark when Sorger stopped at the top of the pass (walking had become harder and harder for him, but his memory had not, as usual, returned); the first trembling lights appeared in the distance, and at length the city, which had almost disappeared, widened into a vast glittering ribbon. The fog had not fully dispersed but had become so thin and translucent as to be scarcely visible in the darkness.

Sorger turned to the midtown section, which unlike the residential areas hardly twinkled at all but formed a rigid luminous design, and saw himself floating along the housefronts. The place where he was standing (the "pass") became as palpable as the ground under his feet, and he sat down on a bench at a bus stop.

In the cars, which were passing in unbroken procession, the drivers were almost always alone; highlighted by the car behind, their silhouettes emerged from the darkness, and after a while the uninterrupted sequence of motionless black busts, passing singly (faceless heads surrounded by wreaths of light), formed a leisurely cavalcade despite the speed at which they were moving and the assortment of engine sounds; as if there were no drivers in the cars, but only silhouettes in identical, evenly lighted frames, unconnected with the seemingly autonomous four wheels that were carrying them through the night.

This otherwise endless, transparent procession was

punctuated here and there by the massive and opaque shuttle buses. Behind their dark-tinted panes, one could only guess at the existence of passengers. Still, an individual or a small group might become visible now and then when the spotlight was turned on above them. Then one would see not silhouettes but clearly delineated human figures, made especially distinct by the surrounding blackness. Most of the passengers thus illumined sat with their heads against the backrest and tilted slightly to one side; seen through the tinted windows, their features were reddish-yellow. These rapidly passing faces were images recalling a forgotten era of peace, an era of "sitting," "thinking," "reading," "resting" figures which provoked a shock of recognition in the eyewitness by suddenly coming very close from far away.

Then a brightly lit city bus turned into the stop, and in it Sorger saw the neighbor woman with her children. The children were talking to each other while the woman looked on in silence. He had noticed her because in the bus she had removed her hand from her forehead with almost the same gesture as he on the bench outside. On her face, he thought, there was a "touch of pain," which (as occurred to him later) he had only sensed in himself. She smiled to herself and took off her scarf as if she were at home, and in the white light her magnificent hair seemed for a moment "a kingdom of its own." He waved. When the bus started moving, she turned her head, saw him, looked at him from top to toe, but failed to recognize him. He jumped up, tapped on the window; but it was a different window with a different face, which looked back at him in surprise as the bus drove off; and then unseen, under the open night sky, Sorger blushed violently.

At first he was only confused, and in his confusion he

spoke to a woman who had got off the bus and was standing there undecided. Without looking at him, she said "No!"; and when he tried to explain, she (her face still averted) showed him her closed hand (not even a fist) and walked away, sauntered off into the darkness without him, a melody unknown to him in her body.

Much later, when Sorger was able to remember and understand that decisive moment in his life, it seemed to him that it would have sufficed to "call a halt," to "slow down" everything (his movements, thoughts, breathing), and then "nothing would have happened." But in that moment, as he followed the woman for a few steps, his only thought was: But I have money. Then the ground at his feet became as distinct as if he had fallen. Silence as after an accident, a barking of dogs. The fall was sudden; the emptiness quite unexpected. Instead of "No one knows where I am," it was now: "I no longer have anyone. Everyone else has someone."

He paced back and forth, incapable of thinking. He had thought himself indestructible. He stood still, sensing that where his projected scientific paper was concerned, he was doomed to failure; perhaps he'd be able to write it, but then no one would hear him. "No chaos!" That was all he could say: then like a rocket of speechlessness he shot out of space, which shrank and was gone.

"Space prohibited!"

The ocean became sinister, unreal, but so did the colony in the pine woods; the whole city was black, but so was every suggestion of nature. "Ye buses, take me away from here."

He paced back and forth; he stopped; he had forfeited not only his "pass" (for a moment it struck him as no more than a "hole" and then as a joke between the knuckles) but also all the spaces and places of his imagination: the table under the eucalyptus trees as well as the northern river, which, with the most poignant parting sorrow, he saw vanishing for all time behind an embankment.

The plan of his life was destroyed: there was no longer a "field"; nowhere; gone was even the possibility of orientation by the stratification of the ground under his feet. Along with the Beautiful Water, he too was drying out; he burst; his skin was pulled off; and from under the earth "the living corpse" rose up into him.

Sorger paced back and forth, conscious of having seen through himself. Hitherto his moments of self-knowledge had shaken him alive, but now, with the loss of "his" places and spaces, which had meant a secure future, he saw himself as a bungling cheat: "Your places and spaces don't exist. It's all up with you."

Who said that? What was this voice that had held him down ever since he had consciousness? For a moment he heard a buzzing inside him, as though he were his own Evil One; and saw a shapeless carcass: his soul, which, if this unceasing voice of condemnation were to be believed, was due to be separated from his body; an afterimage of the cat which he had once taken with him on an airplane and which in its terror had put on a death's-head.

A few years earlier, just after his arrival on the West Coast, Sorger had experienced an earthquake. Sitting on the edge of a swimming pool, he suddenly saw the water slant. The air was full of dust, a strange light prevailed, great mountains seemed to be moving. He felt the tremor, in fact he toppled over, but he couldn't believe it. And now, likewise, he felt that his end was near but at the same time impossible: "Me" die? How beautiful were the smell of food from the houses, the evening light, even the sound of someone spitting in the darkness.

Then, luckily, when the supreme judge went into greater detail, his voice brought up more and more refutable not to say preposterous accusations (finding fault with Sorger's name, reproaching him for not having helped to build the houses in the region, and in the end even accusing him of "failing to offer resistance" in the days of government by violence—Sorger had hardly been born at the time).

Walking back and forth, back and forth, he had gradually lulled himself to the point of saying nothing but numbers.

Then a car stopped alongside him and his neighbor's voice rang out in their common language: "Hey, neighbor." In the next moment, as Sorger got into the happy heap, he thought: "Be thanked, ye powers." He had been waiting so intensely for something that he saw the car as "revelation," and his own skull as a "dome of expectancy." Certain that he would not have found his way home by himself, he put his hand in the crook of the man's elbow. To whom had a man ever been so palpable? "Divine fellow man."

Sorger followed his neighbor to his house. He stood for a long while in the hall, as though that were a special place. As he stepped into the living room, the experience of the "threshold": he was back in the game of the world again.

He even said several times to the wife and children: "It's me." To sit at the table with them; to lift the children up (they let him); to look at the food (ineffable radiance of meat); just to be sitting under a roof. That evening Sorger basked in the joy of certainty. This was the home of a family who unassumingly lived a possible life; and he himself was part of this house where the objects were beautiful and the people innocent.

It was an evening of compliments. He said to the couple: "I cherish you"; and with the same air of almost momentous gravity (to the husband): "In Europe, I shall miss the sight of your striped cotton shirts"; while (to the wife) he praised "the natural polygonal pattern in the crust of your white bread." And he recognized himself in his politeness; that evening it fostered the idea of a "country" embodied by the polite Sorger; indeed, his name suggested the province that the bearer (and countless homonyms) hailed from; and he ended up speaking his almost forgotten dialect so naturally that no one saw anything amiss.

That evening he cast off all the stiffness of the usually rather formal guest; he propped his elbows on the table, plucked his hosts by the sleeve, and studied their faces with candid familiarity. Unable to be alone for a single moment, he followed his hosts all over the house—the husband to the cellar, the children to their room, the wife to the kitchen. The beauty of the threshold! He poured the drinks, he put the children to bed; they told him their most private secrets, things unknown to their parents. Later, while talking, he paced the living-room floor, as if he were the master of the house. "You're so far away," he'd say to his hosts, and ask them to move closer. Provided he took (sole) responsibility for every sentence he addressed to them—keeping his compulsive logorrhea under control—it would help him to make his peace with the human world. With every word that Sorger (with difficulty) uttered that evening (Shape your words slowly, he thought), he gained admittance to this house, to its people—to its "country" (Only if I create the form, shall I be with these people), and he who had lost his large spaces immersed himself studiously in the smallest ones.

In the house, the night was bright; there was a full moon. The children were playing in their room. In the clear light of that evening, where everything settled down in a new stratum of space, the "melancholy gambler" (this formula, he felt sure, was the key to his existence, and not only to this moment of it) saw the face of the woman across from him as he had never before seen any face.

He started—though not for the first time—by noticing her hair; he delighted in its sheer abundance, in her curls, in the line of her part. Little by little the details of her face opened up to him: their beauty was beyond question, but now they became dramatic: one feature guided his eye (he had no desire to be anything more than an eye) to the next. This is happening for my benefit, he thought. But he was not staring at the woman; his gaze, rather, put the finishing touch to his politeness, for in perceiving her he became invisible, converted into a mere human presence. Again he saw himself transformed into a "receiver," as when he had observed the polygonal pattern in the mud of the riverbank. But here, instead of concentrating his powers, he managed, in reconstituting the woman's face, to expend every last one of the energies he found there, until at length the ability to assimilate another person (hitherto dependent on sympathy and confined to particular individuals) became in itself an all-embracing new energy: at present he had no other, but that sufficed.

The first thing to come alive for him in that face was the slightly protruding upper lip, which, by casting a faint shadow on the closed mouth, made it seem open: in any case, Sorger saw it, not as mute, but as prepared to speak. Without fuss or pretense those lips would find the right words to say to someone, and even when done speaking, they would remain eloquent for that person. There was nothing unusual about her cheeks (in inventing this face, his unreservedly receptive glance found nothing more that was striking in it) except that they seemed firm, thus giving Sorger a momentary impression of spaciousness, which he could not hold fast but had to conjure up over and over again. And how helpful were the eyes (they too, with nothing unusual about them, solely as a living fact), darkened by shadow and all-understanding in their mere "darkness"; and how needful of protection the mere fact of the high forehead (calling upon him to act and bring the drama to its conclusion), this sensitively shimmering, one might have said bonelessly vulnerable, ever-luminous curvature. At length Sorger became something more than a self-forgetful beholder of happenings in someone else's face; an overpoweringly gentle manipulation had incorporated his limited personal life into the face of mankind, in whose openness it would go on forever.

All the while, he had been sitting at the table playing chess with the husband, while the wife was reading. Now he stood up and wandered about the house, removing himself from the face, which nevertheless remained close to him. And then from a distance, in the increasing shadow under the lamplight, this woman (just as the people in the darkened shuttle buses had appeared to him as embodiments of "sleeping" or "waking") became a "contemporary," an impression substantiated by the slight double chin resulting from the lowering of her head: "We come from the same region." On the throat a small circle of light: "Strong enough for two"; and though her hand seemed to hover in midair, one finger of it rested firmly on her book: "As down to earth as you."

Sorger resumed his place at the table and, instead of moving his chessman, began to speak. Himself almost invisible, he looked into the faces of the others, as though already separated from them, not by a leap, but by a very gradual lapse of time, which (as he spoke) carried him away, and which, as he told his story, he experienced as an unchangingly gentle contact; and thus, while circumspectly talking himself free, he thought: What I have thought to myself at any time is nothing; I am only what I have succeeded in saying to you.

For another little while the children's laughter in the next room; then the distant cry of gulls. By then Sorger was calm enough to tell them quite simply how space had been "taken away" on his imaginary "pass." "Suddenly one of my faculties failed me, I lost my special sense for earth forms. From one minute to the next, my forms ceased to be namable or even worth naming." At that point he managed to raise his voice and say: "Listen to me. I don't want to perish. At the moment of losing all that, I longed to return, not only to a country, not only to a certain region, but to the house where I was born. And yet I wanted to go on living abroad, in the company of a few people who are not too close to me. I know I'm not a scoundrel. I don't want to be an outsider. I see myself walking in the midst of the crowd, and I believe I am just. I have friendly dreams, even about people who have wished me dead, and I often feel the strength for lasting reconciliation. Is it presumptuous of me to want harmony, synthesis, and serenity? Are completion and perfection an obsession with me? I regard it as a duty to become a better man, a better myself. I would like to be good. Sometimes I feel the need to be wicked, and then I am pursued by the thought of punishment; but then again I feel the need of eternal purity. Today I thought of salvation, but it wasn't God that came to mind, it was culture. I have no culture; I shall continue to have no culture as long as I am incapable of crying out; as long as I whimper my complaint instead of shouting it out loud. I don't want to languish with my grievances, I want to be mighty in my outcries. My cry is: I need you! But whom am I talking to? I must find my fellows. But who is my fellow? In what country? In what time? I need the certainty of being myself and being responsible for others. I am capable of living! I feel the power to Say how it Is; yet I would like to be nothing at all and to say nothing at all: to be known to everyone and no one; pervasively Alive. Yes, at times I feel entitled to a cosmos. And my time is Now; now is Our Time. I therefore lay claim to the world and to this century—because it is my world and my century."

Sorger saw himself move his head like a ludicrous but proud animal (and at the same time pump his elbows in a pathetic attempt to flap his wings). After his long speech he craved something sweet, and the lady of the house brought him a piece of strudel. He wanted music to go with it, and then he asked his neighbors to tell him their story. Probably to show they were on his side, they began with their mishaps, but soon dropped that, and finally—serene narrative gradually turning into excited dialogue, each playing his part and frequently interrupting the other—told him how they had come together. Sorger thanked them for the "hot meal" and added: "Please don't forget me."

Afterwards, as he was leaving (with nothing particular in mind, he took the shortest way through the woods to the beach), it occurred to him that they had laughed at his last words, as though to ridicule the very idea. And so he added, speaking to himself: "I would like to sit under your lampshade soon again."

The night was warm, without fog. While still among the trees, he enjoyed the feel of the sea sand under his feet. Swarms of leaves blew through the pine woods, clung to the grass as to a wire fence, and turned out to be dried seaweed. A bicycle sound in the sand was made by a running dog. The wind roared in the stunted pines as in a forest of tall trees. Sorger had a sensation of air on his face, as though he had rediscovered reality—the air of happiness.

Suddenly, as he rounded a jutting dune (it might have been a street corner), the ocean roared up at him in a white wave. The spray, flung high into the night sky, seemed for a moment to stand still and only then, mingling with new, lighter-colored foam, fell to the ground in brownish flakes. A moment later the ocean, along with the moon and the wave-skimming gulls, resumed its customary aspect; its crashing and pounding made Sorger think of a factory as he walked along. He didn't so much as glance at the water, but looked only at his feet, which plodded over the sand far below him, as though in bird's-eye view. "Shut the doors of your senses."

He began to run; closing his eyes, he ran for a while; then, still with closed eyes, he walked more and more slowly. A streetcar passed through the surf with an old-fashioned screeching of rails. As Sorger went on, the ocean sound changed from the clatter of an old-time farm wagon to the noises of his past. Boards were being unloaded in a thudding, screeching sawmill; heedless moving men were handling heavy furniture. The sounds were irregular, broken now and then by an almost blissful silence, evidently meant to last, within which one could detect only the sounds of a peaceful household, milk rising to a boil, boiling water, the click of knitting needles. But then the handle of a bucket fell off. (As though the sea could be gathered in a saucepan.) Then someone dove into a swimming pool, and someone's face was slapped. Amid the rising street noise, a muffled shot was heard, and a body hit the ground. Cans of milk were loaded onto a platform. A brief clinking of censers, then the screams of the wounded. The rumbling of tanks; a crashing and splintering; a moment of war. Then the stillness of peace; or was it? Sorger opened his eyes, and before them an antique colonnade stretched across the sea into the horizon.

Behind the last column the moon was going down, and for a brief moment there was a moonset sky, a cloud field lit from below, the color of ironstone; and then the whole sky was black, except for the stars vaguely twinkling in the sea mist.

Sorger felt the ocean at the back of his head, which became a large, very cold place. The crests of foam were snow-covered mountain ranges. The air brought him a smell of fire, and for the first time on the coast he had a feeling of autumn. Ocean, autumn, and colonnade: the world was growing old again. There he stood as though the season were his destination. His body became perceptible through the threefold dividing line between earth, water, and air, and he experienced something he had not known for a long time, desire in the form of an enormous longing to escape from his own heart and lungs; while at the same time he looked forward to his bed.

He hurried back to his house. In the neighbors' empty bedroom the bedside lamps had been on since early evening. Husband and wife were sitting in the half-darkened living room; the husband was holding his wife's fingers. The river of return; in the warmth of Sorger's bloodstream, the Indian woman, quivering smoothness, approached. A tiredness came over him in which he wanted only to lie in the dark and listen. A ticking clock sounded like a cat scratching its neck; and then the fabled black-and-white beast filled the countryside with its purring.

Sorger lay down and, while the beam of the Land's End lighthouse flashed regularly into the room, waited without impatience for the ideas that come with dreams. He even ventured to think of his child, something he had been unable to do in all these years; at the first attempt, his head had turned to stone. Now only his face felt heavy; it had a hot clenched fist in it. But his self-pity didn't trouble him; for in it he sensed a desire for a faith that would give him form and enable him to think for more than brief moments of what he loved. "When I see her again, I shall worship her."

Gratefully he pulled up the blanket. Women and children were what made him real. In his sleep, a foam-born woman arose out of the sea and lay down with him. All night they lay side by side, eye to eye, mouth to mouth.

"A few sunrises later" (that indeed is the impression these last few days on the West Coast made on him) Sorger saw himself packing his suitcase in the glow of a still-autumnal morning. He was about to leave for Europe. The house was almost empty, the curtains and carpets were gone; one room still had a wooden table and a folding chair in it, the other just the bed, which had been moved catty-cornered. Sorger had thrown many, and given a few, things away; into his suitcase, along with the carefully stacked photograph albums and notebooks of the last few years, went the few objects of daily use that were dear to him. He began to dress for the trip: a linen shirt frayed with age, which fitted soothingly around his wrists; a solemn-blue "European" worsted suit, the trousers of which clung slightly at the knees; and thin woolen socks, which warmed him pleasantly from bottom to top; and his laced boots from the North. Looking down, he made a speech of thanksgiving to his faithful garments.

The air was fresh and clear: "A fine morning, an American morning." The sun shone on the floor of the emptied room as in the lounge of a ship, and the passenger stood beside his packed suitcase, reading his last mail and casting an occasional look at the house next door, where there was movement in every room. The children were getting ready for school, the husband for the office. With all the hectic excitement, there were moments of perfect calm: the husband bent over the papers he had spread out on a slanting desk like a missal; his wife sipped tea with an elegance that was almost grotesque; and the children, with their school bags already on their backs, stood hypnotized by a top that was spinning on the table.

Lauffer wrote that the river was frozen, that at first he had worn a woolen helmet but had then taken to going about with his shirt unbuttoned like the Indians; that his paper was "amazing" him "more and more" (that he felt obliged to explore every bypath that presented itself, and invariably it stretched out ad infinitum), that he saw himself engaged in a kind of ideal competition with Sorger, since Sorger's aim was to get away from matter and his to increase and enhance it; that his problem, accordingly, was too much "speech," while Sorger was threatened with "speechlessness"; and finally, that the cat was becoming "increasingly regal and unapproachable" and would soon be uttering its first word.

Clouds, which Sorger did not look up at, drifted along with the prospective traveler as he sat at the table reading a book; the crowns of the pine trees swayed as if they were already somewhere else. Meanwhile, behind his back, people who had been sent by an agency strolled about inspecting the house that was up for sale. Not once did he look around at them.

Next door, only the neighbor woman was moving about. Some white cloths draped over her arm shone bright when she passed the spots that were in sunlight. Once she saw him and waved with a carefree, untroubled movement, as though he were already far away; and then she seemed to forget him and herself in a game that she played from room to room.

He was reading a Roman naturalist's two-thousand-year-old attempt to explain the world, the language of which retained the "mild, transitional" quality of a poem. "Therefore solid matter can be eternal, whereas other forms of matter disintegrate."

Three /

The Law

In the plane a deeper roar, remote from death. This was also a flight inside himself. How easy it was to speak; how easy life was altogether. An instantaneous idea: "Something new is beginning in me." The West Coast city on its peninsula receded quickly.

Sorger was flying with the time, and with it, little by little, came daydreams "as changing as the faces of the moon." It was snowing when the plane put down at Mile-High City on the eastern slope of the Rockies. Though booked through, Sorger took his suitcase, left the plane, and boarded an already overcrowded bus which carried him over a snowy highway, through a deserted country-side where he had never been before.

The flakes touched the windshield lightly and flew away. Sorger's radiant daydreams went deeper and deeper. To drive beyond his inner limits: that was his way of thinking of others. He didn't conjure them up explicitly, they came to mind as he gave his imagination free rein.

In the distance, a snow-covered horse stood motionless beside a dead willow tree, the slanting trunk of which had sunk deep into the ground. Schoolchildren pulled up the zippers of their parkas as they got out of the bus; snow blew in through the open door and even on warm hands took a moment to melt. After that, the bus was full of adult silence.

Sorger's daydream produced a face with round, wide-set eyes, from which wrinkles emanated like rays. Now he was sure; he would stop for the night in the mountain village where the bus was going, and surprise his old schoolmate, who was a skiing instructor there.

He remembered him as he had seen him most recently, one summer on the West Coast: the nakedness of his face, with its open mouth as in his schooldays, and its lower lip, which he kept thrusting forward even when he was not talking (but which, when he was talking, spewed words like a milling machine).

Even when at rest, the skiing instructor looked strained, as though trying to get a better grasp of something. He spoke too loudly, but never quite distinctly. Often his speech consisted entirely of exclamations, and then there was a note of fear in his voice. If he trusted you, he would assail you with "ultimate questions" and expect categorical answers. If someone tried seriously to give him such answers, the proud skiing instructor would become that person's servant; and in the summer months, when he was without work, he visited not his "friends" but his "masters" and was only too glad to help them with their household chores. He had no children and had been waiting for years for the woman of his life (whom he could describe with precision); but even the women who at first liked him were soon put off by his weirdness.

In his daydream, Sorger saw the skiing instructor as a man despised for his innocence, and imagined how he would embrace him at their meeting; he saw the man's thick neck, his wide silver belt, and his thin legs between which he always hid his hands when he sat down. Dusk fell on the moving bus, the skiing instructor's Adam's apple bobbed up and down, bunches of dry grass rolled over the snow, and parched corn leaves stood horizontal in the wind.

The bus drove through an area where no snow had yet fallen, nor did anything else seem to be happening there. Later it began to snow, more quietly and with larger flakes. The mountains with their drainage ditches disappeared. Now nothing could be seen but the fallow fields nearby and a solitary herd of buffalo, breathing steam from their nostrils and nibbling at yellowish blades of grass; white fountains rose from the cars, which passed slowly as though engaged in some solemn journey, and clods of muddy snow rolled after their rear wheels. The only human forms on the road were occasional joggers; after a while it seemed to Sorger that they must be in training for a world war.

There were chunks of snow on the floor of the hotel elevator. The hotel was built in the style of an Alpine inn, with a wooden balcony, painted window frames, and a sundial. In his paneled room, with the lights of the great plain far below him, Sorger picked up the newspaper, the name of which was framed in a sketch of the region's mountain peaks. He leafed through it, and almost immediately his eye fell on the skiing instructor's name. He read the item through; it was an obituary. Without thinking, he read the names that followed, and heard a roaring from the shower.

The obituary had been put in by the skiing school. It described him as a "staff member of long standing"; apart from that, it supplied only the address and the hours of the undertaking establishment, here referred to as a "chapel."

Sorger went at once to the chapel, which had long

since closed for the night. Sorger looked through the lace curtains of the gableless row house into the lighted empty rooms: lamps with fabric shades on dark little tables; on the one larger table, a glass ashtray; beside it, an ivory-white telephone. The building was three stories high and had an elevator; the elevator, also lit, was on the ground floor, empty. The wide double door of the building had no handle on the outside. It was a cold, windy evening. The windshield wipers on the passing cars scraped like shovels. Sorger's steps in the snow brought back the sound of meadow grass being mowed. Then he heard nasal Western voices and knew where he was.

He went back to the hotel, his skin numb from the snow. The bones of his face ached. He drank and made merry. He held his wineglass in both hands like a bowl and bared his teeth.

That night he dreamed of the dead man. They were walking together in the country. But then the skiing instructor became shapeless and vanished, and Sorger was alone when he woke up. He saw the deceased in a blue apron; his eyes were sealed with shiny black lacquer. Then Sorger had wonderfully senseless thoughts and fell asleep again, filled with longing for an invented world that would permeate the real world and incorporate it in one vast invention.

In the morning, the sun shone on an empty wooden clock case standing in one corner of the room. Sorger visited the corpse in the mortuary. The skiing instructor lay like a doll in his coffin. The folds of his eyelids extended to his temples; one eye, which was not entirely closed, glistened. He was wearing the woolen cap in which he had almost always been seen, with the inscription: Heavenly Valley; a turquoise amulet hung from his neck.

Sorger stood on the sidewalk outside the building. The porter, in a uniform with brass buttons, was walking back and forth outside the gate; all over the street his discarded cigarette butts were smoking. Over his head hung an American flag; beside it the windblown shoots of a dark-green trailing plant flapped against the wall. A large drum of cable was rolled past. Clearly delineated clouds were piled on other, vaporous clouds, near and at the same time far.

Outside the village, Sorger took a funicular that went up into the mountains. The car swayed as people got in, their ski boots crackled underfoot like burning faggots. Still, there were good faces in this crowd. Out in the snow, children were running around; when they fell, they picked themselves up and ran on, moving like cheerful little wheels.

When he arrived at the top, Sorger attached himself to a group of strangers for no other reason than that they were all wearing light-colored fur coats; but after a while he went on alone. No one had been there since the snowfall. The air was warm but the snow was not melting. It was deep but so powdery that the ground could be seen here and there.

Sorger climbed until there was nothing to be heard. After crossing a ridge, he saw the Rockies proper; they were a dull reddish-yellow, and beyond them a white cloud bank was drifting past. He ran up the slope until his face was plastered with pine needles, then stopped as though he had come to a forbidden precinct. No bird song; only the still-distant Indian shapes of the mountaintops. Ahead of him, at the edge of a deep gully, stood a solitary mountain pine; beside it scrub oak, with snowflakes whirling between the dry leaves. Though there was nothing whatever to be seen, the tree gave off a sound: a faint but distinct whirring, which went on for a while and started up again after a silence. And then the whirring was heard for the third time, not from the same tree, but from another solitary pine far down in the gully. In the next moment, plunging vertically, a flock of shrill, white-bellied birds landed on both trees.

Sorger stood in the deep snow as in an extra pair of boots and looked down into the great, yellow-misty plain, which from the foot of the mountains extended eastward for thousands of miles. In this landscape there would never be a war. He washed his face in the snow and began to whistle monotonously. He put snow in his mouth, but only whistled the louder. He coughed and he sobbed. Then he bowed his head and grieved for the dead man (and the other dead).

When he looked up, he had the impression that the dead were laughing uproariously at him. He laughed with them. The present blazed and the past glittered. The thought of not-being-around-anymore gave him profound pleasure. He had a vision of the thicket on the riverbank. "No ecstasy!" (Never again.) To conjure up ecstasy, he looked about for a landmark. In the snow-covered, sunlit gully he distinguished a shimmering furrow—the most beautiful woman he had ever seen. Involuntarily he cried out, and a faint echo came back at him from a bush. He was overcome with melancholy and lust.

Again, on the way back to Mile-High City, bunches of hard grass rolling over the frozen snow. A single bush cast an enormous shadow on the bare plain. Fervid expectation. But even if nothing happened, that would be what he expected. That would enable him to play a game: everything is (perfectly) possible, and just as an earthquake gave rise to a human dance, meaningless being-alive engendered a meaningful game.

Was there no one else in the plane that carried you farther east that night? Your row of seats was empty, and the backrests in front of you were upright in the dim light reflected from the roof of the cabin. —The even hum in the deep, half-darkened cavern provided a background music that preserved the passenger's connection with the past few hours. He thought of "his people" and made plans to see them soon; he was determined never to be late again. The dead skiing instructor brought the members of Sorger's own family alive for him. Once upon a time he had felt responsible for his brother and sister. There had been a bond between them that linked them all in a circle. Of late they had had little opportunity for a language in common (they hadn't lost it, but it had become a kind of memory exercise that they just reeled off). Brother and sister had embraced for the first time at the death of their parents. That, at least, was how it looked to the daydreamer, who saw the lights of the towns below him as paths in a cemetery and then as constellations. Then they had fallen silent for many years, at first in indifference, then in hostility. Each regarded the others as lost. When his brother and sister came to Sorger's mind, it was in the form of a sudden death notice (and they too, he felt sure, expected nothing more of their brother than the news of his death). True, they often appeared in his dreams, sometimes talking to each other as they had never done in reality; but more often they were malignant corpses, lying around the house where they were born, impossible to get rid of. Because they had never become explicit enemies, there was no possibility of reconciliation.

It didn't even occur to Sorger that his relations with them might become "as before." He wanted only to be as clear as he was now that the outside world had become a living dynamic space behind his forehead—then perhaps different social forms would be self-evident. After that, he saw the other villagers, most of whom he had hitherto regarded as a group of people malevolently looking forward to his death; and now he knew that the opposite was true—they had always sided with him in spite of his going away; they had thought he was in the right.

He wrote mental letters to his brother and sister and added friendly insults. Question: "Aren't these plans too contrived?" And the self-assured answer: "I'll just have to make them come true."

The sound of the plane changed. The traveler's exhilaration left him; and he went on speaking in silence (putting down each word in his thoughts, as though writing it): "What of it? If there is no universal law for me, I shall gradually give myself a personal law that I shall have to observe. Before the day is out, I shall frame its first article."

Clouds puffed past the window, and then at the edge of his field of vision the City of Cities emerged from the gray of dawn like a field burned over and still dimly glowing here and there, while the plane circled over the vacant stormy ocean and the sun rose above the sea mist. When the wheels touched down, the lights went on in the cabin and some of the passengers clapped their hands. In applause for the landing or for the city? And then it came to Sorger that he had not been traveling alone.

The man ahead of him on the way out looked familiar. The man turned around, both nodded, and only then did they realize that they were unknown to each other.

At the exit the stranger stopped Sorger, made a slight bow, and invited him to share a cab with him. It turned out that they came from the same country. "Actually, I was intending to go straight on to Europe," said Sorger. But then he followed the man as if that were a part of his law. In the cab, he looked up at the relaxed faces in the buses alongside, and thought: Actually, I'd rather have . . . The man looked him in the eye: "Forgive me. Have you a little time for me? I need your goodwill. You look so available."

They parted company in midtown, surrounded on all sides by panting joggers, and arranged to meet again later. In attempting to visualize the man, Sorger, who had not had enough sleep, saw only a half-eaten apple in the man's hand—seeds glistened on the core.

As a rule, Sorger had to "work" himself into a new place; it was some time before he felt at home there. But in the megalopolitan hotel he immediately felt sheltered. His corner room in the tapering tower-like edifice had two windows, one facing west, the other south. Westward, the eye flew to the reservoir in the great mid-city park and rested there—southward, it passed over an intricate pattern of rooftops, below which the network of streets remained invisible, and leapt straight to the horizon, which was barred from end to end by giant office buildings, and it was as though the true metropolis began only with this distant blue. The varicolored area of flat-roofed apartment houses between Sorger and the barrier seemed a region apart, from which the cars, honking their horns but hidden in the chasm-like streets, seemed much farther removed than the numerous planes roaring overhead. Turning away from the west window and the reservoir, Sorger, in an instantaneous dream, saw this self-contained system as a shut-down factory. Gulls skimmed the light-gray surface of the reservoir; in the other window appeared the two spires of a cathedral, not nearly as high as the surrounding high-rise buildings, and Sorger felt his fatigue, which only a moment before had bordered on exhaustion, metamorphosed into self-mastery and strength. He saw the stranger's face distinctly: the cheeks looked as if all their muscles had been knotted together, a strand of hair cut across his forehead and seemed prolonged by the notch of his lower lip; he heard his voice abruptly rising and falling as though he were looking for the right pitch. The severe lines of the high-rise buildings, the glitter of the planes, the wailing of the police sirens—Sorger had the impression that a lasso had been thrown: the whole city was being hoisted into his room.

He was staying at a so-called residential hotel. Many of the guests lived there for a quite a while, often with their families. Forgetting his need for sleep, he rode down to the lobby under the auspices of an elevator man in a braided uniform. At every floor, grownups got in, accompanied by children (with flexed knees), all talking at once in different languages. By the end of the protracted descent Sorger had become "one of the elevator crowd" and as such he bounced out into the street.

He had time for detours. As he made his way in the sunlight, his sleepy grogginess turned to erotic self-assurance. Was it his fatigue which, more intensely at each detour, made many places seem like repetitions, separated by wide, flashing expanses?

By way of getting ready for the stranger, he walked slowly into the park and stopped, facing one of the granite boulders which jut out of the grass like the wing tips of buried airplanes. Looking up, he saw people passing through a wide, still-shady hollow between two hills, like Indians in the Far North; here and there in this unbroken procession he saw reminders of his dead. Not because of similarities; it sufficed to immerse himself in the big-city crowds as they moved this way and that, to dwell on an insignificant gesture, the outline of a cheek, a rapid glance, a headband, and quite naturally, without dream or evocation, the departed would enter into the picture, but without obstructing the general movement (as often happens in dreams); on the contrary, giving it new life. Unlike any other landscape, the Big City swept "his people" along in its movement, not only the living, but the resurrected dead as well.

Seeing his dead walking sprightly in the crowd, the survivor involuntarily rubbed his hands against the grooves in the granite, for joy at his new understanding of time, which until then he had thought of as purely and simply hostile. Here time no longer meant loneliness and death, but reunion and shelter; and, for the length of one lucid moment (when would it slip away?), he conceived of time as a "God" who was "good."

Yes, he had the word, and time became a light in the middle of the city, shining in the glass globe of a park lamp lit up by the morning sun. The thick, cloudy, dusty glass, containing the shadow of an electric light bulb enlarged by the sun, flared up in the city mist and led his gaze onward to running dogs, from these to a bright-colored pile of clothes in the fork of a tree, and from these to the children playing ball down below and the still shadowy-dark ball at their feet.

Like primeval man, he moved on to partake elsewhere of the daylight that was beginning anew on every object. The eyeball of a man coming toward him, a shimmering metal box, and the pale moon seemed joined into a triangle. Too much light. Alone and released from his ties with the disciplined gravity of natural forms, how was he to avoid the folly and incoherence of ecstasy?

He went into a coffee shop and read the paper. It had a weather map on which the various regions were indicated only by "Bitter cold," "Snow showers," "Mild," "Foggy, then sunny." As he immersed himself in the map, amid the clatter of china and the soft radio music, these coalesced to form a cozy late-autumn continent in whose biggest city he was "drinking coffee" and "reading the paper" like a citizen of long standing. And here, as he glanced at the sunlit buses outside (the passengers sitting on benches placed lengthwise were visible only from behind as glossy hairdos in different colors), Sorger, more confident of the future, experienced his second return to the Western world. And with that the place in which he then happened to be began to take on importance.

The coffee shop was very narrow, with a single row of seats, which led deep into a kind of tunnel. (At the end of the tunnel a luminous sign read: "Women / Water.") The subway entrance was directly outside the front window, and some of the people passing horizontally on the street would suddenly vanish down the stairs, moving obliquely out of the picture, while others rose head first into the rectangle of the window.

Behind Sorger were Big City voices, not always free from accent, but even when there was an accent, so very self-assured. He was struck by the number of children, which here, of all places, seemed surprising. A child came in and wanted to buy something they didn't have. Sorger heard the child sigh. At that moment someone at the cash desk behind Sorger was making out a check in a loud voice. As he said the date (all sounds died away, only the radio music went softly on and the steam from the coffee machine seemed to move through the date), a general breathlessness set in and time became increasingly active (for a brief instant Sorger saw an enormous silhouette over a river landscape) and irradiated the room with a warming wave of light.

For all this the eyewitness had only the words "century" and "peacetime"; he saw calendar leaves falling as in a silent film. The goddess Time did not remove the coffee shop, which suddenly began to glitter along with the tin ashtrays and sugar bowls (which became gold and silver), from that day's date, but connected it with the dates of past days, until the room (becoming not strange but more and more homelike) encompassed all those inventions, discoveries, sounds, images, and forms down through the centuries which make for a possibility of humanity.

All those present breathed as one. Light became matter, and the present became history; at first painfully convulsed (for this moment there was no language), then calm and matter-of-fact, Sorger wrote, to give the force of law to what he had seen, before it vanished: "What I am here experiencing must not pass away. This is a law-giving moment; absolving me of my transgression, for which I alone was responsible and which has weighed on me ever since, it puts me, as an individual capable of participating only by chance, under obligation to intervene as consistently as possible. At the same time, it is my historic moment: I have learned (yes, I am still capable of learning) that history is not a mere sequence of evils, which someone like me can do nothing but despise—but has also, from time immemorial, been a peace-fostering *form* that can be perpetuated by anyone (including me). I have just found out that I, hitherto a mere witness (though sometimes thinking myself completely into others), belonged to this history of forms, and that, along with the people in this coffee shop and those passing by outside, I, inspired with new life, am actually playing a part in it. Thus the night of this century, during which I searched my face obsessively for the features of a despot or a conqueror, has ended for me. My history (our history, friends) shall become bright, just as this moment has been bright—up until now, it could not even begin; conscious of our guilt, yet giving allegiance to no one, not even to others conscious of their guilt, we were unable to vibrate in harmony with the peaceful history of mankind; our formlessness only engendered new guilt. For the first time I have just seen my century in the light of day, open to other centuries, and I had no objection to living at the present time. I was even glad to be the contemporary of you contemporaries, and to be a citizen of the earth among others; and I was sustained (beyond all hope) by an exultant feeling not of my immortality but of man's. I believe in this moment; in writing it down; *I make it my law.* I declare myself responsible for my future, I long for eternal reason and will never again be alone. So be it."

Sorger stared at himself in the coffee-shop mirror, empty, exhausted, petrified, as though emerging from the depth of the centuries; on that day he was moved by his own face.

Looking up, he was not at all surprised to see, in the throng of people outside, the two women he had met in Earthquake Park on the West Coast. He smiled, and after gracefully giving him their sign, the two women vanished into the subway: they would often meet again.

Then a strange transformation occurred: the crowd outside the window began to move faster and faster, became more dense, face pressed against face, and at length—each individual in hurrying past almost frighteningly showing all his characteristics—filled the whole street. Thousands of eyes came glowing toward him. The image reeled and he knew that he had once again slept for a few moments. He felt the warm blood in his arms as a bond with his forebears, and looked forward to seeing the man from the plane: "Shall I recognize you? And what will you tell me?"

Still in the coffee shop, Sorger, in observing the scratched tabletop, found his way back to "his" earth forms. As he sat there in the low, dark, ground-floor room as though walled off from the towering Big City on all sides of him, a shimmer of the frozen river emerged from the wintry night; the shuttle buses crossed the newly regenerated West Coast pass and drove into the eastern morning light as over a continental divide, and behind them, clearly visible in the rising mist, the ocean waves rose and fell. Not only the bruised tabletop but also the floor of the coffee shop imitated the surface of the earth. Near the cash desk it formed a slight hollow, and for a terrifying moment Sorger felt that the ground was gone from under his feet, as though the floorboards had been laid on the bare, unleveled earth; and through this irregularity of the room the city became, in its very depths, a living and powerful natural organism. Going out into the street, where the humped sidewalk extended the coffee-shop floor, Sorger seemed to inhale the whole rocky island in one breath. Moving on the concrete slabs of the sidewalk intensified his conquest of space and gave it permanence. He experienced the subsoil of the city, which only a short while before had risen into the air from lifeless pavement. Now the buildings no longer seemed to have been plunked down in the landscape, they had become an integral part of it, as though the skyscrapers were really at home on this rocky island. Indeed, the city gradually became a village-like settlement in which small houses with bay windows stood side by side with high-rise buildings. A woman with a polka-dot scarf on her head, carrying a loaf of bread in a string bag, was waiting for the bus, holding by the hand a child with a school bag. The summer lived on in a brick sunk deep into the tar, and the rain-filled holes in the asphalt foreshadowed the rural winter with its vast expanses of ice.

At one point Sorger stopped among towering buildings in the awareness of being at the geographical summit of New York. There he saw a locust tree, losing not only its leaves but whole branches as well in the mountain wind.

In the city on the West Coast, Sorger had never been on his way to see anyone; now he had this man from the plane, and he was going to see him. The stranger's name was Esch, and again he looked at Sorger as unswervingly as that morning in the cab, as if he had had Sorger's face before him throughout his absence.

They sat in a spacious restaurant, at first almost alone, with many empty tables around them, but these were soon occupied by the swarm of diners who swept into the restaurant with the coming of night. All evening the subway shook the ground under them. They were sitting in a corner booth, and when they raised their heads, they came into contact with the leaves of a potted rubber tree. The far end of the room was white with steam from the kitchen; sometimes the dishes moved like paddle wheels.

At first sight, the stranger's lips were very pale, but after a while Sorger stopped noticing them. Much of the time, even in speaking, eating, and drinking, the stranger held his head propped on one hand. He said (repeatedly sticking his tongue out): "You mustn't imagine that I want to ask you questions. I don't want to get acquainted with you. When I thought about our appointment during the day, I regretted my impulse. I toyed with the thought of not showing up—and I'm certain it was the same with you."

Involuntarily, Sorger hung his head. When he looked up, it seemed to him for an eerie moment that he was looking into his own wide-open eyes; only then did he realize that the stranger was crying. At the same time, the color of those eyes became a thing apart (as did his bare forehead). The two men moved deeper into the booth, until no one else could see them. The stranger asked Sorger for a handkerchief, blew his nose, and said: "Listen to me for a while." He spoke of "business failure," "inability to compete," "wife and children," "money," and the "impossibility of returning to Europe." He summed up his story in three outcries: "I know nothing!" "All I can do is clench my fist." And in the end, simply: "Poor me!"

Sorger summoned up his power, transformed himself (with difficulty) into the booth where they were sitting, and surrounded his chance acquaintance, who shook his head in surprise at the state he had got into and from time to time politely asked for (and obtained) Sorger's handkerchief. Sorger (as booth) enfolded the stranger until little by little the man's rigid torso came to life, put on the at first grotesque but then winning face of a child, and finally rubbed his arms, out of which, as he said, his "fear flew away." And then in the deep space of night Sorger felt a shudder of creation pass over him and, surprised at himself, wished to be physically united with this man, as though there were no other way of keeping him alive. But then one of those glances that want everything to be different proved sufficient, and in it the stranger was able to lean back, as it were. Later Sorger deliberately looked the other way, as though one could cure the sick world just by disregarding it for a while.

From the start he had the impression of listening to his own story—not because of any resemblance in the stories, but because in this man's words of self-accusation he recognized the voice that had often denied him, too, the right to live. But speaking from another man's mouth (and no longer a silent litany within himself), this voice did not condemn him, Sorger; it was identifiable as the absurdity which sometimes stifled others as well as himself. And so Sorger, opening the "gates of his senses" and stepping back from himself and his companion, was able to become the "laughing witness," who fitted them both into a serene order; though moved by the stranger's misfortune, he felt, as he listened and watched him, the carefree pleasure of a sympathetic audience. From time to time, he even smiled, and noticing his smile, the still hesitant Esch took heart and spoke freely.

To describe his despair, Esch displayed it; not that he acted it out; he merely commanded the only fitting gestures and words for it and had the presence of mind to use them at the right moment. Portraying himself, fervent and at the same time laconic, he pictured his misfortune and became the prophet of truth; in this way (with Sorger as the indispensable opposite), he averted panic and even, though without overdoing it, showed himself attentive to his audience, anticipating—while going on imperturbably with his lament—his every move, pouring wine, reaching for the check, etc. In the end, he mastered his condition so fully that he was able to frame it in a sequence of burlesque signs. He said: "I could cry the whole time—just watch me!" And true enough, he actually produced a tear or two. In the next moment he displayed his trembling hands—whereupon beads of sweat appeared on his forehead and immediately disappeared. There followed a calm interval, which the narrator (again at the proper moment) broke off by whispering in his listener's ear: "I've nearly finished"—then picked up the plate with the check and a pencil on it and, looking down at it, calmly told the end of his story: "In the afternoon, the cliffs of death were still rising from the park and in the zoo the animals' cages were empty. But now in the evening, what a pleasure to hold a plate with a pencil rolling on it. I wish us all a long life."

He concluded his performance with a parody of himself. He pointed to an aquarium, where small chunks of granite served as decor for the ornamental fishes; and then, earnestly, with nothing offensive in mind, called Sorger's attention to the neighboring booth, where—there was little else to be seen—a woman's shapely leg was swinging up and down, and swore, without batting an eyelash, "to die a natural death." (Previously, when he was asked if he wished to die, only his pupils had darted to one side.)

Then the stranger got hungry. He ate, not greedily, but with almost ceremonious movements, drinking his wine in small sips, contemplating every morsel at length and putting it into his mouth with a look of affection. He said that he felt food and drink literally "sparkling" in his mouth. Then he smiled, and sustained the smile for several minutes, as though storing up energy.

Sorger watched him eat and, learning from him, felt warmth on his forehead. His face was covered over by the stranger's face, and in the end there was no other.

They sat in the booth as on a bridge; it sufficed to

exchange a grin of complicity now and then. Each sank into his private thoughts, but they enjoyed them in common. "A god had his sport with them." Once Sorger fell asleep with his eyes open and was awakened by his companion's voice, but heard only the final sentence: "I've never told anyone that before." What had the man said?

Once more, to be sure, the stranger's misery resumed its hold on him. On his way back from the toilet he got lost and without noticing sat down at another table, with other people. There he sat motionless, staring into space, until Sorger went and got him.

But before that, hadn't Esch missed several times when reaching for his wineglass? Hadn't he put on his jacket inside out? "Power, come back to me." Sorger became his advocate, commanding, forbidding (and in his retrospective fear the other was glad to obey), releasing him from pain, predicting good things—and in the end gave him his blessing, whereupon the last vestige of blackness poured out of the man's mouth and, as the hatcheck girl later remarked, the "gentleman's" face revealed only a "sad contentment."

They did not go out "into the night"; rather, they passed from the restaurant to the street as from one city room to another. In the doorway leading into the open, Esch, as though he were the owner of these rooms, made a gesture of invitation to Sorger.

Sorger had once heard of a strange sacred mountain in China which was forbidden to foreigners. From its summit, the natives (when the weather was right) could see their shadows on the clouds below and read their future in the shape of the shadows. A special shadow appeared that night on the yellowish-lit street along which the two of them took each other home, from south to north, from downtown to uptown, traversing half the length of the city. This shadow showed itself on one of the many clouds of dense white steam which, smelling of hot rolls and often hissing softly, rose through the asphalt and, in the corners of Sorger's eyes taking on the form of fleeing dogs, were driven swiftly into the darkness by the night wind. Near an underground work site from which an uncommonly large sheet-metal ventilator protruded far above the surface of the street, the white steam was much thicker; and it did not seep off to one side, but high in the air formed a persistent but constantly renewed mass, upon which one of New York's intensely bright streetlamps cast the shadow of a small tree. When, ceding to the wind and the rhythmic bursts from below, this mass of steam broadened or lengthened and narrowed, the tree shadow on it expanded or shrank with it—for a moment it was bloated and blurred and in the next it was small, shrunken, deep black, and clearly delineated. Though neither a word nor a sign was exchanged, the two men stopped in unison to contemplate the shadow branches (on which a few individual leaves were discernible) on the clouds of steam. True, the playful silhouette answered no questions about the future, but thanks to their perception of this commonplace sight (a sight not "forbidden," not "sacred," but accessible to all) the rest of their walk was dominated by a present which encompassed them both without distinction, and with every step on the pavement they sensed the beneficent hardness of the earth.

Was this beauty on the humpbacked avenue ephemeral (did the two foreign nightwalkers encounter it by mere chance)? Would the unique scene—the yellow light, the glaring white steam, the tree shadow that moved back and forth on it—soon vanish for all time in Eternal Formlessness?

The Avenue of the Present, where Sorger and Esch continued on their way, jogging now and then along with the many night joggers, took on life before them as a place in itself, with its own unique nooks, vistas, and eminences, just as a neighborhood takes form for people who have lived there for years: and, indeed, a number of shop windows displayed signs reading "Sunday Brunch on the Avenue," as though this avenue, leading straight through the metropolis, were a traditional sightseer's goal. On the left, the park appeared at the end of every cross street, as though inclining downward into the darkness, but here and there a light arose from its rocky hillocks; on the right, the waning moon, which at every street corner appeared slightly higher in the sky. Gradually—the air had grown noticeably cooler—the moon put on a wide halo, and at a crossing where the two walkers stopped outside an all-night grocery store (as though this were the place to part) vanished in a great cloud that reflected the city lights. Then swarms of vague shadows raced across the pavement, soon followed by the bodies belonging to them—great snow crystals, which descended with a softly crackling sound from the night sky. Each man said: "An hour ago I'd have taken these shapes for rats."

They were now in the vast American region of "Snow Flurries" (vision of hilly countryside with wagon tracks and a single fence post) and had time to stand side by side in the snowfall. It was past midnight; but everywhere, far up and down the avenue, people were still afoot; some were even scraping the snow from car tops and trying to make snowballs.

Close by the two walkers, a woman hugged a man, who merely responded with a smile. But when, after a short conversation, the man tried to fondle the woman, she turned away. Speaking softly, he tried again, drawing her whole body to him; she stiffened and he turned away with a gesture of discouragement. His cheeks went violently red; and Sorger, who now noticed for the first time how young the two of them were, thought of the skiing instructor, whose face in the "chapel" had worn an expression of bitter disappointment. And he drew the young fellow entirely into himself—that is, into the shimmering worldwide snowy night, into the healing wintry space, to make him well again.

Then, behind the window of the grocery store, the sad people reappeared—a grotesque, mocking world—in the form of two elderly men (the one sitting behind the checkout counter, white; the other, standing in front of it, black). They avoided each other's eyes as though—aside from the actual circumstance (which undoubtedly played a part) of their being "clerk" and "customer," "black" and "white"—something more, something worse than personal enmity had erupted between them: the wretched incomprehension that blurs the features and muddles the mind—something that neither wanted and that made them both miserable.

Unlike the young couple on the street outside (where the man, with face averted, was timidly tickling the woman), the faces of the two old men in the grocery store were deeply pale. They did not speak; they hardly moved (except that the black man kept crumpling a brown paper bag). Both kept their eyes lowered; their lids quivered; not once did either appeal for support or help to the other customers, who stood congealed with their purchases, not even impatient, just as pale, silent, and forlorn as the protagonists. Only when the black man, soundlessly moving his lips, finally opened the door, did the clerk raise his face to the next customer, but he did not grin (as the witness outside had expected); he merely showed (to no one in particular) his dark, desperately wide-open, and for a moment earnestly imploring eyes.

Immediately thereafter, while Sorger's eyes followed the black, who, occasionally throwing up his hands, disappeared down the avenue, a beam of light flashed over the two companions and all those who were still abroad, including a group some distance away, waiting in the darkness for a bus—and then continued down the street like the beam of a searchlight, though no cars were passing just then. The trembling of the ground and the wind that followed made it clear that the flash rising through the street grating came from the subway below.

Sorger looked at Esch, who had turned into the half shadow; Esch answered his look, and glancing at each other from time to time, both went their common way: first helplessly rounding their eyes in a fervent plea for counsel, then half closing them like "enlightened ones," then almost roguishly winking at each other, and finally bidding each other goodbye with pure veneration (as if they knew that they could also have been enemies)—until their eyes turned away from each other into the nocturnal city, where snow and the autumn wind pursued the people descending the stairs into the subway, and where night plane followed night plane, occasionally flaring up in the sky, as though their course were just one more avenue.

In the end, Esch held out his calling card (the card of a "sad businessman") and jangled his "European keys" as a sign that he was capable of going home (it passed through Sorger's mind that he himself no longer had any keys at all); thrusting a positively puckish face into Sorger's, Esch castigated him for his "absentmindedness" and recited a few lines from a poem: "The passage of beauty was as brief/as a dream in the snowy light," and as a farewell gift gave his "compatriot" his hat.

Had the catastrophe only been postponed for a short time? No one would die. Sorger had the power to wish, and the repose of the horizontal world set in. The wind changed. Snow and leaves danced up the street: "There fly we all!"

Strange to say, the hotel entrance was below street level: from it a few steps led to the dazzlingly bright though deserted lobby, in a far corner of which the elevator man had fallen asleep on a stool, while the voice of the night clerk, who was himself invisible from the entrance, welcomed Sorger, whom he had recognized in the hall mirror, with the words: "Got in late?" For a moment the air from outside poured in through the slowly closing door. Then it was suddenly very still in the lobby, and Sorger put in a transatlantic phone call.

He sat down to wait on a red-upholstered chair along the side wall, next to the sleeping elevator man, whose white hair was combed smoothly back. Only the house sounds were still audible: the rattling of a ventilator and the clicking of an ice machine as it spat out more and more cubes. A runner, as red as the chair, extended to the rear wall, and the brass cage of the elevator diffused its patina of age throughout the lobby, which at first sight (like the whole hotel, for that matter) seemed only sturdy. When had he last had time for such humble, undramatic, merely heartwarming objects? "Do I want anything more? Is it not my dream to live content, surrounded by the worldly-heavenly charm of things?"

Then the phone rang and Sorger staggered to the booth; he talked excitedly and at the same time felt a strange pain, which cut through him like a scalpel, from the center of his chest to the top of his skull, accompanied by a tormented sound, which was his own special and personal laughter. ("You having a party over there?" he was asked.)

After phoning, he remained seated in the dark booth, without feeling, barely alive. He hadn't even spoken of a homecoming, and no curiosity had been shown. The only response to his expression of his feelings had been an embarrassed laugh. Sorger learned that he was not needed. He didn't even mind; he sat sweating, preserved the other voice in his ear, and wanted to keep saying the same word. At the same time, he silently counted the stairs leading from the street down into the entrance hall. He wished for those he loved, and they came (they had all been in the adjoining room the whole while); and at the same time the ocean stretched out between them.

"He's just an animal."

Who said that? He opened the door of the phone booth and through an opening in the key panel saw the night clerk talking with the telephone operator, who was sitting caged at her switchboard. The words seemed to refer to none of those present; yet in spite of himself, Sorger looked at the dozing elevator man, and instantly noticed that he had a bleeding wart on his cheek and that the epaulettes were missing from his uniform. And again the night clerk said to the woman through the opening: "He's just an animal—an animal gone mad. And there's only one way to deal with mad animals: exterminate them."

A deeper night descended like a sudden (and soon incomprehensible) foreboding over the cheerfully lighted basement. The ventilator rattled for a moment as though the four characters present were riding in a ghostly train:

a space-time jolt turned their faces into murderers' masks, from which poured the invariably evil slogans of the violent past, not only of other countries but also of this one, which the foreigner had sometimes looked upon in all its length and breadth as "God's country." That slight jolt sufficed to transform the day-bright lobby, along with the City of Light outside, into a jungle bristling with the shadows of bayonets. A train screeched, the ticking of teletype mingled with the sound; and in the shadowy face of the night clerk Sorger recognized an Indian mask signifying a man "losing his soul": two mice sitting on the cheeks were eating up the soul. But then it turned out that the clerk had only been reading the newspaper out loud.

Which then was the truth: the beautiful prelude or the hideous cacophony of the end? "What do I want? What is real for me?"

Real was the child's drawing over the key panel; real were the tired, unmoving eyes of the telephone operator; real was the ceremonious gesture with which the elevator man, awakened by the loud voice, invited Sorger into his elevator with its glass chandelier and red-velvet bench; real were the almost parallel strands of the old man's hair stiff from wet-combing, his sloping shoulders, and the shiny patent-leather shoes. Standing with his back to his passenger during the leisurely ride to the penthouse, the man treated Sorger to an incomprehensible sermon, at the end of which he raised the two fingers, between which he was holding the bank note Sorger had given him as a tip, in a gesture of dismissal: "*That* is something!" Real was what was peaceful.

The short corridor smelled of paint. Sorger noticed that his door, which had been green that morning, had been painted dark red. Wasn't there a store that had shone bright with pyramids of food the day before but on his way home last night had changed into a burned-out hole, where the only sign of food were a few apples with burst skins lying in the ashes? (And the back of his coat showed deep gashes that seemed to have been made by razor blades.)

Sorger entered the room with one of the singer's songs in his head. It was about a man who, "to keep away from the hole of death," had even been willing "to ferret and pry like a cheap detective": "Born to win." The bed was turned down as though for two, and the bedside lamps lit. The folds in the sheet figured a map of the world. In one breath Sorger experienced the time from his birth far away in Europe to the present, as a gentle, steady upward movement, and felt himself grow strong.

He opened the curtains and blinds (flakes scraping against the glass and the blackness) and looked through his notes of the past few years. In the process, he saw how radically his ideas about his projected paper had changed: his interest in enduring natural forms had been augmented with a feeling for the episodic configurations that can crop up anywhere (and not just in nature) when "I, Sorger" became, in a manner of speaking, "their moment"—and could there be a terminology for unique happenings that slip away, leaving, at the most, words and images in the memory?

The smooth heavy thing which Sorger now saw in front of him and which was also taking up space inside him was a glass mountain, which barred his way home, and he looked across at the white bed as a possible escape. Would it not be fitting to narrate these brief dreams, which could not be substantiated because they were too bound up with his innermost being? Did this brief "circuit of forms" not on every occasion fill him with enthusiasm as a lucky insight, which then demanded permanence in a *form* and thus communicated to him an idea of true human work, which would eliminate feelings of disgust and the sorrow of parting between him and the world? But how would it ever be possible to "narrate" forms which knew no "little by little"?

Sorger spread out his notebooks, each with its special color, on the table. The tabletop became a sort of geological map, with different colors indicating the different geological eras. He was seized with an intense but vague feeling of tenderness: naturally, he wished for "more light"! He stood motionless, bent over the varicolored pattern, which in places was pale with age, until he himself became a tranquil color among the others. He leafed through the notebooks and saw himself disappearing in the writing; in the story of stories: a story of sun and snow. Now he would be able to win everyone to his view, and the dark terrestrial globe revealed itself as a machine that could be mastered and even understood down to its innermost core.

"Falsification!" But this was no longer an accusation; rather, it was a salutory idea: he, Sorger, would write the Gospel of Falsification; and he triumphed in the thought of being a falsifier among falsifiers. (An isolated individual was capable only of patchwork.) Still, he saw himself capable of facing up to failure, and already he was vanishing through "his" arcade. In the brook there was water, in the water there were pieces of ice.

In bed, with the feel of the mattress, he threw off the last traces of forsakenness and, while turning out the light, wished everyone well. The objects in the dark room spoke with the voices of relatives. He saw two eyes by which he felt loved; and a voice that was far away or quite close to his ear said: "I love you." He didn't breathe, desire came to him, and then he was asleep.

Europe stretched out below him, a labyrinth loud with night sounds, strident with auto horns. He saw the Great Manuscript in which his life was laid bare, and actually read a sentence in it (which stood out bright from the rest of the writing): "He could only be himself, and the mirror, nothingness, and gravity touched one another."

It was a sleep of metamorphoses: the arm thrust between knees became a tree, the fingers were roots growing into the earth. And he was not alone: Lauffer's unwieldy shoulder twitched under a wide suspender strap in the telephone room of the Indian village in Alaska; the neighbor woman on the Pacific Ocean arched her eyebrows. Each charmed the whole earth with the face of a famous actor, and Sorger was the joker which encompassed them all.

Then they were together in a snowfield under the bright sun, sitting at a table and holding a family council (which included the stranger). A fruit tree, with branches like elk's antlers, was laden with large, yellowish-white early apples, many of which were under the snow.

Yet his senses remained alert: through closed eyelids he saw the graying dawn, and through the connecting door listened to the man in the next room, who, without a letup, cursed all men and all things between heaven and earth in a litany that became more and more violent.

His pillow felt like the touch of a baby's bare foot, and as he woke there was within him a child who quietly, without batting an eyelash, playing with its own breath, looked out of the window. Everything in him that he wanted to be organic was organic; and everything that he wanted to be inorganic was inorganic.

"It's me!"

Once Sorger had conceived the idea of a successful day: on such a day the fact of morning and evening, light and darkness ought to be beauty enough. During his last hours in New York he had an intimation of such a day. He got up quickly and quietly, washed "in the water of this city," savored the long dawn in a calm yet festive mood, as though the daylight were being delayed a little just for his benefit. He was naked and would have liked to show himself in that state. He felt freedom in his armpits, and a Latin sharpness in his mind; even if he collapsed, it would not be death. The snow had stopped, and as the sky cleared, something that resembled a runaway house pet that was just coming back appeared in the west ("There you are again"): it was the declining, deep-yellow moon; the stars glittered all about as though to show the way. He saw near and far at once, so that, along with the dawn-black birds flying past the penthouse windows to the left and right, the day-bright hills of New Jersey appeared on the horizon. But from the unseen avenues far below, a yellow glow extended over the first floors of the buildings which were otherwise steeped in shadow, and here and there the headlights of hidden cars circled the upper rows of windows. The park had sunk into the city, and the gray of the reservoir rose to view; the soft color made the oval surface large and soothing; the dark gulls resting on the water showed the white of their feathers whenever they rose for a moment into the air. The fringe of snow on the curving shore looked like frozen surf. The first joggers were already circling the reservoir, perceiving the world with their thighs, as it were, as reliable as the water itself, which with the rising sun quickly turned blue and glittered, now traversed by shady wind trails, which thrust forward, halted, and changed direction—until at last the radiance of morning detached itself from the water, became daylight, and evenly filled the whole city. In his thoughts Sorger was down by the reservoir, looking up at the room where he stood breathing the thin, invigorating air. Over all the roofs, smoke passed like a man, and powdery snow fell from all the trees in the park.

"This is the present!"

Every glance over the city, it seemed to him, was a recurrence (and confirmation) of happenings experienced elsewhere and believed lost. The hotel room was traversed by the quavering shadows of birds (and airplanes), and on the top floor of the neighboring building someone moved through rooms spotted with sunlight, carrying a pile of sheets, which turned bright and dark in their passage like the water of a brook flowing over brightly colored pebbles. A jogger with a dog running behind him rose into the air, turned into a sea gull, and was reflected in the water. "Build up a feeling for repetition. Go down and mingle with the people." But first a chambermaid came in and said: "God bless you. Touch home soon." (And, breathing loudly, looked at him.)

Sorger went to a church where, personally led to a seat by a man clothed in black, with a white carnation in his buttonhole ("Where do you wish to pray?"), he attended Sunday Mass. (Sunday had made its first appearance with a small number of cars rocking like boats on near-deserted, water-gray Madison Avenue far in the distance.) The faces of the faithful were reflected in the bronze covers of the collection boxes, and in making his contribution Sorger felt himself to be one of the community of money, while the hands of the ushers, tapping on the railings, made the sound of bakers taking bread out of the oven. The whole world swayed when the bread was transformed into the Lord's body and, *simili modo*, the wine into the Lord's blood.

"In like manner," the people took Communion. In like manner, "I, Sorger," turned server, stumbled over the edge of the carpet. Resolutely the adult knelt. In like manner he was greeted by strangers; passed a merry funeral party on the morning-bright street; watched the rather military costumed parade of a South Slavic ethnic group, to which his forebears had belonged (the tiniest tots, barely able to walk, stumbled along in national garb), and in the park watched the inexorably passing joggers (time and again, the patter of feet and violent panting behind him), who, unlike the swarms of people just walking about, never took on the features of acquaintances. Among the joggers, he actually recognized the exhausted face of a man with whom he had made friends during his student years in Europe. For a moment his eyes followed the sweat-darkened back of one who had become a stranger; while the other, staring at him as he ran past, had only said: "*Like* Valentin Sorger!" They would never meet again.

Sorger had his last vision of the other continent in a museum. Still fortified by the works before which he had gradually pulled himself erect as one does in the presence of stern (and brazenly vital) models, he stood at the top of the monumental inner stairway, and in a single mighty impulse of the heart took in the great lobby, black with people crowded head to head; while at the same time he looked through the enormous glass doors, down the whole length of granite-gray Eighty-second Street, at the far end of which (the street was intersected by several heavily traveled avenues) he discovered a gray-blue shimmer of the narrow arm of the sea that bounds Manhattan and is known as the East River, and above it a whitish flock of birds flying back and forth and becoming transparent at each change of direction.

Again snow began to fall; children spun about beneath the flakes and stuck their tongues out in the snow; the pretzel stands smoked; and then came another dusk. In this populous, civilized, lively area, where it was no distance at all from the marble interior steps in the foreground to the arm of the sea on the horizon, automobiles drove ahead and turned, pedestrians stood and walked, joggers idled and sprinted in all directions—all together a loving order, merging with the evening, to which Sorger longed to attach himself, since his gaze, sharpened by his past history, was now capable of penetrating to the depths of space and of participating in the peaceful beauty of this present and in the dark paradise of this evening.

"O slow world!"

But why was his yearning—which had just been rising from his innermost self to the outermost world, striving to hold his individual self and the universe together once and for all—immediately followed by a pale, soundless lightning flash, in which what he had longed for so passionately receded from him almost imperceptibly, leaving behind it the emptiness of an earth-spanning streak of death, which weakened him and made him abruptly stagger back into himself? Cleansed of all self-interest till nothing remained but presence of mind, desirous only of completing the world ("I want you and I want to be part of you!")—he was struck by the consciousness of an incurable deficiency, which was neither grounded in himself nor attributable to the present epoch of the earthly planet, which he loved in any case. He no longer wished himself in any other epoch—but that part of the world which, even with the purest, most fervent passion, he attained and staked out was still *far too little.*

Hadn't he once felt rich? He sat down on the stairs, the edges of which were full of resting people, and very slowly tied and untied his shoelaces. Already attendants were clapping their hands and the people were taking short steps toward the exit.

For a moment it seemed to you, Sorger, that the history of mankind would soon be ended, harmoniously and without horror. Yes, there was such a thing as grace. (Or was there?) Unimaginative, bloodthirsty misery was releasing you, and you felt your eyelids anointed by an eternally wild need for redemption. A deep sigh passed through you, and through the whole crowd as well, and you looked up with new strength and sought the gaze of other eyes as heavy as yours. You felt sorrow and then bitter pain at the thought that you would soon have to leave this area of peace, and you wanted to be among the last to leave; but the beautiful thing about your pain was that through it the earth was transfigured (as in prehistoric times heat and pressure had turned limestone to the marble that gleamed at your feet).

In the night plane to Europe it was as though you, my dear Sorger, were taking your "first real journey," the journey on which, so it is said, a man learns "what his own style is." Behind and in front of you, babies were screaming miserably, and when they finally calmed down, they stared like dark-eyed prophets. You no longer knew who you were. Where was your dream of greatness? You were no one. In the first gray of dawn you saw the blackened wing of the plane. The passengers' bleak, weary faces were smeared with marmalade. Already the stewardesses were putting on their city shoes. The blank movie screen, shimmering in the sunrise only a moment ago, darkened. Roaring, the plane burst through the clouds.

> *Vanishing face!*
> *The stones at my feet bring you closer:*
> *Immersing myself in them,*
> *I weigh us down with them.*

The Lesson of Mont Sainte-Victoire

This evening I promise you a tale which, I hope, will remind you of everything and nothing.

GOETHE, *Das Märchen*

for Hermann Lenz and Hanne Lenz

with thanks for January 1979

The Detour

On my return to Europe, I needed my daily ration of written matter and read and reread a good deal.

The inhabitants of the remote village in Stifter's *Rock Crystal* are set in their ways. When a stone falls out of a wall, the same stone is put back; new houses are built like the old ones, damaged roofs are mended with old shingles. Such setness seems justified by the striking example of the animals, "which never change their color."

And then one day I was at home with colors. Bushes, trees, clouds, even the asphalt of the road, had a shimmer, which came neither from the season nor from the light of that particular day. The world of nature and the work of man, one with the help of the other, gave me a moment of ecstasy, known to me in the images of half sleep (but without their menacing quality, their augury of terrible things to come), which has been called the *Nunc stans*, the moment of eternity. The bushes were yellow gorse, the trees were singly standing brown firs, the earth's vapor made the clouds look bluish; the sky (as Stifter was still able to say so calmly in his stories) was blue. I had stopped on a hilltop on the Route Paul

Cézanne, leading eastward from Aix-en-Provence to the village of Le Tholonet.

I have always found it hard to differentiate colors and even more so to name them.

The Goethe of the *Color Theory*, who sometimes made a show of his knowledge, speaks of two persons, in whom I partly recognize myself. These two, for instance, "wholly confused pink, blue, and violet"; in viewing these colors, they seemed to distinguish only slight nuances of lighter, darker, weaker, or more intense. In black, one of them noticed a tinge of brown, and in gray a tinge of red. They were both extremely sensitive to the gradation of light and dark. Their condition was probably pathological, but Goethe regarded them as borderline cases. Nevertheless, when he conversed with them at random and questioned them about the objects round about, he became utterly bewildered and feared that he was going mad.

Quite apart from mere identification, this note of Goethe's helped me to perceive the unity between my earliest past and the present: in another moment of the "standing Now," I see the people of those days—parents, brothers and sisters, and even grandparents—in the company of today's people, all laughing at my remarks about the colors of things around me. A kind of family game consisted of letting me guess at colors; the confusion, of course, rested not with the others but with me.

But, unlike Goethe's two cases, my disorder is not hereditary. There is no other example of it in my family. Over the years, however, I have learned that I am not suffering from classical "color blindness" or from any of its variants. I sometimes see colors and see them correctly.

Not long ago I was standing on the snow-covered summit of the Untersberg. Not far above me, almost within reach, a crow was gliding on the wind. I saw the characteristic bird yellow of the retracted claws, the golden brown of the wings shimmering in the sun, the blue of the sky. These three moved across the sky like the passing of a large, airy surface, in which at the same moment I saw a three-colored flag. It was a flag that stood for nothing, a thing of pure color. But through it I have at last become capable of looking at actual flags (which up until then had only cut off my view), because now their peaceful prototype exists in my imagination.

Twenty years ago I was examined for fitness for military service. Though ordinarily rather shaky about colors, I came off rather well in the color test, which consisted in making the right selection from a jumble of numbered dots of color. When I got home and reported the outcome ("Fit for armed service"), my stepfather spoke up (for ordinary purposes, we had stopped talking to each other) to say he was now proud of me for the first time.

I write this because my oral reports of the incident have always been incomplete and misleadingly ambiguous. In speaking, I have always said the man was "slightly tipsy." Though accurate in itself, this detail falsified the story. Would it not be closer to reality to say that on that day I viewed the house and garden with a sense of homecoming? My stepfather's remark struck me at once as revolting. But why is it connected in my memory with the fresh reddish-brown of the garden which the man had just spaded? Hadn't I, too, been partly proud of the news I brought home?

In any event, the color of the soil was what lingered in my memory. When I now search for the moment, my view of it is no longer that of an adolescent; I find myself, that is, the self I wish to be, timeless and contourless in that reddish-brown, and it is through that reddish-brown that I can clearly understand myself and the soldier I was. (Among Stifter's earliest memories were the dark spots inside him. Later he realized "that they were woods outside" him. Now, time and again, his stories show me colored spots in unspecified forests.)

During the Franco-Prussian War of 1870–71, Paul Cézanne's father, a wealthy banker, ransomed him from military service. He spent the war period painting at L'Estaque, then a fishing village in a bay west of Marseilles, now an industrial suburb.

The place is known to me only from Cézanne's paintings, but in my mind the mere name L'Estaque gives body to a vision of peace. Regardless of what has become of it, the region remains "a place of refuge," not only from the war of 1870, not only for the painter Cézanne was then, and not only from a declared war.

In the years that followed, Cézanne often worked there, preferably in intense heat and under a "sun so fierce" that "all objects seemed to be massive shadows, not only in black or white, but also in blue, red, brown, and violet." Nearly all the paintings done in his "refuge" had been black and white, their mood for the most part wintry; but later the village, with its red roofs against the blue sea, gradually became his "Card Game."

It was in the letters from L'Estaque that he first appended the word "pictor" to his name, as the classical painters had done. This was the place "which I shall leave as late as possible, because there are some very beautiful views." The postwar paintings no longer convey moods, nor are particular seasons or times of day discernible. Time and again the forms disclose only the archetypal village on the Clear Blue Sea.

Toward the turn of the century, refineries sprang up around L'Estaque, and Cézanne stopped painting there; in a few hundred years, he wrote, living would be altogether pointless. Only on geological maps are the region's colors unimpaired; and a small patch of mignonette-green still bears the name Calcaire de l'Estaque, and no doubt will for a long time to come.

Yes, it was thanks to Paul Cézanne that I was standing amid the colors of the open country between Aix-en-Provence and the village of Le Tholonet, and that I saw even the asphalt highway as color.

I grew up among peasants. Paintings were rare, except in the parish church and in wayside shrines; from the start, I regarded them as mere accessories and for years expected nothing of importance from them. Sometimes I even sympathized with the religious and political proscription of images; what with my halfhearted way of looking at pictures, I would even have welcomed such a proscription for myself. Since endlessly repeated ornament fell in with my need for the infinite, wasn't that the right thing for me? (I once managed, while looking at a Roman mosaic floor, to think of dying as a beautiful transition, without the usual limitation known as "death.") And is it not a perfectly colorless and formless void that can most miraculously come to life? (A sentence spoken by a priest in another "remote" village—no layman would be likely to venture such a statement—fits into this context: "An endless soaring of love between the soul and God—that is heaven.")

I ought to have been more grateful to the painters of pictures, because often enough these supposed accessories had at least taught me to see, and not a few became recurrent images in my thoughts and daydreams. True, I scarcely perceived forms and colors as such. What counted was always the special object. Colors and forms without an object were too little—objects in their everyday familiarity, too much. But I shouldn't say "special object," since what I was looking for were, precisely, commonplace things, which, however, the painter had revealed in a special light. Today I can call them "magical."

The examples that occur to me are all landscapes of a type suggesting the depopulated, silently beautiful, menacing phantasms of half sleep. Strangely enough, they always occur in series, sometimes embodying a whole period in the work of the painter: de Chirico's metaphysical Piazze; Max Ernst's devastated, moonlit jungle cities, each one of which is titled *The Whole City*; Magritte's *Realm of Lights*, that repeated house under leafy trees, in darkness, while all the rest of the picture is irradiated by a bluish-white daytime sky; finally, and above all, Edward Hopper's wooden houses amid the pine woods of Cape Cod, in paintings with titles such as *Road and Houses* or *Road and Trees*.

But Hopper's landscapes are not so much nightmarish as desolately real. One can find them on the spot, in broad daylight; and when a few years ago I went to Cape Cod, a place I had long been drawn to, and tracked down the scenes of his pictures, I felt for the first time in my life that I was in an artist's country. Today I could still trace the curves, the uphill and downhill stretches in the road across the dunes. The details, often entirely different from those painted by Edward Hopper, are distributed to the left and right as on a canvas. At the center of one such afterimage, a reed protruding from the thick ice of a pond "goes with" the tin can beside it. I went there for reasons of my own, and realized when I came away that in the work of a painter and the landscape forms of New England I had laid the groundwork for a travel guide: far from being deserted, the wooden houses I had seen at night were dream-houses blinking between the pines, and there I found a home for the hero of a tale that remained to be written.

Poets lie, says one of the first philosophers. And indeed, it has long been held that reality means hard times and disastrous happenings; and that the arts are faithful to reality when their central and guiding content is evil or man's more or less ridiculous despair over evil. But how is it that I can no longer bear to hear, see, or read such thoughts? Why is it that as soon as I myself write a single complaining sentence, a single sentence accusing myself or others—unless there's a sacred fury in it!—I literally see red: though, on the other hand, I shall never write about the good fortune of having been born or about consolation in a better world to come. Mortality will always be my guiding principle, but never again, I hope, my central theme.

At first Cézanne painted horror pictures, such as his *Temptation of St. Anthony*. But in the course of time his sole problem became the *réalisation* of pure earthly innocence: an apple, a rock, a human face. His reality became the form he achieved, the form that does not lament transience or the vicissitudes of history, but transmits an existence in peace. Art is concerned with nothing else. But what gives life its feeling becomes a problem in the transmission.

What was beginning to happen inside me when, still in the era of magical pictures, we, the woman and I, drove through another countryside in the South of France?

As part of that journey I now count the walk I took the night before in the wild hill country where the woman lived. It was one of the last days of the year, and for once the mistral, the ordinarily cold fall wind from the Massif Central, was warm; it blew strong but steady, without the abrupt blasts that produce the effect of hallucination. Though the path had dwindled to next to nothing, I still felt that the house with the woman in it was near. It was she who had first shown me Hopper's pictures; she was capable of affection for simple things and she knew "who I am." I sat down in a grassy clearing, the whole of which quivered. The bent treetops were almost motionless. The air was clear, and on the bright western horizon, streaks of cloud kept shooting up into the sky and vanishing. "In my reflection on things seen" (as Cézanne once described his working method), the moonrise that then followed enters into an analogy with a second moon, which, on a similar calm evening, I glimpsed above a nearby horizon and identified as the gleaming yellow arch of a barn door. I sat in the murmuring wind as once in childhood I had sat in the murmur of a certain pine tree (and as later on, in the midst of the city's roar, I managed to hear only the murmur of the river that flows past it).

The car ride the following day was the start of a journey that took us to the coast. The mistral had died down; a balmy, spacious winter's day. Scant Mediterranean pines in a stony landscape. The woman taught me their name, which, accompanied by the date 1974, has often come back to me as a refrain: *pins parasol.* Sloping gently downward, the road led past them. There (not "suddenly"), along with the road and the trees, the world opened out. Besides, "there" became somewhere else. The world was solid, sustaining soil. Time stands still, eternally and day by day. The openness can also, repeatedly, be I. I can wish all barriers away. I should always be so calm in the outside world (amid forms and colors). It is my fault when, in danger of closing up, I reject the presence of mind that is always possible.

In a story I had written five years before, a landscape, though flat, arched so close to the hero that it seemed to push him away. Yet the radically different, concavely widened world of 1974, which relieves pressure and thinks the body free, still stands before me as a discovery to be communicated: the umbrella pines and my joy of life, those are valid reality. In any case, the *pins parasol* often came in handy when the entrances of strange houses arched up at me, though the "I" of that earlier world may time and again become distraught and bewildered (there *is* an intrinsic guilt).

Was it only then that something began to happen inside me? Wasn't it much earlier, in the presence of other southern trees, that I first conceived of a rational joy? Among the dark cypresses of the summer of 1971 in Yugoslavia: what was it that, more each day, gave way in me, until someone finally opened her arms for the first time? (Here, too, I place the mulberry tree, in the shade of which we often sat, and the light-colored sand at its feet, sprinkled red with the juice of fallen berries.) It was then that the transformation occurred. The man I was came of age, but at the same time demanded to go down on his knees or to lie with his face down, and in all this to be no one.

The transformation was natural. It was the desire for reconciliation which, as the philosopher put it, comes from "desiring another's desire." This desire struck me as perfectly reasonable, and from then on, it has carried over into my writing.

Yet it was not a good time. (In mortal terror, my mother sent me appeals for help, and I didn't know what to answer.) Consequently, I read the ancients' magical trees of death into the cypresses. "Dream yourself into things" was long a writer's maxim; imagine the objects to be dealt with as though seeing them in a dream, in the conviction that there alone they will acquire their true essence. And then they formed a grove around the writer, from which, of course, he had difficulty finding his way back to life. True, he repeatedly found an essence of things, but this essence could not be communicated; and in stubbornly trying to hold it fast, he became unsure of himself. No, magical images—and that went for the cypresses—were not the right thing for me. Within them lies a not at all peaceable nothingness, to which I never want to return. Only outside, in daylight colors, *am* I.

The state has been called the "sum of its norms." I, however, know I am committed to a different system, the realm of forms, in which "true ideas," as the philosopher said, "coincide with their objects," and every form is powerful as a paradigm (even though the artists themselves in more recent times "are half shadows and now, in the present, are almost entirely unreal").

But what justifies one in contributing to this realm? The question torments me every time I start a new piece of work; I keep thinking that I am no more than a benevolently silent reader. Still, once—before I had ever written anything—I felt justified. I had a vision of the theme, of the "book" I longed to write, of many books. Not in a dream, but on a sunny day; nor was this a lapse brought on by southern cypresses; no, I was right here and my subject right there. We were driving through gently rolling country on a fairly straight road, on a late-summer Sunday in Upper Austria. There was no one on the road. Just once, I saw a man in a white shirt and black suit, walking on the other side. His trousers were loose, they flapped against his legs when he walked. Later, when we drove back, the man, to my delight, was still walking, with his trousers flapping around his ankles and his jacket unbuttoned, on a Sunday in Upper Austria. At the sight of this man walking along, the "I" of my first book felt an obligation to go among men and tell them something. He resolved to go among them with might and main, and convince them. Should I then suppose that nothing new happened in connection with the *pins parasol* of 1974, but rather that something came back, which I was able to welcome as "Reality"?

There is a painting by Cézanne which has been referred to as *The Great Pine*. (He himself never gave his paintings titles, and seldom signed one.) It shows a tall, solitary pine by the Arc River southeast of Aix. This was the river of his childhood. After bathing, he and his childhood friends would sit in its shade; later, at the age of twenty, he asked Emile Zola, who had been one of these friends, in a letter: "Do you remember the pine on the bank of the Arc?" He even wrote a poem to the tree. In it the mistral blows through the bare branches; and the picture, too, suggests the wind, particularly in the way the lone tree slants. That tree, more than just about anything else, might be titled: "Out in the Open." It transforms the ground from which it rises into a plateau, while the branches, twisted in all directions, and the infinitely varied green of its coat make the empty space around it vibrate.

The Great Pine is depicted in other paintings, but never is it so solitary. In one of them (which is signed) the bottommost branch seems to wave in the direction of the landscape. Along with the branches of a neighboring pine, it forms a vaulted gateway leading into the distance, where the slopes of Mont Sainte-Victoire lie stretched beneath the bright colors of the sky.

Before my encounter with Cézanne (but after I became acquainted with Edward Hopper), there was another painter who carried me away from mere opinions about paintings and taught me to view them as paradigms and to honor them as works.

At the time, I had been reading a description of a German village in the nineteenth century by a Swabian peasant turned poet. Wishing to avoid all petty views of man, he called his poems "Gospels of Nature, written by her reader." (At the sight of a distant snowfield, which often in hazy sunlight is distinguishable from the sky only by a faint glow, his words in turn come home to me, his reader: "Yours are all things—the heavens themselves, and even the stars, if you have radiance for the radiance in the distance.")True, when he wrote prose, he took a paltry view of people, of his villagers, and he knew it. Sometimes it grieved him that "the body fatigued by farm work could neither hear nor see." (The life of this man, Christian Wagner, in whose poems the spirit spoke, but who, as the philosopher said, owes his enduring fame to his unity with "his subject, the body," deserves the word "tragic," which is so often used meaninglessly.)

It was then that I first looked seriously at the paintings of Gustave Courbet, many of which portray the life of peasants in the mid-nineteenth century, and was moved by the lofty silence of these pictures, especially one entitled *The Peasants of Flagey (Doubs), Returning Home from Market.* And then I knew: these are the right pictures—and not only for me.

Courbet, as his precisely localized titles show, regarded the subjects of genre paintings, these scenes of everyday life, as the true events of history. And so it is that to the sympathetic mind his peasants—as they sift grain, stand at a graveside, prepare a dead woman for burial, or return home from market at dusk (and those as well who only sit and rest, sleep and dream)—form a self-contained procession, which today includes "my" genre painting of an old woman, who on a warm sunny day much later walked slowly down a back street in West Berlin with her shopping bag and, during a brief silence that made her everyday reality more profound, revealed to me the housefronts as our shared and still happily enduring peace procession.

During the Paris Commune of 1871, the painter Courbet was one of those chiefly responsible for having the victory column on the Place Vendôme razed. For, he said, the square at the end of the rue de la Paix is no place for "a monument to war and conquest." At the fall of the Commune, he spent several months in prison for this offense, and many pictures of the ensuing decade (his last) show nothing but a wild green sea, a wild sky, and very little beach. One of this series is titled *The Great Wave.* It shows hardly anything but water and air, but the rock colors give the effect of solidity, and the numerous interrelated forms make it dramatic.

As Cézanne saw it, Courbet had "the sweeping gesture and grand manner of the Masters." He called *The Great Wave* "one of the discoveries of the century." While looking at Courbet's paintings in the Louvre, he would call out the names of the objects in them: "There, the hounds, the pool of blood, the tree. There, the gloves, the lace, the shot-silk coat."

Ever since I began to think, I have felt the need for a teacher. Sometimes a word sufficed to spark off a desire to learn and make me feel drawn to someone. Today I am grateful to the few professional teachers who over the years have had something to communicate to me; but I would not call any of them "my teacher." There was one man at the university who inspired me with a hitherto unprecedented thirst for knowledge. In a lecture on law, he formulated the ethical implications of things in enigmatically simple mathematical sentences; I should have liked (I truly longed) to be his "student." Unhappily, he was only a guest lecturer, and after a short week he was gone. The writers whom I read seriously are dear to me more as brothers than as teachers—as brothers they are sometimes too close to me. The only person whom now, in retrospect, I sometimes regard as a kind of teacher is my grandfather (a common enough phenomenon, I believe). Whenever he took me for a walk in the country, that walk stayed with me as a lesson (though not at all in the same way as present-day "nature walks").

Time and again I am afflicted by my ignorance, and this feeling gives rise to an aimless striving for knowledge which engenders no idea, precisely because it has no "object" with which to "conform." But then one small thing may convey a message and thus instill the "spirit of the beginning"; then I may start to study in earnest, when previously, however busy and active, I had only longed to.

The Cézannes that I saw at an exhibition in the spring of 1978 struck me as such things of the beginning, and I was overcome with a desire to study such as had hitherto been inspired only by Flaubert's prose style. These were works of his last decade, when he came so close to his aim of "realizing" his subject that the colors and forms alone sufficed to do it honor. ("By reality and completeness I mean one and the same thing," said the philosopher.) And yet these paintings show no added light. The fêted subjects owe their effect to their own colors, and sometimes the overall effect of the lighter landscapes is one of darkening. The nameless Provençal peasants of the late nineteenth century, the heroes of the portraits, loom large in the foreground; with no particular insignia of royalty, they dominate an earth-colored ground, which is their land, their country.

Darkness, lines, composition, reinforcement, darkening eyes; yes, I was shaken. And after two years of "study," an appropriate sentence fits itself together: the silence of these pictures seemed so complete because the dark lines of a composition reinforced an overall tension, which (as the poet put it) I could attain by "darkening over" to it, that is, by a leap, in which two pairs of eyes, separate in time, met on a painted surface.

"The picture has begun to tremble," I jotted down at the time. "What freedom, to be able to sing someone's praises."

One portrait in particular moved me, because it pictured the hero of the story I had yet to write. It was titled *The Man with the Folded Arms*: a man, whose picture would never bear a proper name (but who was not no one or just anyone), seen in the corner of a rather empty room defined only by its wainscoting; sitting there in the darkness of the earth tones that also modulate the man himself; a man, it seemed to me, at "an ideal age: already substantial, but still capable of yearning." (True, when I studied his posture, I was put off by the hand tucked back under the arm, and it took an effort of will to unbend it.) The man's eyes looked obliquely upward, without expectancy. One corner of the mouth was slightly distorted by a thicker shadow line: "humble sorrow." His open white shirt was bright, as was his large rounded forehead under his deep-black hair—vulnerable in its nakedness. I did not see this man in my own image, or as a brother; I saw him, rather, as an accomplice, who, now that I have finished his story, is once again the inviolate *Man with the Crossed Arms*, radiating a silent little smile.

There were so many similar portraits that I had little mind to spare for the other pictures on exhibition. In a separate room, which seemed circular, one picture after another showed the top of Mont Sainte-Victoire, which the painter depicted from different angles, but always from below, from the plain and from a distance. He himself said: "The same motif, seen from different angles, offers an object of study of such extreme interest and such diversity that I believe I could keep busy for several months in the same spot, just turning now a little more to the right, now a little more to the left."

At the exhibition the mountain did not stop me for long. But in time it darkened in my mind, and one day, much later, I was able to say that I had an aim.

The Mountain of Colors

Mont Sainte-Victoire is not the highest mountain in Provence, but it is said to be the steepest. It does not consist of a single peak but of a long chain, the crest of which describes a relatively straight line at an almost constant altitude of a thousand meters above sea level.

It looks like a sheer peak only when seen from the valley of Aix, situated half a day's walk almost due westward. What from there looks like a single summit is in fact only the beginning of the high crest extending another half day's journey eastward.

This mountain range, which rises gently on the north and on the south descends almost vertically to a high plateau, is a gigantic anticlinal calcareous fold, and the crest is its upper longitudinal axis. The western view of the three peaks seems especially dramatic, because it offers, as it were, a cross section of the whole mountain range with its different strata, so that even someone who knows nothing about this mountain can hardly help forming an idea of its genesis and regarding it as something very particular.

This one great block, jutting into the sky from the plain, is surrounded by a number of flatter ones, which are separated from one another by clefts and can be differentiated by the changing colors and patterns of the rock; and they too, under lateral pressure, have formed folds, thus on a smaller scale extending the forms of the mountain into the plain.

An astonishing and disturbing feature of Mont Sainte-Victoire is the light color and dolomitic luminousness of the limestone, described in a pamphlet for mountain climbers as "rock of the finest quality." One cannot ride to the top. There is no practicable road on the whole mountain, not even on the gently sloping northern flank; nor is there any inhabited dwelling or inn (there is still a deserted seventeenth-century chapel on the crest). The south wall can be negotiated only by mountain climbers, but from all other directions one can climb it without great difficulty and continue for a long way on the ridge.

Even from the nearest village, the expedition calls for a full day.

I had hardly left Aix on that July day, walking eastward on the Route Paul Cézanne, when I began, in my thoughts, to give travel pointers to an indeterminate number of people (and yet I was only one of the many who had undertaken this journey since the beginning of the century).

For a long while I myself had only toyed with the thought of seeing the mountain in the flesh. Wasn't it an *idée fixe* to suppose that because a painter had once loved it there must be something intrinsically remarkable about it? It was only on the day when a spark leapt from thought to imagination that I made up my mind (and my decision was accompanied by an instant feeling of pleasure): yes, I would go and see Mont Sainte-Victoire! Thus my journey was not so much a quest for Cézanne's motifs (most of which, moreover, I knew had been blocked by buildings) as a response to my own feeling: that mountain attracted me, as nothing in my life had ever attracted me.

Under the plane trees on the Cours Mirabeau, the crowns of which join to form a roof, Aix had been positively somber in the morning. The arch and the white fountain at the end of the long avenue glittered in the background like a small mirror. It was only as I left the town that I was surrounded by a mild gray daylight.

The day was hot and sultry, but I walked in airy warmth. The mountain was not yet in sight. At first the road curved gently over the rolling country, more uphill than down. The road was narrow, and lost its sidewalk while still within the city limits, so it was sometimes difficult to keep out of the way of the cars. But after a good hour's walk, after Le Tholonet, it opened out.

In spite of the traffic, I had a feeling of stillness, just

as the day before, in the midst of the Paris noise, I had felt stillness in the street where we had once lived. I had thought of taking someone with me; now I was glad to be alone. I was walking on "the road." In the shady roadside ditch I saw "the brook." I stood on "the stone bridge." Here were the cracks in the rock. There, bordering a side road, were the pines; large, at the end of the road, the black-and-white of a magpie.

I breathed the fragrance of the trees and thought: Forever. I stopped still and noted: What possibilities there are—in the present! Stillness on the Route de Cézanne. A summer shower passed quickly. Drops glistening singly in the sun; then only the road seemed wet, the pebbles in the asphalt bright with color.

I was going through a period of transition; a year without fixed residence. The story of the man with the folded arms had mostly been written in an American hotel room. Its dominant color, since I looked out day after day at a small lake, had become the morning gray of the water (I felt at the time that I had been "plowing below the earth's surface"). It had been decided, in part by the development of my story, that I would go back to the country I started from—though I was occasionally troubled by a pronouncement of the philosopher. To uproot others, he said, was the worst of all crimes; to uproot oneself, the greatest of achievements.

I still had a few months' time before going back to Austria. In the meantime, I lived only in other people's homes. I was torn between joyful anticipation and dread of a narrowing.

It had often been my experience that a new place, which may not have provided a single noteworthy moment, let alone a happy one, can in retrospect confer a sense of spaciousness and appeasement. In such a place I turn on a water tap and a broad gray boulevard at the Porte de Clignancourt in Paris unfolds before me. Thus I felt impelled, as Ludwig Hohl put it, "to take the long way around" in returning home, to circle through Europe.

In this project, Homer's Odysseus was my hero, as he had been for many before me: like him, I had provided myself with (temporary) security by calling myself No-Man; and at one time I had thought of having the protagonist of my story carried in his sleep (as Odysseus had been by the Phaeacians) to his homeland, which at first he would not recognize.

Sometime later I was actually in Ithaca. I spent a night on a bay, from which a path led to a totally dark interior. A child, whose weeping can long be heard, is carried off into the darkness. Light bulbs are burning in the eucalyptus leaves, and in the morning steam rises from wooden planks wet with dew.

In Delphi, once thought to be the center of the world, the grass in the stadium was all aflutter with butterflies, which the poet Christian Wagner took to be "the redeemed thoughts of the holy dead." But in the face of Mont Sainte-Victoire, when I stood amid the colors of the open country between Aix and Le Tholonet, I thought: Isn't the spot where a great artist worked the center of the world—rather than places like Delphi?

The Philosopher's Plateau

The mountain comes into sight before you even get to Le Tholonet. It is bare and monochrome, more radiance than color. The outlines of clouds can sometimes be mistaken for high mountains: here it is the other way around. At first sight the shimmering mountain looks like something in the sky, an impression favored by what would seem to be the just congealed falling movement of the parallel rock faces, extended horizontally by the stratified fold at the base of the mountain. One feels that this mountain has flowed from above, out of the almost like-colored atmosphere, and condensed in midair.

A strange phenomenon often occurs in the observation of distant plane surfaces; formless as they are, these backgrounds change when something, a bird, for example, appears in the empty space between us and them. The planes recede and at the same time take on discernible shapes, while the air between them and the eye becomes material. All at once, a localized and sickeningly familiar landmark (whose popular names have also distorted its reality) is placed at the right distance; all at once, it becomes "my motif," which I now know by its real name. This applies not only here, where I am writing, to that gleaming snowy surface high up in the Tennengebirge, but also to the Sunday café on the Salzach, which a circling flock of gulls once identified as the "house across the river"; just as on another occasion, thanks to a single intervening swallow, the Kapuzinerberg unexpectedly opened up its depths and stood there, newly understood, as the House Mountain—always open, never veiled.

In the seventeenth century, the Netherlands developed a type of "world landscape" designed to guide the eye into infinite distances; and to this end certain Netherlands painters used the trick of putting soaring birds in the middle ground. ("And there was not a bird to save the landscape for him," writes Borges in one of his stories.) And can't a bus driving over a bridge, with its window frames and the silhouettes of its passengers, move a distant sky closer? Doesn't a spot of tree brown suffice to give form to a patch of shimmering blue? But Mont Sainte-Victoire, without a flock of birds (or anything else) between us, was at once close to me and far in the distance.

It was not until after Le Tholonet that the three-pronged mountain proved to be a range extending from west to east. For a time, the road is straight and level, skirting the mountain; then it climbs in zigzags to a calcareous dome, which forms a plateau at the foot of the steep face, and then runs parallel to the mountain ridge.

It was midday when I climbed the zigzagging road; the sky was deep blue. The rock face formed an unbroken band extending to the horizon. In the red sandy clay of a dried brook bed I saw children's footprints. Not a sound except for cicadas screeching at the mountain. Pitch dripped from a pine tree. I took a bite out of a fresh green pinecone which had already been gnawed by a bird and smelled of apple. The cracks in the gray tree bark formed a natural polygonal pattern, which I ran into wherever I went, ever since I had seen it in the dry mud of a riverbank. From one of these cracks, very close to me, came a cheep, but the gray of the cicada that belonged to it so resembled the gray of the bark that I saw it only when it moved and began to climb down the tree trunk backwards. The long wings were transparent, with black thickenings. I tossed a stick at it, and it was two cicadas that flew away, screeching like ghosts that are given no peace. As I followed them with my eyes, the pattern of the cicadas' wings was repeated by the dark bushes that grew in crevices in the mountain wall.

On top, at the western edge of the plateau, lies the village of Saint-Antonin. (In his later years Cézanne, as he says in a letter, often went there in his wanderings.) The place has an inn, where one can sit in the open, under the shade trees (*Relâche mardi*); the acacia branches form a kind of latticework against the shimmering mountain walls.

The plateau, over which the Départementale 17 plunges eastward as into an unexplored interior, seems barren and is almost uninhabited. On the whole elliptical patch of the map, the only village indicated is Saint-Antonin-sur-Bayon on the western edge. The nearest town of any size is Puyloubier, two hours' walk, and off the plateau, on the slope leading down to Lower Provence. I call this large platform raised above the landscape the Philosopher's Plateau.

Irresolutely, I started down over the deserted road. (From there there was no bus back to Aix.) But then I decided to go on to Puyloubier. Not a single car passed me. A silence in which every slightest sound suggested a spoken word. A faint generalized humming. I was in sight of the mountain all along; now and then, I stopped without intending to. I saw a trough-shaped gap in the crest as the ideal pass. The dry upland meadows extending to the foot of the cliffs were whitened by snail shells clinging to the grass. They formed a fossil landscape, to which for a moment the mountain belonged, for suddenly, at a glance, it disclosed its origin, a monumental coral reef. From one side came the afternoon sun, from the other a light fall wind. What had been written with a plow under the earth's surface the year before now blossomed and sent forth an intense glow. The grass blades by the roadside passed in majestic flight. My pace was deliberately slow, as I walked in the whiteness of the mountain. What was happening? Nothing. And there was no need for anything to happen. Freed from all expectation, I was far from ecstasy. My even gait became a dance. I was an outstretched body, carried by its own steps as on a litter. In this perfect hour the walking dancer, who happened to be me, expressed "extension as a form of existence and the idea of this form of existence," which, according to the philosopher, are one and the same thing, expressed in different ways. But the walking dancer expressed them in one and the same way—rule of the game and game of the rule—as did the walker with the flapping trousers in Upper Austria. Yes, in that moment I myself knew "who I am"—and consequently felt a still undefined obligation. The philosopher's work, after all, had been an Ethics.

A photograph shows Cézanne leaning on a heavy cane, carrying his painting materials tied to his back, with the mythical legend: "Setting out for the motif." But striding joyfully over the plateau, I was no longer concerned either with setting out or with a motif—for I knew that this painter never needed a special "flock of birds" to hold the world together in his pictures. His only animals, and those only at the start, were the crouching mongrels in his demonic picnics and nude scenes, which have been interpreted as grimaces put in to counter his spiritual yearnings.

All the same, I was glad on reaching Puyloubier to sit under the plane trees of a Provençal village and drink beer among strangers. The roofs between me and the outline of the mountain had a soothing effect. A sunny street was named rue du Midi. On the café terrace an aged "war veteran" tenderly displayed his juniper-wood cane to the rest of us; he reminded me of the great John Ford. Two young women, setting out with knapsacks and hobnailed boots to climb the ridge and follow it westward, were straight out of his old movies.

Wolf's Leap

But Puyloubier was also the place where I encountered "my" dog. I'll have to get rid of him before I can go on.

There were no dogs in our house except when we took in a stray, to whom I became greatly attached. One summer he was run over. It was several days before we loaded him onto a little cart and started for the knacker's in the neighboring village. It was rather slow going, because we kept having to run away from the stink. In the end we abandoned the cart in the middle of a field. (That was the only time in my childhood that I felt anything like despair.) Later, in a city, I looked on as a black mastiff and an equally black Doberman pounced on a white poodle from behind and tore it in two.

But it was only when I took to going about the country on foot that I conceived an undying hatred for most dogs. Now, however friendly a countryside may be, I expect to meet a monster like the one in Puyloubier. Cats lurk discreetly in meadows; fish scatter darkly in brooks; the buzzing of hornets is a mere warning; butterflies will always be "my dead"; dragonflies display Easter colors; birds: an ocean in the morning, by evening reduced to a whirring in the ferns; snakes are just snakes (or empty skin). But oh, the dog standing motionless in the darkness, which turns out, as you come closer, to be a fence post, and then, after all, a dog—

On the outskirts of Puyloubier there is a Foreign Legion post. Circling around the village on my way back, I passed it. The grounds are paved in concrete, without tree or bush, and surrounded by a high barbed-wire fence. Both grounds and buildings seemed deserted, as if the soldiers had just moved out.

But then I heard a jangling of metal, like somebody running with a drawn sword. Then came a growling, or rather a distant muttering, and scarcely an instant later a roar directly in my ear; the most evil of all sounds, death cry and war cry, springing straight to the heart, which for a moment bristles like a cat. No more colors or forms in the landscape: only white fangs, and behind them, bluish-purple flesh.

Yes, behind the fence stood an enormous dog—a kind of mastiff. I immediately recognized my enemy. Other dogs from all over the post came running, scratching the concrete with their claws. But the others remained at a distance from me and the first dog, whose voice and stance marked him as the leader.

His body appeared to be motley-colored; his head and face were deep black. There stands evil, I thought. The skull was broad and seemed foreshortened despite the drooping chops; the triangular ears were drawn like small daggers. I looked for the eyes and found a glow. During a break in the roaring, while he was struggling for breath, slaver dripped soundlessly. Meanwhile, the others barked, but their efforts seemed dispirited and rhetorical. His coat was shorthaired, smooth, and streaked with yellow; the anus was a papery white circle; the tail flagless. When the evil sound started up again, the landscape vanished in a whirl of bomb craters and shell holes.

Looking back at the dog, I saw that I was hated. But I could also see the beast's torment; a damned soul was rattling around inside him. No part of his body could hold still. Only once, as though bored with me, he stopped moving, blinked hypocritically to one side, and even played patronizingly with his acolytes (whom he could just as well have bitten to death)—and in the next moment he leapt cinematically at the fence, so high that I actually recoiled.

After that, he stood menacingly still. He stared at me long and attentively, but all he was looking for were signs of fear and weakness. I realized that his hostility wasn't directed at me in particular; here on Foreign Legion territory, where military law reigned supreme, his bloodthirstiness was trained to attack anyone who, bearing neither arms nor uniform, simply *was who he was.* (At least one person in the world ought to remain unarmed, a mere "I" of this kind once wrote.) He, the watchdog inside the army post, and I outside (in a realm for which he, by definition, had no eyes, because for him only his restricted territory had reality); between us, as in the old poem, the barbed wire like an *everlasting, accursed, cold, heavy rain,* through which I, dreaming but alert, viewed the enemy and saw how in his homicidal frenzy, possibly exacerbated by the ghetto he lived in, he lost every characteristic of his race to become, exclusively, a brilliant exemplar of the species executioner.

I remembered how once, when I was out walking with my grandfather, he showed me how to keep dogs at a distance; even when no stone was available, he would bend down as if to pick one up, and the beasts would shrink back every time. Once he even threw earth into a dog's mouth; the dog swallowed it and let us pass.

I attempted something of the kind with the mastiff of Puyloubier, but he simply roared at me out of a vastly magnified mouth. As I bent down, a yellow Paris Métro ticket, canceled and covered with my jottings, fell out of my pocket; in a moment of exuberance I tossed it through the fence. Instantly, the dog turned himself into a marten (a marten, as everyone knows, will eat anything) and bolted my paper: greed, but also revulsion incarnate.

In my fancy, the worms inside him that lived on him flung themselves in dark turmoil on the ticket—and, lo and behold, the dog excreted an inverted little tower, as pointed as its dagger ears. It was only then that I noticed that he had staked out his official territory on the concrete with comparable dried and bleached formations (a grandiosely scribbled hieroglyphic).

Gentle suasion (or speech of any kind) would have been inconceivable in the face of such unreasoning animosity. I therefore crouched resolutely down, and the Legionary mastiff fell silent. (Actually, he was only startled for the moment.) Then our faces moved so close to each other that they vanished as in a cloud. The dog's eyes lost their glimmer, and the dark head turned blacker than crepe. Our eyes met—or rather one eye met another; one-eyed, I looked into his one eye. Then we both knew who the other was, from then on we could only be mortal enemies forever; at the same time, it dawned on me that the beast had long been mad.

The dog's next sound was not a bark but a desperate panting, which increased in violence and finally became the whirring of the wings he had just sprouted and with which in another moment he would fly over the fence. It was accompanied by the general howling of the pack, no longer directed against me alone but against the white of the mountain wall in the background, or perhaps against everything outside the animal kingdom. Yes, now he was out for my blood, and I, too, was looking for a magic word that would make him dead and gone.

Speechless with hatred, I left the Legion post. At the same time I was conscious of guilt: "With a project like mine, I have no right to hate." Forgotten was my gratitude for what I had seen thus far; the beauty of the mountain was expunged; only evil was real.

Thus stricken dumb, I had difficulty in walking. The enemy within me quivered for a while, then began to stink. Nothing recognizable and, worse, nothing namable was left in nature. The word that now occurs to me for my bewildered, one might say war-haunted, stare is a Germanism taken over into French: "*vasistas*" (from *Was ist das*); this word is said to have originated with the Prussian occupation troops in 1871, and refers to the transoms they found—they had never seen anything like them—in certain attic rooms.

Outside Puyloubier, now heading westward, I sat down on a grassy path leading through a vineyard, and basked in the sun. Tired no doubt from so much walking, I dropped off to sleep. I dreamed about a dog who turned himself into a pig. Light in color, firm and plump, he was no longer a caricature of a man, he was an animal as he should have been. I grew fond of him and fondled him—yet awoke unreconciled and, in the words of the philosopher, "purified for holy works by orgies of knowledge."

In the still day-bright sky, the moon was rising. That helped me to imagine the "Sea of Silence," and Flaubert's "appeasement" made its way into my heart. The clayey path smelled refreshingly of rain. As though for the first time, I saw the white of a birch. Every row of vines was a path leading somewhere. The vines were beacons of peace; the moon, an ancient sign for the imagination.

I walked with the last rays of the sun, refreshed by the wind on my face; the blue of the mountain, the brown of the woods, the carmine red of the clay embankments were my color guides. From time to time I ran. Once on a bridge over a ravine I even took a jump, a pretty high and long one, gave a roguish laugh, and named the place Wolf's Leap; then I went calmly on, looking forward to the food and wine that awaited me in Aix.

When I got there late in the evening, I saw crabs crawling on what was left of the cobblestones of the Cours Mirabeau, and cigarette smoke that turned out to be a blue balloon buffeted by the night wind. I was so tired I didn't think much more than "Long-Day Blues."

Mulberry Lane

I spent another few days in Provence. Occasionally, on top of much else, I lost my sense of humor, and my colors faded; pallid formlessness (always when walking downhill). One night a man crossed over to me from the other side of the street and said: "I'm going to kill you." I looked at his hands, which were empty. "No, not with a knife." I managed to catch his eye, and we went a short way together—false friends.

In Cézanne's studio on the Chemin des Lauves, his belongings had become relics. Beside the shriveled fruit on the windowsill, my grandfather's thick black jacket had been carefully hung. In the café on the Cours Mirabeau, I saw *The Card Players*; they had spread a square of baize on the table and were different from what they were in the pictures—and yet exactly the same (their eyes glued to their cards). I sat near them, reading Balzac's story "The Unknown Masterpiece," about Frenhofer, the unsuccessful painter, with whose longing for a perfect and therefore real picture Cézanne identified himself, and discovered that French culture had become the home I had always longed for. The Jas de Bouffan (House of the Wind), the family's old country home, where the painter had worked and which he often painted, now borders on the superhighway to Marseilles; a housing development behind it has taken its name. "*Réussir votre isolation*" says a billboard advertisement for a home-insulation firm. But a little later I misread the "Omniprix" on a supermarket sign as the "Omnipotens" that occurs in one of Cézanne's letters.

Once I got lost out in the *macchia* and suddenly found myself looking down on a man-made lake which lay far below me, as blue and deserted as a northern fjord; over its turbulent waves flew a flock of withered leaves. A gust of wind struck a tree like a bomb, and a maquis bush glistened as though swarming with ants. Nevertheless, time and again, I felt the embrace of beauty so intensely that I, in turn, longed to embrace someone.

On the last day, I finally made up my mind to climb the mountain, which until then I had only circled. My starting point was Vauvenargues, a village in the northern syncline of the mountain ridge, where the philosopher by that name made the observation: "It was the passions that first taught man reason."

The climb to the crest, where the abandoned chapel is situated, was long but not difficult. (I put some apples in my pockets to ward off thirst.) A strong wind was blowing at the top; I sat in the cleft which from below I had looked upon as the "ideal pass"; far to the south I saw the Mediterranean, to the north the gray flank of Mont Ventoux, and to the northeast, far in the distance, the snowfields of the northern Alps: they were "really pure white" (as someone once said of white hyacinths). The former Garden of the Monks was nestled deep in the rock like a dolina, a shelter from the wind; high above it, a whirring of swallows' wings (which recurred indistinctly on my way back, accompanied by a swaying of spiderwebs). Higher up, on the crest, hardly distinct from the rock of the mountain, a tiny stone military hut, manned by two soldiers, who had to stoop to go in and out, and equipped with a radio telephone, which could be heard crackling a long way off.

But it was something more than this military installation or the limestone, which looked dull gray as one came closer, which made the mountaintop so unreal. There was no summit feeling; and my thoughts turned to a famous mountain climber who, in describing his ecstasy at the highest point on earth, drew on the observations that another man (not a mountain climber) had jotted down while strolling through almost level suburban streets, barely a hundred meters above sea level. Consequently, I didn't stay long but started on the westward descent, taking pleasure in the upland meadows, the valleys, and the Provençal roads, which Cézanne had praised for being Roman roads. "The roads of the Romans are always admirably placed. They had a feeling for landscape. At every point, there's a picture." (One more reason for walking on traveled roads rather than cross-country trails.)

When I looked around at the mountain from the first plateau, its flanks had again taken on a festive radiance (one spot glowed like a vein of marble); and when I next looked back, from deep in a pine forest down below, its brightness shone through the treetops as though a wedding dress had been hanging there. As I went on, I threw an apple and it curved through the air, connecting my path with the forest and the rocks.

It is that expedition which gave me my justification for writing a "Lesson of Mont Saint-Victoire."

In the great painter's territory I had grown more invisible from day to day—to others as well as to myself; the strangers around me helped by amiably overlooking me. After a while I could choose, or so it seemed, to be "the invisible man" whenever I pleased. I felt, not that I had vanished or dissolved into the landscape, but that I was well hidden among its objects (Cézanne's objects).

But hadn't this always been the case; wasn't there even in my childhood something which, like L'Estaque later on, was for me the *place*, the *thing* of concealment? Cézanne has nothing to do with this thing (but another painter does, no doubt). It took on meaning for me through the legend of a saint (in which it is not even mentioned).

The thing is a woodpile; the legend is the story of St. Alexius under the stairs; and the other painter is Pirosmani, a Georgian peasant painter who died penniless under the last of the Tsars and is now famous. There is a connection, which cannot be explained but can be told.

In my grandparents' house there was a wooden stairway, and under it a windowless room. In that room "under the stairs" (so I believed at the time) St. Alexius, returned unrecognized from foreign parts, lay reveling in the thrills of concealment (which were my own). Later I saw similar stairways in other houses, with storerooms for tools or neatly piled firewood under them. Much later I daydreamed that my ancestors, about whom I knew next to nothing, came from Georgia; and just as I had found in Cape Cod the house for the man in the story that was still to be written, I hoped that in the East I would learn something of his origin—in this, my point of departure was Pirosmani's pictures, which kept pace with his own life. The Georgian painter had moved about the country a good deal, earning a livelihood chiefly by painting the signboards of inns, and had spent the last years of his life unrecognized, in a woodshed, which in my fancy was "under the stairs" . . . And (closing the circle?) I as a writer longed at one time to become with my writing a corduroy road for someone else (who could, however, be myself), or, precisely, a light-colored, tightly-packed woodpile.

The justification for writing—needed for every new work—made its appearance on that descent from Mont Sainte-Victoire, when I succeeded for once in criticizing myself (instead of sinking into myself and losing my sense of humor as usual when walking downhill). At the sight of a shimmering meadow, which instantly made me think: Garden of Eden, and where even the molehills appeared to me at first as "in the blue distance," I took myself to task: "Why at the sight of beauty must you draw celestial comparisons? Look at the earth, speak of the earth, or just of this spot here. *Name* it with its colors."

I deliberately slackened my pace and bowed my head, to avoid looking into the distance. In the dusk, I looked into a side path, but only out of the corner of my eye. At present, I don't remember whether I stood still. Most likely I went on without stopping, but in a state of joyful calm; once again imbued with my justification for writing, once again a self-confident scribe and storyteller.

Why do I say *justification*? Because there I experienced the moment of unspecified love without which there can be no justified writing. Far down the side path I saw a mulberry tree (what I actually saw was reddish spots of juice in the light-colored dust of the path), in fresh, radiant conjunction with the juice-red of the mulberries of the summer of 1971 in Yugoslavia, where for the first time I had managed to conceive of true joy; and something—the thing seen? my vision?—darkened; at the same time, every detail appeared round and clear; and all this in the midst of silence in which my usual self became strictly No One, and I, in a sudden transformation, became something more than merely invisible, namely, *a writer*.

Yes, this twilit side path now belonged to me and became namable. In addition to innocently uniting the fragments of my own life with the mulberry spots on the dust, the moment of fantasy (in which I alone am real to myself and know the truth) revealed to me anew my kinship with other, unknown lives, thus acting as an unspecified love and striving to communicate itself in a form conducive to fidelity, namely, as a justified project aimed at the cohesion of my never-to-be-defined nation as our common form of existence: this was a moment that relieved me and cheered me, the daring moment of my calling as a writer, and in it I became as serene as when thinking "the idea of a ship." But then the usual torment (which, however, is the opposite of despair) returned: "But what is form? What has the innocent man I am here (I do not feel myself to be good, only innocent) to tell? And who is the hero of such a story?" (For, unspecified reader, who but the subject of a picture or the hero of a story ever proposed anything to you in your life?)

A car stopped (there was a quiet little dog in the back seat) and gave me a lift to Aix, where I arrived with a passionate resolve; in pursuit of a dematerialized but substantial language, with which I hoped to tell of the long overdue return of the man with the folded arms. No, it was not a torment; it was work.

The Picture of Pictures

Thus far, I have been speaking of a painter and a writer; of pictures and writing. But now it is time to tell how I came to see the painter Paul Cézanne as a teacher of mankind—I do not fear to say: *the* teacher of mankind in the here and now.

Stifter formulated the eternal law of art, as follows: "The blowing of the wind the murmur of the stream the growing of the grain the rolling of the sea the greening of the earth the glowing of the sky the light of the stars—these things I regard as great . . . Let us try to find the gentle law by which the human race is governed." Yet one is struck by the fact that Stifter's stories almost consistently end in catastrophe; indeed, the situation in itself, without dramatic accent, becomes a menace. At first, the snow falls "peacefully, tranquilly"; it is a "lovely white cloak"; then, to the children, when they venture up to the at first "beautiful," then "terrifyingly blue" glacier, it becomes a "white darkness"; for weeks the "radiant sky" over the village remains a radiant sky, but in the end it transforms the "soft blue air" into a "sheer cliff." Explanations for this transposition of things into the realm of the sinister have been sought and found in the person of the writer. But the time element in the narrative is also responsible for providing the gently murmuring stream with those dangerous pits—into which, moreover, no one sinks for good, so that the opening sentence of *Limestone* applies to all the other tales: "I am going to tell a story a friend once told me, in which nothing unusual happens, but which I have nevertheless been unable to forget." (Stifter, who was also a painter, never depicted a catastrophe in his paintings; at worst, they show trees felled by the wind.) At the Musée du Jeu de Paume in Paris, there is a Cézanne painting whose meaning—not only to him, the painter, and not only to me, a writer—I thought I understood.

It was painted in the last years of his life, after the turn of the century. Like many of his earlier pictures, it depicts rocks and pine trees. The site is named in the title: *Rocks Near the Grottoes Above the Château Noir.* (The Château Noir is an old manor house above the village of Le Tholonet.)

It is hard to say exactly what I understood. My strongest feeling at the time was one of "nearness." Today, in my need to communicate my experience after long "reflection on things seen" (it would be more accurate to speak of a brainstorm), a scene in a film comes to mind: Henry Fonda dancing with his mother in *The Grapes of Wrath.*

All those present are dancing to ward off a grave menace: driven from place to place by landlessness, they are defending the bit of soil on which they have finally found a home and refuge, from the enemies all around them. Although the dancing is purely a stratagem (while whirling each other about, mother, son, and all the rest exchange wily, vigilant looks), it is nevertheless a dance like other dances (and as none before it), a dance of warmth and solidarity.

Danger, dance, solidarity, warmth—these were the components of my feeling of "nearness" as I stood looking at the painting. Suddenly magnified, the pines and rocks were deep within me—just as a flushing bird momentarily flies through one's body with giant wings; but instead of passing as such phantasms of horror do, they remained. Yes, my feeling of nearness was an insight. In the year 1904, when this picture was painted, something irrevocable happened, a cosmic event; and the cosmic event was this picture.

Once, when Cézanne was asked to explain what he meant by a *motif*, he slowly joined the outspread fingers of his two hands together, folded, and interlocked them. Reading about this, I remembered that in looking at this picture I had seen the pines and rocks as intertwined letters, their meaning as clear as it was indefinable. In one of Cézanne's letters I read that he did not paint "from nature"—that his pictures were "constructions and harmonies parallel to nature." Then, taught by the canvas itself, I realized that in that historical moment the pines and rocks, on a plain surface but—irreversibly dispelling the spatial illusion!—in colors and forms bound to the actual spot ("above the Château Noir"), had joined hands to form a coherent picture writing unique in the history of mankind.

Thing-image-script in one: that is the miracle—and yet it does not fully communicate my feeling of nearness. Here I must also mention the house plant which, looking through a window, I saw against the landscape as a Chinese character. Cézanne's rocks and trees were more than such characters; more than pure forms without earthly traces—in addition, they were woven into incantations by the painter's dramatic brushstroke. At first my only thought was: So near. Now they seem to me related to the first cave paintings. They were *things*, they were *images*, they were *script*; they were brushstrokes—and all these were in harmony.

In a few hundred years, the painter had written from L'Estaque, the whole world would be flattened. He had added: "But the little that remains is still very dear to the heart and eye." And thirty years later, he said: "Things are in a bad way. We shall have to hurry if we want to see anything. Everything is vanishing."

Has everything really vanished? Didn't it come to me, in those days at the Jeu de Paume, that Cézanne's great thing-image-script-brushstroke-dance, that miracle unique in the history of mankind, will open the world to us mortals for all time? Didn't I recognize those pines and rocks as the picture of pictures, in the presence of which (and of others near it and elsewhere) the "good self" could continue to find new strength? Didn't I, even then, regard the still lifes on the opposite wall as well cared-for "children"?

The Jeu de Paume is a rather commonplace museum—but this wall radiant with beloved objects is exemplary in its beauty (not to mention the fact that the window opens out on the Place de la Concorde, which to Cézanne's mind was "the square of squares"). The pears, peaches, apples, and onions, the vases, bowls, and bottles strike one, in part because of the slight distortions and inclined planes, as enchanted things, which in another moment will come to life. And yet it is obviously the instant before the earthquake: as though these things were the last of their kind.

There is a comparable wall in a museum in Switzerland. Three large portraits hang side by side: the painter himself, his wife, and the boy with the red vest. These nameless persons seem to be looking out of the window of a train that is standing still but traveling through the ages. They have been traveling a long time and still have a long way to go. Only the child props his head on one hand and seems tired; the grownups are erect, expressionless, and alert. Their wall now forms an intersection with the still-life wall at the Jeu de Paume: the Zürich train with the three people in it stops at the avenue of fruit in Paris.

Are Cézanne's works, then, messages? As I see it, they are proposals. (Ludwig Hohl once said that Van Gogh's visions "could also have been told," whereas Cézanne's "could only be painted.") What do they propose to me? Their secret lies in producing the effect of proposals.

For, obviously, almost everything has vanished. In a pile of fruit, the dull yellow of one waxed orange is enough; after that I can imagine nothing more. Where today is the color that comes from the substance of the thing itself? What thing today is *food for the eyes*? That is why I search so needily for intact nature. Time and again, what I find may be sublime, yet time and again I dread the horizon that will devour me. Consequently, in my need for continuity, I willfully immerse myself in everyday, man-made things. Didn't I just see a beech copse reflected in the gray-blue of the asphalt? Doesn't the roar of the evening plane occasionally make a day start over? Isn't the tin star on the child's sweater a time-honored tradition? And don't the plastic bags from which the newspapers have finally been removed flutter in the sun like light-colored pleated skirts? Yes, but that isn't everyday life. It can be said that everyday life has become evil. Nothing is left but a sad, episodic beauty surrounding man-made things, and that is unreal because there is no certainty of its recurrence. (True, once after leaving Aix I saw a shimmer of Mont Sainte-Victoire clay in the red plastic floor of the Marseilles airport . . .) Happy the man whom a pair of eyes awaits at home!

Here in Austria I once heard two village elders say:

"If they have no faith in anything—then what are they here for?" They were not referring to me, yet I felt concerned. For I had long been troubled by the thought that "it takes faith to keep things for any length of time." What was this secret of faith that the village elders seemed to know? I could never have described myself as a believer, in childhood still less than now; but didn't I, very early in my life, have a "picture of pictures"?

I'm going to describe it, because this is the place for it.

This picture was an object in a receptacle in a large room. The room was the parish church, the object was the chalice with the white wafers, the receptacle was a gilded tabernacle, which opened and closed like a revolving door and was kept in a recess in the altar. This so-called holy of holies was for me the *reality of realities*.

And this reality had its recurring moment: the moment when, by virtue of the words of the consecration, the particles of bread, which had, in a manner of speaking, become God's body, were enclosed in the tabernacle along with the chalice. The tabernacle was opened; already wrapped in its cloth, the object, the cup, was placed in the glorious colors of its silken grotto; the tabernacle closed—and behold the golden radiance of its rounded exterior!

That is how I see Cézanne's *réalisations* (except that I stand before them, instead of kneeling): a transformation and sheltering of things endangered—not in a religious ceremony, but in the form of faith that was the painter's secret.

The Cold Field

Unlike the streets of Paris, even those I knew only briefly, which time and again appear to me when I least expect them, Mont Sainte-Victoire has never once turned up in my daydreams. On the other hand, the mountain returns to me almost daily in an analogy of forms and colors. Almost imperceptible slopes can lead to solitary peaks and adventurous high plateaus; and then, even without specific knowledge, I feel that I understand the country around me.

But of course the aftereffect of this mountain goes far beyond a refreshing understanding of nature.

There is a hill on the outskirts of Paris which, unlike Montmartre, can scarcely be seen from the city. I am referring to Mont-Valérien, in the western suburb of Suresnes. Barely distinguishable from the chain of hills running westward parallel to the Seine, Mont-Valérien is the site of a fort where, during the Second World War, the German occupying forces carried out mass executions.

I had never been there, but after seeing Mont Sainte-Victoire I was drawn to the place. One fine summer afternoon I went up and saw a stone cemetery against the blue sky; I picked blackberries that were hard and sweet; and glancing at the numerous little houses on the surrounding hills, where here and there a dog barked and a wisp of smoke arose, I perceived nothing but a ghostless present. Slowly, I descended the eastern slope, crossed the Seine, and on my way back to Paris passed through the Bois de Boulogne. There I climbed another scarcely noticeable hill which also has its associations with the war and is known as the Mont des Fusillés; the trees (beneath which, as everywhere else, Sunday excursionists were lying) still show bullet holes. That afternoon was the only time I ever thought of Cézanne in such a connection, though his paintings have often been likened to music; namely when, to preserve the present, I wanted to shake it "like a marimba."

Later, at nightfall, I stood on an overpass at the edge of the city and looked down at the Boulevard Périphérique, which appeared to me in mobile gold colors; and the thought that then crossed my mind still strikes me as reasonable: namely, that someone like Goethe should envy me for living at the end of the twentieth century.

Without my intending them to, the circles around Mont Sainte-Victoire grew wider and wider.

My stepfather came from Germany. Before the First World War his parents moved to Berlin from Silesia. My father is also a German; he came from the Harz Mountains (where I have never been). But all my mother's forebears were Slovenes. In 1920 my grandfather voted for the inclusion of southern Austria in Yugoslavia, which had just been established, and the German-speaking people of his village threatened to beat him up. (My grandmother flung herself between them; scene of action: "The turn of the plow"; Slovenian *ozara.*) After that, he seldom opened his mouth about public affairs. As a young girl my mother acted in a Slovenian amateur theater group. Later she was proud of her ability to speak the language, and in Russian-occupied Berlin after the war her Slovenian was a big help to us all. True, she never really felt like a Slovene. The Slovenes have indeed been said to lack a sense of nationality, because unlike the

Serbs and Croats they never had to fight for their country; and indeed, many of their songs are sadly introverted. I'm told that Slovenian was my first language. Later the local barber told me over and over again that when I came for my first haircut I hadn't known a word of German and our whole conversation had been in Slovenian. I don't remember that, and at any rate I've almost forgotten the language. (I'd always had a feeling that I came from somewhere else.) At the country school in Austria I was sometimes homesick for Germany—which to me meant postwar Berlin. When I heard about the Third Reich, I knew there had never been anything more evil, and when possible I acted accordingly. But it never occurred to me that the Germany I had known as a child was in any way involved.

Later on, I spent almost ten years in various towns in the Federal Republic, which struck me as brighter and more spacious than my native country; and in Germany, in contradistinction to Austria, where, so it seemed to me, hardly anyone spoke my language, I was sometimes able to express an opinion with passion (though in so doing I often felt that I was betraying something else). I can still conceive of living in Germany, for I know that no other country numbers so many "incorrigibles" who hunger for their daily reading matter; so many of the dispersed and obscure nation of readers.

But it was in Paris that I first encountered the spirit of the crowd and disappeared into the hubbub. Thereafter, from the remoteness of France I moved to, as I couldn't help seeing, an increasingly evil and sclerotic Federal Republic. Much as German groups might speak of "tenderness," "solidarity," and "mutual encouragement," they behaved like mobs; as individuals, they went sentimental. ("Obstinacy, sentimentality, and travel" is the motto of a German friend of mine.) Regardless of age, the people in the street seemed worn out; their eyes had lost their color. Instead of growing, the children seemed just to shoot up. Fragments of painted high-rise buildings drove down the desolate streets in the form of bright-colored cars, and in those cars headrests had taken the place of people. The typical sounds were the whirring of parking meters and the popping of cigarette vending machines; the corresponding words were *Abfluss-sorgen* (drainage problems) and *Fernsehkummer* (television trouble). The signs on the shops were not "Bread" or "Milk" but pretentious acronyms. Almost everything, in newspapers and books as well, bore a spurious name. On Sunday, the flags on the department stores fluttered over emptiness. The many dialects, once the "accents of the soul," had become a soulless garble which (in Austria, too) turned my stomach. True, there were mailboxes for "Other Destinations"—but no feeling for north, south, east, and west. Even nature seemed to have lost its reality; the treetops and the clouds over them moved spasmodically—the fluorescent tubes of the double-decker buses were aimed straight at me, dog chains jangled behind front doors, the people at the windows were on the lookout for accidents and nothing else; an intercom shouted into a deserted street: "Who is it?"; newspapers advertised artificial turf; and only here and there, in the vicinity of the public toilets, might one glimpse a sort of mournful beauty.

Then I understood violence. This world with its "functional forms," labeled in every detail, yet totally speechless and voiceless, was not in the right. Maybe it was pretty much the same somewhere else, but here I saw it naked, and I wanted to knock someone, anyone, down. I hated this country, with as much enthusiasm as in my childhood I had hated my stepfather, whom in my imagination I often hit with an ax. And the statesmen there (like all artists engaged in politics) struck me as ham actors—never an utterance that came from a center—and my only thought was of "failure to atone."

At that time, I even detested the geology of Germany; its valleys, rivers, and mountains; yes, my loathing reached deep into the subsoil. It was therefore my intention that in his book *On Spatial Configurations* the man with folded arms, a geologist, would describe a West German landscape, which would be known as the Cold Field. In prehistoric times two rivers had "disputed" the watershed. The one, taking advantage of its steeper gradient, had moved back its starting point beyond the original watershed and "piratically" tapped the other river. "Beheaded," as it were, by the blade of the first, the valley of the second was laid waste. Below where it was tapped, the river became "stunted"—with the result that the valley seems much too wide and has for that reason become known as the Cold Field.

But even before setting foot on European soil, the geologist had turned himself back into me, and since then I had been living in Berlin. I reread Hölderlin's *Hyperion*, finally understood every sentence, and was able to look on its words as images. In addition, I often stood looking at the paintings in Dahlem. Once I stepped out of the Underground onto the little round Platz of Dahlem-Dorf, saw it edged with composite street lamps like the Place de la Concorde in Paris, glimpsed the beauty of a "nation," and even felt a certain longing for something of the kind. And, in Germany, the word "Reich" showed me its new meaning when, on my long way around, I crossed the northern "flatlands" described by

Nicolas Born and was once again reminded, by the curving sand roads and dark patches of water, of seventeenth-century Dutch landscape paintings. The new meaning came from a distinction: those landscapes, if only they had a stunted tree or a single cow in them, showed the radiance of a "Reich"—while here I was moving in an utterly lackluster "district."

Until then, moreover, it had never struck me that Berlin is situated in a broad glacial valley (previously the fact would hardly have interested me); the houses still seemed to have been scattered at random over a steppe-like plain. Then I discovered that a few streets away was one of the few spots in the city where the receding ice had formed a discernible slope. There lay the Matthäus Graveyard, the top of which, rising high above the surrounding country, is said to be the highest point in the Schöneberg district. (The artificial rubble mountains thrown up after the war don't count.) One afternoon I set out to visit the place. The sultry air and distant thunder were just what was needed. The first barely perceptible slope in the road put me in a state of expectancy. But it was only in the cemetery that the rise became visible. The level hilltop provided a kind of terrace among the graves. There I sat (the tombstone beside me bore the names of the Brothers Grimm) and looked down into a large hollow. The city I saw looked entirely different, and from the bottom of the valley, far in the distance, a river feeling rose up to me. The first drops of rain fell warm on my head, and today I feel justified in applying a sentence from the old novels to the man who was sitting there: "In that moment no one was happier than he." On my way down, in the gently sloping Langenscheidtstrasse, I felt the flow of the primordial waters: a clear, gentle feeling. In the evening my graphite pencil point glowed, and for a few days the flags on the Kaufhaus des Westens waved at the bottom of the valley.

Then at last I made my way to the Havelberg, barely a hundred meters above sea level, said to be the highest point in West Berlin. In a grassy clearing I saw sacks, which stood up and proved to be sleepy soldiers. By a roundabout route I reached the summit, which I myself determined, because the Havelberg forms a fairly level ridge. There I lay down under a pine tree and once again breathed the air of the present. From a shooting blind, with wild boar running about below it, I looked down in the dusk on East Berlin, where we had lived after the war.

It was by pure chance that I also went to see my father that year. We hadn't heard from him in a long time, and I was surprised when he answered the phone. He was living in a small town in northern Germany. As we had done on our few previous meetings, we made elaborate arrangements to meet, missed each other as usual, and spent the whole evening trying to figure out why. Since the death of his wife, he lived alone in the house; he didn't even have a dog anymore. He saw his likewise widowed woman friend only on weekends; in between, one called the other's number each evening and let the phone ring briefly as a sign that he was still alive. (But here neither house nor man will be identified in the usual way.) In his eyes I saw the fear of death and suspected a belated sense of responsibility. Here, it seemed to me, was someone's son. Halfhearted inquiry was swept away by the spirit of questioning, and I was able (wanting to was enough) to ask about what had long been kept silent. And he answered me, partly for his own sake. Casually, he told me that mornings, when he looked at himself in the mirror, he felt like "smashing his face," and then for the first time I discovered in him the forlornness, bitterness, and rebelliousness of a hero. When late that night he took me to the train, a poster fastened to a tree outside the station was ablaze; some unemployed taxi drivers had set it on fire.

Once after that, I caught sight of another Germany, not the Federal Republic and its Länder, nor yet again the ghoulish Reich, nor the half-timbering of the petty principalities. It was earth-brown and wet with rain, and it was on a hilltop; it was windows; it was urban, devoid of people, and festive; I saw it from a train; it was the house on the other side of the river; it was humorously quiet and was called Mittelsinn; it was "the silent life of regular forms of silence"; it was enigma; it was recurrent and real. The man who saw it had a crafty feeling like Lieutenant Columbo after solving a case; yet knew that there could never be lasting relief.

The Hill of Spinning Tops

It was now certain that I had a communication to make about Cézanne's mountain. But what was the law of this communication, its self-evident, necessary form? (For of course I wanted to accomplish something with my writing.)

I couldn't be satisfied with a dissertation that would merely look for relationships in my field of inquiry—my ideal had always been the gentle emphasis and appeasing flow of a narrative.

Yes, I wanted to tell a story (and I enjoyed studying dissertations). For often, in reading and writing, I had seen the truth of storytelling as a clarity in which one sentence calmly engenders another and in which the truth—the insight that came before the story—is perceptible only as a gentle something in the transitions between sentences. Moreover, I knew that reason forgets, the imagination never.

For a time I thought of treating particular aspects—the mountain and me, the pictures and me—and setting them down side by side as unconnected fragments. But then I rejected such fragmentary treatment because it would have resulted not from a possibly unsuccessful striving for unity but from a deliberate method, known in advance to be safe.

Then, in Grillparzer's *The Poor Minstrel*, I read: "I trembled with a longing for unity." A desire for the One in All was rekindled in me. For I knew that unity is possible. Every single moment of my life hangs together with every other—without intermediate links. I need only reconstitute them with the help of my imagination.

At the same time, a well-known restriction occurred to me; for I also knew that analogies must not be arrived at lightly; quite unlike the daily muddle in our minds, they are the golden fruits of the imagination after passionate upheavals, they are the true comparisons, thus, as the poet said, forming "the far-shining brow of the work." It therefore seemed presumptuous to trust in such analogies to hold a story together.

The next problem was when. When was this tale to unfold? It had long seemed to me that there were no longer any fitting places for a story to happen in. For the story of the man with folded arms I had to reach far back into the wilderness, and such things as an airplane or a television set came close to wrecking my project. I therefore considered relegating the action to the turn of the century and choosing as my hero the young painter and writer Maurice Denis, who had once actually visited the revered Cézanne in his home country; and, if only because of the thick black coat in the studio, which resembled my grandfather's, I *felt* the atmosphere of the time.

But wasn't it part of my truth that the protagonist should be German-speaking? This led me to imagine a young Austrian painter in the period between the wars, who moves to Provence in 1938, shortly before his country is annexed by Germany. I already had a deeply etched image of such a man: one of my mother's brothers, who was blind in one eye and whose letters from the war, written in a clear script, I had read over and over again as a child. He was killed on the Russian front. I had dreamed of him all through my adolescence and now I felt a longing to be him again, and to see the blue background color of a wayside shrine through his eyes.

In the end, however, I hoped it might be "me" (I had transformed Sorger, the geologist, into myself, and besides, he persisted in many of my perceptions). The "lesson" told me not to "invent" but to "realize" (*réaliser*) (which of course called for invention at every step); and my personal certainty was to trust in Goethe's "good self" as the inner light of my story; as the bright and ennobling quality which inspires confidence in the reader. Nothing else is worth reading.

I then decided to take a second trip to Provence, where I expected to find the solution. But I didn't want to be alone there again. More and more keenly I felt the need for someone who would be right for me; not someone with a certainty, but someone who was himself groping, the kind of person who, like certain children, can still be asked the great questions.

So I arranged to meet D. in Aix. D. comes from a small town in Swabia and is a dressmaker. On leaving school, she moved to Paris and rented a two-room apartment. Though at first humiliated by the buyers and shopkeepers, she was soon making a living. She still goes back to her childhood home for such things as the dentist. Her parents are members of the "hidden nation" (of readers), and from the start she has looked upon pictures as more than accessory.

Her pictures are her "creations," each one of which represents an idea of its own. Her two-room apartment is at the same time a studio, resplendent with many-colored materials. She takes her work more seriously than anyone else I know, prides herself in it as only an artist can, and has no patience with anyone who interferes with it.

Once, she told me, she decided to create the "coat of coats." She was sure she had the strength for it, but in the end she had been defeated by the problem of "connections," which I "as a writer must have come up against." (That, so she said, was the end of her megalomania.) But the unfinished coat of coats had been so beautiful that people who had seen it on the Métro had been stricken with awe.

It was D. who kept bringing me messages in Paris about "conquering enemies through self-control" or "how your sensibility can give you power over others"; that kind of thing. After seeing Hitchcock's *Under Capricorn*, she spoke of Joseph Cotten's lips, lying "so quietly in his face"; and after seeing Ozu's films, she spread out a newspaper when cutting her nails, because that was what the Japanese master's favorite leading man had done.

There is nothing womanly about D.; she seems child-like or mannish or girlish, and when she feels free to speak her mind she reminds one of the slave girl who knows more than any master. Once I recognized her in Rembrandt's *Jacob Wrestling with an Angel*; she was the angel who in Genesis is referred to merely as "a man." Many people reveal a selfless, demonic, evil emptiness when you get close to them; but D. remains impenetrable—and can't bear for anyone to touch her. Yet, when I asked her what she needed her lover for, she replied: "Words alone aren't enough comfort to me."

Her eyes are bright and have rings under them. Once when I was sick, she came and stared at me mercilessly until I shooed her away. In other respects as well, she makes me think of a shaggy flightless bird; she doesn't gesticulate and seldom makes faces, she either sits very still or moves about (rather awkwardly). Still, she is always alert; never a moment's daydreaming; when she is with you, all her thinking is *with* you. This thinking-with makes her Voltaire's *bonne compagnie*: "He spurned men of science, and resolved from then on to live only in good company."

Yet D. doesn't open up to many people; she is shy and often embarrassed. Her power is at its best when she is alone, at work, or in her nightly wanderings through the streets of Paris, where someone occasionally lays a hand on her head (her parents, it seems, had been "in love" with her head).

As a rule she is silent (but once in a while she talks profusely or emits peculiar sounds of emotion or tenderness). She is—unusual for a woman?—a good walker. We had often gone for walks in the deciduous forests between Paris and Versailles, where here and there one sees dark, wide-branching cedars.

It was nearly winter. I had just seen a friend die, and was again beginning to take pleasure in my own existence. This friend, who thought of himself as the "first man to experience pain," had nevertheless tried up to the last moment to wish death away. I was thankful for all things and decreed: Enjoy yourself, take advantage of your days of good health.

At the airport the people were standing for once in dignified darkness; shadowy faces, without the usual hellish quality. When the name of someone I had once known well was called out, it seemed to me that all the people I had ever known had ceased to be anything but names over polyglot loudspeakers.

As the plane was putting down in Marseilles, Mont Sainte-Victoire plunged below the northern horizon like a whale. The plane trees on the Cours Mirabeau had lost almost all their leaves, the street had become a bare-bright row of bones. The avenue of Aix's summer glory was now wet, gray, and bare, and had been incorporated into the street network of Paris. We had the "two comfortable rooms" customary in old novels. I looked into D.'s bright, impenetrable eyes. She was already wearing the right kind of shoes. The very next morning we struck out eastward.

In my quest for unity I had discovered yet another clue, to which I felt committed, though I had no idea where, if anywhere, it might lead. In the preceding months, every time I had looked at Cézanne's paintings of his mountain, I had come across this clue, and it had become an obsession with me.

Seen from the west, where the mountain shows three prongs, it reveals its strata and folds in a geological cross section. I had read that Cézanne as a young man was friends with a geologist by the name of Marion, who in later years accompanied him on many of his expeditions in search of "motifs." As I studied the maps and descriptions of the mountain, my thoughts began, involuntarily and inexplicably, to revolve around one and the same point: a fault between two strata of different kinds of rock. This occurs on the gently rising ridge path leading from the west to the actual crest, and it can fittingly be called a "point" because here, where one stratum penetrates most deeply into the other, it also intersects the line of the ridge. This point, which in nature cannot be discerned with the naked eye, nevertheless recurs time and again in Cézanne's paintings, where it is indicated by a shadow line of varying length and thickness; even in the pencil sketches, the indentation is indicated by shading or at least by a delicate outline.

It was this spot more than anything else—I was about to start working—that impelled me to repeat the trip to Provence. From this new trip I expected the key; and even if my reason tried to talk me out of it, I knew that my imagination was right. By the time I got to Aix, to be sure, I was just looking forward to the expedition.

A bus took us as far as an aqueduct, and from there we hiked up the Chemin de Bibémus to the Plateau du Marin, an upland heath. From there, at first sight, Mont Sainte-Victoire seemed to jut out of the prickly heather like an erratic boulder. This is a quieter itinerary than the Route de Cézanne; it does not pass through the village but leads straight to the crest. After a while there is neither asphalt nor cars.

In town the sky had been veiled with rain; here on the plateau it was vast and soon turned to blue. We came to a sparse evergreen wood where the sun shone through the boughs and the pine needles sparkled on all sides. After a while, I asked D. cautiously why working on the coat of coats had dispelled her megalomania. She answered only: "I've got it back since then."

On the way up, there had still been oaks, losing their leaves in swarms. Now there were only evergreens, the air was balmy, and on the horizon the seasonless shimmering of the mountain. The screech of branches rubbing together took the place of the summer's cicadas. At the end of a side path the black-and-white magpie turned up again, fluttering like a paper glider. In time it grew so still on the plateau that the faint sounds from other levels suggested a ringing of bells. I peered between the open scales into the dark interior of a pine cone, and simultaneously at the gauze-blue cracks in a layer of cirrus clouds drifting high overhead. The thought of a bird's voice became that voice itself.

We passed runners, hunters, and soldiers, but they all seemed to be within their rights. The Foreign Legion dog existed no longer; or perhaps he was just a lump of clay lying in a gully. There were uphill and downhill stretches, twists and turns; the plateau is not an "unbroken level expanse" (as it has been described on the basis of Cézanne's paintings); it is crisscrossed by ravines and faults. Determined to familiarize myself with every detail of this landscape, I kept looking for shortcuts, with the result that we often got lost, looked separately for the right path, and saw each other standing like idiots on two different hills.

We hadn't meant to climb to the top; but then, without deciding anything, we kept on climbing until we were there. It was as windy as in summer, and neither warmer nor colder. Late in the afternoon, we stopped at

Le Tholonet and sat tired and contented in the Auberge Thomé, alias L'Etoile d'Or. It was good to be able to say, simply, that we were hungry.

We looked out at the mountain where we had just been. In between there is a chain of low hills, at one point broken by a hollow. One part of it had been left bare by a forest fire. Not even bushes were growing on the slopes, and the rain had dug deep grooves in the naked clay. These grooves in the otherwise even slope twined themselves into an inextricable tangle; here and there the runoff had shaped the earth into conspicuous towers and pyramids with big bluish stones on top of them. On a small scale, this whole bare patch, with its tangle of runnels leading nowhere, was very much like the vast wilderness in South Dakota, the scene of countless Westerns, to which discouraged wanderers gave the name of Badlands. The other part of the chain, spared by the fire, was covered by a dense growth of pine trees, which rose up in tiers, branch over branch, as far as the hilltop. In her dress pieced together from different-colored materials, which was at the same time a coat, D. sat between me and the view.

Only then, thinking back, did I remember the point which my imagination had circled for so long. I looked up to the mountain ridge and looked for the gap. It was not visible to the naked eye, but I knew that the place was marked by a power pylon. The place even had a name: it was called Pas de l'Escalette. And below it, in flatter alluvial land, there was a small abandoned hut, shown on the map as the Cabanne de Cézanne.

Something slowed down. The longer I looked at my gap, the surer I was—of a solution? an insight? a discovery? an inference? a finality? Gradually the gap in the distant crest transferred itself to me and became a pivot.

My first feeling was deadly fear—as though I were being crushed between two strata of rock; then—if ever—one of openness, of a single all-enveloping breath (which could immediately be forgotten). The blue sky over the hilltop grew *hot.* In the densely wooded area beside it, the variegated green of the pines; the dark shadow lines between the branches were rows of windows in a world-wide hillside colony; and then every tree in the forest was separately visible, spinning in its place, an *everlasting* top; and with it the whole forest (and the whole great colony) spun and stood still. Behind it the true and trusted silhouette of Mont Sainte-Victoire, and between it and myself D. in her colors, a comforting human form (for a moment I saw her as a blackbird).

No one threw up his arms in amazement. Someone slowly joined his hands and boldly knotted them into a fist. I would go all out and risk all for all!—I saw the realm of words opening up to me—with the Great Spirit of Form; the sheltering cloak; the interval of invulnerability; throughout "the indefinite prolongation of existence," as the philosopher defined time; I had stopped thinking of any "reader"; I only looked at the ground in passionate gratitude. Black-and-white pebble mosaic. Over the stairs leading to the upper story of the inn floated a blue balloon, fastened to the banister. On a table out in the open stood a bright-red enamel pitcher. Far in the distance, above the Philosopher's Plateau, the air was that unusually fresh blue that Cézanne so often used in painting this countryside. Over the mountain face itself, cloud shadows flew as though someone were drawing curtains over and over again, and at length (the early mid-December sunset) the whole mountain stood still in a yellow glow, as though turned to glass, yet did not, as another mountain would have done, cut off my homecoming. And I felt the structure of all these things within myself, as my armor. TRIUMPH! I thought—as though the whole thing had already been successfully written. And I laughed.

Once again D. had thought with me and was immediately able to answer my question about the problem of connections and transition. She had even brought samples of the different materials intended for her coat: brocade, satin, damask.

"So you want me to tell you about the coat. It began with my calling what I had thought up the Great Idea. The coat was to embody it.

"I began with a sleeve. From the start I had difficulty forcing the firm rounded form I wanted on the soft, yielding material. I decided to back the material with a stiff woolen fabric.

"The sleeve was finished. I thought it so priceless, so beautiful, that I despaired of having the same strength for the other parts of the coat.

"I thought of my idea; of nature's moments of tension and sudden softening; how the one merges with the other.

"Every day I thought for an hour or two of the coat I had begun; I compared the parts with my idea and pondered: how was I to go on?

"The upper part was finished. When I started on the lower part, the unity was lost. The pieces I made had no connection with the upper part. At this point the weight of the thick and thin materials I had fitted together made my work more difficult. I had to hold them up in the sewing machine to keep them from slipping.

"I laid the pieces down in front of me side by side; none of them went with the others. I waited for the moment when suddenly my picture would hang together.

"During this time of examining and testing, I could feel myself growing physically weak and incapable. I forbade myself even to think of the Great Idea.

"Pictures and blueprints of Chinese roof construction, the problem of relieving the strain of heavy weights by proper distribution, filled me with excitement. I saw that connections are important no matter what one is doing.

"Then one day I stopped thinking about it and just sewed the pieces together. I made the coat curve inward at one point. It excited me to feel so sure of myself.

"I hung the coat on the wall. Every day, I tried it on. I began to think well of it. It was better than anything else I had done, but it wasn't perfect.

"In making clothes, you have to remember every form you use for reference as the work goes on. But you shouldn't have to quote it to yourself, you must automatically see the final form you are aiming at. In every instance there is only one correct one; the form determines the color and must solve the problem of transition.

"A transition must clearly divide and at the same time bring together."

The Great Forest

In the Vienna Kunsthistorisches Museum, there is a painting by Jacob van Ruisdael titled *The Great Forest.* It shows a spacious deciduous forest. In among mighty oak trees one sees the striking white of the birches that are so frequent in Ruisdael. The darkly mirroring water in the foreground is also a familiar feature of his work. Here it is a river ford so shallow that you can see the traces of the yellow sand road, which on emerging turns left and leads on into the woods. The picture probably takes its name from the dimension of the canvas, because what can be seen of the forest is small; immediately beyond it, an open space begins. It is a forest inhabited by peaceful folk: in the foreground, a wayfarer with hat and stick who has laid down his bundle and is sitting by the roadside; in the background, a man and woman who, lightly dressed and carrying an umbrella (there are grayish-white clouds in the sky), emerge from the curve in the road. But the picture may actually represent a segment of a "great forest"; for possibly the point of view is not outside but inside it—perhaps the wayfarer, as seems quite natural, has turned to cast a last look before going deeper into the woods. The feeling of spaciousness is further intensified by a peculiarity of seventeenth-century Dutch landscapes: for all the minuteness of their forms, they nevertheless, with their patches of water, their roads over dunes, their dark woods (under spacious skies), begin to grow as one beholds them. The trees grow perceptibly, and with them grows a quiet, overall twilight. Even the two horsemen who have stopped to rest grow as they stand there.

There is a forest of this kind near Salzburg; it is not one of those great forests one finds at the edge of large cities; it is no forest of forests; yet it is wonderfully real. It takes its name from the village of Morzg at its eastern edge. The road to it begins in a pass-like hollow between the Mönchsberg and the Festungsberg; known as the Schartentor, this hollow forms a kind of dividing line between the inner city and the southern plain, with its housing developments extending to the foot of the Untersberg. The forest can be seen through the arch at the city limits: a band of apparently tall trees crossing the plain from east to west on this side of the two-humped rocky hill of Hellbrunn. Though hardly an hour's walk distant, it appears, seen from the city, to be veiled in faint distant blue, as though there were a river in between (actually, the Salzach is farther east). First comes an urban sort of "meadow," traversed by concrete walks and resounding with footsteps—in the middle of it, all by itself, the former "keeper's house"; in the evening, one of its windows glows with an almost imperceptible inner light and muffled singing can be heard from within; then comes an intersection guarded by three successive stop-lights; and then a "quiet zone" (the Thumeggerbezirk), where there are no shop windows to distract one, or any other mark of city life. A brook, actually the arm of a canal, runs parallel to the road, in the opposite direction; sometimes its glitter extends a long way and evokes vague memories. Here most of the trees are birches; they appear to be native to the spot, as in the woods of far-off Russia. The bushes are light-red willows, a tangle of many-armed candelabra when the sun shines through.

The road across the plain rises gently—just enough to make cyclists lift themselves briefly out of their seats—and then runs level again. The slight increase in altitude makes it possible to speak of a plateau. There is nothing citified about the meadow here; it is an open field with a lone farmhouse in it. A fall wind from the Untersberg that towers in the background is now discernible (on the way back, at a scarcely lower level, the sudden warm stillness of the air is even more evident). Over the strip of peat bog at the foot of the mountain there is often a fine haze, out of which, when it thickens to fog, the crowns of the trees blossom. The meadow in the foreground is also a peat bog; the molehills are black (with white pebbled in them); chickens from the farm, often with windblown ruffs, are scratching about in it. Through a concrete culvert another small canal passes under the road leading to the next housing development.

The unusual thing about this development is the crooked pines at the entrance to it—not at the edge of the road, but forming an island in the middle of the asphalt, a forerunner to the row of pines which appear, often in a harsh reflected light, at the end of the street. Many of the houses look out on empty fields, this village has nothing urban about it, but neither is it rural. The two rows of houses seem to be marching into the fallow fields. The houses are low, of distinctly different colors, many partly of wood; almost all have espaliers, suggesting raised ornaments, running along their fronts. In part because of the black tundra soil in the gardens and the voices, which often change language from one house to the next, this long, straight street suggests a pioneer settlement in the Far North. Except that here innumerable cats, sauntering noiselessly back and forth between the rows of houses, replace the whimpering, howling dogs chained to stakes.

The row of pine trees at the end of the street proves to be the entrance to a cemetery. Now and then a drunk is shoved out of the nearby inn, stands at the door for a while singing defiance, then suddenly falls silent and goes away. It is a large cemetery. Several parallel paths lead through it to the south. Over them towers a statue of Christ on the cross, who—as in no existing painting—is first glimpsed from the side. The paths are long and narrow, and in the archway at the end of them the approach to the Morzg Forest shimmers green. Now and then a slow funeral procession moves past, bells toll, and for a moment a stranger walking behind the coffin becomes a friend or relative of mine.

This approach is a wide, flat, almost treeless meadow,

suggesting a recently dried-up lake; windy and, after the balmy stillness of the cemetery, often wintry cold. Part of it is used for sporting events, and a random passerby may be called upon to play the role of referee. All in all, the children here are more trusting than anywhere else; they draw grownup strangers into conversations about the weather, which usually begin with "Cold today, isn't it?" At one point, one skirts the long wooden poles of a paddock, and on foggy days one seems to be looking through Japanese sliding doors. An old farmhouse has been preserved and fitted out with old-fashioned trappings, a well, a watering trough, a wooden bench, and a great pile of firewood—but all that doesn't add up to a farm. Now the forest can again be seen: brown (inky at dusk), and taking up most of the horizon; yet narrow; in places, that is, one can see through to the other side. To the right, high above the forest, the truncated pyramid of the Untersberg; to the left, farther in the background, a jagged cliff which, with its regular fluting, shines in the sunlit haze like a giant scallop shell. The road leads straight into the forest; the meadow is part of it, a vast clearing.

The first indication that one is in the forest (apart from the wooden benches) is the hazelnut bushes with their catkins, which wave in the slightest breeze—fine, densely parallel lines, falling like rain in diagrammatic sketches. The trees are dark, intermeshing spruces; each tree—and consequently the whole forest—is about to start spinning.

A wide, straight road—apparently the main entrance—leads into the forest. The threshold feeling is a calm that leads one onward without purpose. Once inside, you find that the forest, which looked level from outside, conceals a low chain of hills running eastward (visible from outside the forest only when there is snow on the ground and the rising ground shows through). The people of Salzburg are familiar with the hill of Hellbrunn, with its park and the castle at its feet; they go there on excursions. But few have heard of the Morzg Forest in between, and hardly any know that a part of this forest lies on top of a rocky hill. Here there are only logging roads and irregular paths, and you seldom see a walker; at the most you may hear a jogger's panting and see the skin of his face, mask replacing mask, change from dead to alive and back again at every step. A picket fence in a large bomb crater; a part of the wood—a circle the size of a face, suggesting yet another mask—seems to have been gnawed by rodents. On closer scrutiny, what seemed to be a wooden partition proves to be a target, and what looked like a bench in front of it is the shooting stand that goes with it. In origin, this rock is closely related to the civilized Hellbrunn hill. In an interglacial period, the melting ice deposited masses of rubble in a Garda-sized lake and with the calcareous water cemented them into the present rocky hill. This one, however, is not nearly as high (perhaps four stories) as the one in Hellbrunn, and scarcely longer than a long city block. In a schematic drawing it would be represented as an escarpment to the south of Salzburg, rising gently and then descending steeply (with sheer cliffs at the top).

From the road, you first glimpse the western foot of the hill and at the same time, like an enclave of color in the mass of spruces, a lighter-colored, almost parklike zone of acacias, alders, and hornbeams, through which a number of possible paths lead uphill; here the only conifers are larches, under which the grass is unusually soft and thick. At the edge of this deciduous copse there is an enormous beech tree. Its roots rise like cliffs, twining around an old boundary stone and almost concealing it.

Directly behind it, still at the bottom of the hill, a water hole is partially hidden beneath a thick layer of leaves. At first sight, one takes it for a rain puddle, but this water is clear and rises in almost imperceptible jets through the blackish leaves from deep underground. It is drinkable (a secret supply in case of emergency). One is struck by the rounded stones under the grass, ordered as regularly and compactly as cobbles in a road. They are many-colored, and on each one the lichens have etched a distinct picture script, as different from one to the next as traditions originating in different continents. A red, bell-shaped hump is a replica in miniature of Ayer's Rock in Australia, the largest monolith on earth. Another shows an Indian hunter's tale. At dusk, when the vegetation above them disappears, these stones reveal their secret writing and become a somber-white Roman road, leading into the forest.

Up the hill the cobbles lose themselves and the Roman road becomes a sunken lane with wagon tracks. The village children have made clay balls, which have dried in the meantime, but now when breathed on give off a fresh smell of rain. Often, when I look up, a lone bird is sitting in a larch tree; small as it may be, it seems strangely large silhouetted against the slender branches of this kind of tree. The rust-brown windward sides of the tree trunks, which point the way from east to west, remain white for a long while after a snowstorm, and it looks as if these trees were all birches. When it rains, there is nothing blacker than the elephant legs of the beech trees.

The gully into which autumn leaves float at any time of year ends at a woodpile; at that point a night-black thicket begins—the only place where the forest shows anything like depth; the black hole tempts one to enter, but not even a child could squeeze through the dense growth. In addition, numerous alders rise abruptly from the ground; these are not trees with trunks and branches but crisscrossing poles (which in a storm are not uprooted but break in the middle); joined and reinforced by creepers, they form a kind of barrier before the underbrush.

This network catches the leaves, which in retrospect stand for the whole forest. They are windblown beech leaves, light-colored and oval—the oval shape accentuated by the grooves, which in every leaf radiate from the center to the edge, the color an even light-brown. For a moment, playing cards seem to be hanging on the bushes—and then they are lying on the ground all over the forest, sparkling and fluttering in the slightest breeze, reappearing wherever you go—a reliable game, whose only color is a gleaming light-brown.

The next strip of pines is rather wide-spreading for the species. Through them one sees, hardly a stone's throw away, the steep ridge, which instantly strikes me as "something fought for." Here the collective cry of a flock of birds flying overhead can sound like a burst of gunfire. Part of the sound is the sharp click of a stone falling somewhere in the silence—the ground is covered by moss all about—on another stone. The little white clouds flitting between the trees have turned out to be deer escutcheons, more of them with each glance. (They are part of the card game.) Or behind the trees appear the village children's faces, strangely separated from their bodies, like the faces of saints in old pictures. In the spruce woods, often said to be frightening or sinister, it is fairly quiet and dry in time of wind and rain, and palpably warmer than in the open country (powerful heartbeat when you lean your forehead against a tree trunk). In the course of time, the fallen pinecones begin to shimmer light-brown.

On the hilltop there is neither a panoramic view nor the benches that ordinarily go with one. But the tree roots invite you to sit down and rest, and you can let your legs dangle over the cliff. The city to the north is invisible; to the south, only a broad grassy meadow shows through. The little cliff, as pale gray as a termite's nest (it obviously provided the material for some of the tombstones in the cemetery just crossed), merges directly with the steep southern slope. Here the space between the trees is studded with stones that seem to have been carried down by landslides. At first sight, the white of the many birch trees suggests a snowstorm. In time, the green of the empty field below becomes warm and deep, and extends far beyond the city. Across it cuts a path on which a child once ran after a man, jumped up on his back, and was carried from there on. Another time, a real horseman merged with his horse in the darkness, to form a single gigantic creature. From a distance, the dialect of the people walking down below sounds like all the languages in the world rolled into one.

On the hilltop the village children are about the only passersby. With their varied costumes, they are the bright color in the forest. The forest is their big playground, and they are bursting with information about it. Question: "Do you know the forest well?" Answer: "Sure do!" Even if you don't hear a thing and there's no one in sight, the hill is certain to be full of them. At the first peal of thunder, figures can be seen running homeward between the trees.

The pale-gray crest road running straight westward looks something like a military highway. Bare saplings screech as they rub together in the wind, or send out muffled messages in Morse code. The resinous spots on the bark of the trees mark bullet holes. Lightning has struck off the main branch of a solitary beech, and the bare trunk shows three bright patches of color: white where the limb broke off, the blue-gray of the southern lee side, the rust-yellow of the windward side (black in the rain). The white flowers in the grass turn out to be animal teeth. And maybe a dog will come running out of the thicket, his tongue flapping from side to side like a whiplash, and silently sniff at the hollows of your knees from behind. The sharp-edged nagelfluh niches along the road repeat the pattern of the ancient cliff tombs. But they are empty. Light-brown beech leaves have blown in. With their ovals and parallel lines, they radiate eternal peace.

Then comes the slope, where the only perpetual spring in the forest has its source (today a trickle, tomorrow a torrent). Farther down, it has formed a little valley, with the three classical terraced steps. Now, at the eastern foot of the hill, the long-awaited cave, sealed by an iron door. Dripping is heard from within, mingled with vibrant sounds, as of someone beating a drumskin lightly. Again the children provide information: they've been in there "lots of times"; no bats; mushrooms are grown in there.

Here, on the level stretch just before the village (already its houses can be seen through the trees), lies the pond the wanderer has been looking forward to. The spring runs into it, and the road widens. Until early spring, the pond is sheeted in whitish-gray ice. My progress is deliberately slow. The remains of a corduroy road under my feet are another vague memory. One is struck by the contrast between the numerous elder bushes and the towering spruces. Early in the year, the branches put forth shadowy-green leaves, often bluish at the tips. It is only here in the vicinity of the village that birds gather. Their complicated calls turn the forest into a railroad station. Some sound like call signs: a long-drawn-out whistle like the swishing of a cowboy's lasso. The songs change with the seasons, and one is reminded of the slowly revolving sky in a planetarium. At dusk in the bright, intricately twining elder thicket a glow appears, as though rising from the ground. The last children pass, many of them barefoot. The pattern of a spruce bough suggests a palm frond.

In the round pond, now free of ice, the water circles almost imperceptibly. It teems with fish. Pieces of something that looks like volcanic tufa, but is actually polystyrene, are floating on the surface. At the edge of the pond, a raft hammered together from doors is rocked by a sudden wind squall as on an ocean wave. An evening shower taps lightly, kindly, on the wanderer's forehead.

On the threshold between forest and village, the cobbles of the Roman road reappear. Here there's another woodpile, covered with a plastic tarp. The rectangular pile with the sawed circles is the only brightness against a darkening background. You stand there and look at it until nothing remains but colors: the forms come later. They are gun barrels pointed at the beholder, but each of them individually is aimed at something else. Exhale. Looked at in a certain way—extreme immersion and extreme attention—the interstices in the wood darken, and something starts spinning in the pile. At first it looks like a scarred piece of malachite. Then the numbers of color charts appear. Then night falls on it and then it is day again. After a while the quivering of unicellular organisms; an unknown solar system; a stone wall in

Babylon. World-spanning flight, a concentration of vapor trails, and finally, a unique blaze of colors, taking in the entire woodpile, reveals the footprint of the first man.

Then inhale. And away from the forest. Back to the people of the present; back to bridges and squares; back to streets and boulevards; back to stadiums and newscasts; back to bells and department stores; back to drapery and glittering gold. And the pair of eyes at home?

Child Story

And so the summer ended.

In the following winter . . .

1

Often, in adolescence, he thought of living with a child later on. He looked forward to an unspoken sense of community, to quickly exchanged glances, to sitting down with the child, to irregularly parted hair, to being close together and far apart in happy unity. The light of this recurrent image was the darkening just before the onset of rain in a courtyard strewn with coarse sand, bordered with grass, outside a house that was never clearly seen but only sensed behind his back, under a dense cover of wide-spreading, sporadically murmuring trees. The thought of a child was taken as much for granted as his two other great expectations—the woman who, he felt sure, was destined for him and had long been moving toward him over secret pathways, and the professional life, which alone, he held, could offer him the freedom worthy of a human being. But these three yearnings had never once appeared to him together, joined in a single image.

On the day when the longed-for child was born, the adult stood in a football field not far from the hospital. It was a bright Sunday morning in spring; in the course of the game the puddles in the grassless space between the goalposts had been churned into mud, which sent up swirls of vapor. At the hospital he learned that he was too late; the child had already been born. (He had probably been none too eager to witness the obstetric proceedings.) His wife was rolled past him down the corridor; her lips were white and dry. The preceding night she had waited alone in the little-used labor room, on a very high rolling bed; when he brought something she had forgotten at home, there was a moment of profound gentleness between them, the man standing in the doorway with a plastic bag and the woman stretched out on the high metal bed in the middle of the bare room. It's a fairly large room. They are at an unaccustomed distance from each other. On the way from door to bed, the bare linoleum floor gleams in the whitish, humming fluorescent light. In the flickering glow as he switched it on, the woman's face had turned to him without surprise or fear. Behind him—it was long after midnight—the spacious, half-darkened corridors and stairways of the building were bathed in an aura of unique, inalienable peace, which carried over to the deserted city streets outside.

When the child was shown to the adult through the glass partition, what he saw was not a newborn babe but a complete human being. (The usual baby face made its appearance only in the photo taken later on.)

He was glad when it turned out to be a girl; but—as he later realized—his joy would have been the same either way. The creature held out to him behind the glass was not a "daughter," let alone "progeny," but a child. The man's thought was: It's happy. It's glad to be in the world. The mere fact of being a baby, without particular characteristics, was a source of good cheer—innocence was a form of the spirit!—which passed by stealth to the adult outside: those two, once and for all, have become a pair of conspirators. The sun shines into the room, they are on a hilltop. What the man felt at the sight of the child was something more than responsibility; it was also the urge to defend it, the primitive feeling of standing on two legs and of having suddenly grown strong.

At home in the empty apartment, where everything had been made ready for the newborn babe's arrival, the adult took a bath, more copious than ever before, as though he had just gone through the hardship of his life. And true enough, he had just finished a piece of work in which he thought he had attained to the self-evident, casual, yet reliable law he had been aiming at. The newborn babe; the satisfactory completed work; the fabulous midnight moment of oneness with his wife; for the first time in his life, the man reclining in the steaming hot water considered himself and saw a kind of perfection, small, unimpressive perhaps, but just right for him. He felt an urge to go out. The streets, for once, were those of a hospitable metropolis; to walk them alone that night was a feast. But on one condition: that no one should know exactly who I am.

That was the last oneness for a long time. When the child came into the house, it seemed to him, the adult, that he was falling back into a cramped childhood, when he had done little else but keep an eye on his younger brothers and sisters. In past years, movie houses, open streets, and the footlooseness that went with them had passed into his flesh and blood; these alone, he felt, left room for the daydreams that made life look like something adventurous and worth mentioning. But in all those footloose years, the handwriting on the wall said to him time and again, "You must change your way of life." Now, inevitably, his life underwent a radical change. He who had been prepared at the most for a few minor adjustments found himself a prisoner in the house, and all he could think, while pushing the crying baby around the apartment for hours, was, unimaginatively, that his life was over for a long time to come.

In the preceding years he had often been at odds with his wife. He respected the enthusiasm and conscientiousness she devoted to her craft—it was more magic than work, an outsider could detect no sign of exertion. And on the whole he considered himself responsible for her; yet often, in his secret heart, he was convinced that they were not right for each other, that their life together was a lie and, measured by the dream he had had of himself and a woman, utterly trivial. There were times when he cursed this marriage as the mistake of his life. But it was with the coming of the child that this episodic disunity became a definitive breach. Just as they had never been really man and wife, they were never, from the very start, real parents. He took it for granted that you went in to the child when it was restless at night; in her opinion this was wrong, and that in itself could provoke her to sullen, almost hostile silences. She went by the specialists' books and precepts, all of which, however grounded in experience, he despised. They infuriated him as presumptuous violations of the secret between him and the child. Hadn't the child, in its first appearance—the little face behind the glass partition, scratched by its own fingernails and yet so peaceful—been so world-shatteringly real that anyone who had even glimpsed it would surely know what was to be done? Just this was the woman's recurrent complaint: in the hospital she had been cheated out of that guiding vision. Through the fault of others, she had missed the moment of birth, something had been forever lost to her. The child, she said, was unreal to her; that was why she was afraid of doing something wrong, why she observed other people's rules. This the man failed to understand: hadn't the child been put into her arms practically the moment it was born? And besides, he couldn't help seeing that she handled it not only more skillfully than he but more patiently as well. Didn't she concentrate on what she was doing and follow through, whereas he, no sooner had he achieved the brief moment of bliss in which it seemed that with a stroke of the hand, thanks to the one crucial pulsebeat that was still needed, he had imparted the soothing, life-giving magic of his own self to a sleepless or sick little being, than as often as not he ran out of energy and the best he could do, bored and positively yearning to escape into the open, was to sit out his stint with the baby.

To make matters worse, the hostility of the outside world seems inevitable in such situations. No sooner was the child brought home, for instance, than ground was cleared for a high-rise building directly across the street; the days and nights resounded with jackhammers, and most of the adult's time was spent in writing letters to the builders, who reacted with expressions of surprise, alleging that "this is the first time," etc. etc.

Still, it takes an effort to recall such moments of unpleasantness or even depression. What preserved its reality and importance was in every case an image to which the memory, with no attempt to transfigure it but with the certainty that "This is my life," returned in grateful triumph; and even in connection with that period which, to judge by the dates, was one of apathy more than anything else, these flashes of memory revealed a vital energy, which nevertheless endured and gave promise for the future. The woman soon went back to her work, and the man took the child for long walks around the city. Avoiding his accustomed busy boulevard, he went the other way, exploring those old, uniformly dark districts where, more than in any other part of the city he had known, the pavement takes on the coloration of the earth below it and the sky above. Thus, as the adult maneuvered the baby carriage from roadway to sidewalk and back, the city became the child's native place. Leaf shadows, rain puddles, and snow-fraught air stand for the seasons, which were never before so distinct. The all-night pharmacy, where, after a race through driving snow in a spacious, festive light, the needed medicine is procured, becomes a new sort of landmark. On another winter evening, the television is switched on in the apartment; there sits the man with the child, who after crawling all over him finally falls asleep on top of him; with that warming little burden on his stomach, the TV becomes for once a pure joy. A late afternoon in a deserted S-Bahn station far out of town even leaves him with a Christmas Eve feeling (Christmas was indeed imminent): though alone on the platform, the adult is not the lonely young man or curiosity-propelled gadabout of old, but a prospector in search of lodgings for those entrusted to his care (yes, they were planning to move). The unusually large, glass-bright waiting room; the closed but well-stocked newsstand; the snowy air in the hollow below, where the curving tracks glistened in the beams of oncoming trains: all these are good tidings, which he will take home with him.

All his images of the life of that first year relate to the child—who, however, is physically present in few of them. Indifferent reminiscence might prompt the question: "Where actually was the child just then?" But when memory is warmth and its content is a dark color feeling outlasting the times of day as in an arcade, it can be assumed that the child is nearby, safe and warm. One such glance passes through the concrete gateway deep down into the still-empty grass of a giant stadium, blooming an unseasonable fresh green in the floodlight—white breath-clouds over every row of seats—where a famous foreign team will soon come running in for a friendship match; or from the top deck of a city bus through the rain-sprinkled windshield onto the urban colors which, reduplicated in the course of the ride, end by transforming little by little a chaotic jumble of streets into something like a hospitable city. In retrospect, the period when man and wife were still living alone became the time before the child. His vision of the two of them resembled one of the painter's pictures, showing a young man standing with bowed head at the seashore, hands propped on hips, waiting; behind him, only a bright sky, marked, however, around the bent arms, with distinct whorls and rays, which one viewer has likened to the winged spirits that hovered around the central figure in the art of former times—and true enough, when later the man looked at a photograph of himself and the woman, it seemed to him that the unborn child was winging its way through the empty air between them.

What determined the course of events in that first year was not harmony but a conflict exacerbated by the spirit of the times. For most members of their generation the traditional social forms had become "death," and the new forms, though not ordained by any external authority, imposed themselves with the power of a universal law. Their closest friend, whom until then one could picture only resolutely alone in his room, on the street, or at the movies (and who possibly was so close to them for that very reason), suddenly took to living with a group, and to strolling down the boulevard arm in arm with any number of people; now he who had often been embarrassingly mute spoke with uncanny ease in the name of all; he, who for a time had actually thought of himself as the preposterous "last of his kind," seemed justified in his opposition to the lone individual. The adult then began to look on the child as his work, as a pretext for turning his back on history. A pretext, because he knew that, even without a child and without work, he would never have been willing or able to play an active part in the manifestations of "history." He halfheartedly attended a few meetings, at which every sentence uttered was a spirit-deadening crime, and regularly delivered a flaming speech forbidding these people, once and for all, ever to open their mouths again—to himself on the way downstairs. Once, he even attached himself to a demonstration, but vanished after the first few steps. His main feeling in the new social groupings was one of unreality, more painful than before in the old ones. In the old ones, it had been possible to imagine a future—the new ones set themselves up as the sole possibility, as a compulsory future. And since the transvaluation was taking place mostly in the city, there was no getting away from the innovators. Perhaps because of his indecision, he became an address for these people. He had long recognized them as one more hostile power, and his only reason for not expressly repudiating them was that the enemies they were combating had always been his own sworn enemies. Be that as it may, he soon drew away from them. But in their daily forays through the city, groups were always dropping in on him. He will never forget the look which his intruders from the hostile system (as he then saw them) cast on the child—if they so much as noticed it; though without particular intent, that look was an insult to the creature lying there, to its meaningless sounds and movements, and signified contempt—as palpable as it was infuriating—for the trivia of everyday life. He was in a quandary; instead of showing these utter strangers the door, he usually went out with them—their presence in the apartment would impinge on the child's air supply—and spent the evening in their "pads," either, like them, sitting with earphones in front of the soundless television screen or witnessing in polite silence their mildly conspiratorial but in a way official deliberations, in which the slightest candid, spontaneous utterance would have been a source of embarrassment; in either case, feeling guilty and depraved, because, convinced as he was that he sometimes knew the truth and was in duty bound to transmit it, he was by his mere presence giving aid and comfort to these phonies.

It was a friendless period; his own wife had turned into an unfriendly stranger. The child became all the more real, thanks in part to the remorse with which he literally fled home to it. Slowly, he passes through the darkened room to the bed, meanwhile watching himself from above and behind as in a monumental film. This is his place; shame on all those spurious communes, shame on me, for denying or making a secret of my one true allegiance! Shame on my lip service to your modern world. And so, little by little, it became a certainty to him that the only history his kind of man could acknowledge was the history he saw in the lines of the sleeping child. And yet, in retrospect, his diagonal passage through the balmy-warm room was associated with the concerted roar—never has anything more hellish and inhuman been heard—of a charging squad of riot police in the street below.

All this contributed to the story of the child; what the adult chiefly remembered, apart from the usual anecdotes, was that it could show pleasure and was vulnerable.

2

The child's arrival seems to have sparked off thoughts that would soon call for a decision. As usual, the adult was slow to make up his mind, but when in the following winter he finally arrived at a decision, it was, as so often, an irresistible suggestion: the three of them would go away for a time, they would go to a foreign country. At this idea, the adult for once saw himself, his wife and child, as a family (something not ordinarily in his good books).

A glorious day in March, when the white enamel of an empty kitchen shines with the light of the City of Heart's Desire, which unfolds its far-famed rooftops outside the window. The newfangled metal tips on the light switches blink, and the electrical appliances brought from home buzz to no avail because the voltage is too low. This was more than a move; it was an emigration, once and for all, to the right place, for the child as well as for themselves. At the table by the balcony door, night falls and the morning rises like nowhere else in the world, and there they sit, a wee bit frightened, but clearly outlined, at their first family meal. They have begun a new life.

The city turned out to be totally different from the metropolis that had shown itself on their short visits. Instead of the miles and miles of movie houses, cafés, and boulevards they had looked forward to, it reduced itself to a small circle of pharmacies, self-service stores, and laundromats, smaller than any circle in their previous experience. The spacious *places* they had known gave way to the cramped little *squares* of the residential quarter, shaded by trees and housefronts, which day after day, when he went out with the child in his arms, resounded with the clanging of heavy iron gates and in time came to stand for a specific neighborhood consisting of sandy, dusty patches of bare ground studded with dog turds. The more distant goals are the woods in the west and southwest, accessible only by long rides on the Métro; and that one *square* where there are not only benches but also a miniature amusement park with booths and merry-go-rounds. This *square* lies deep in another neighborhood, beyond the inner ring of boulevards; the expedition takes all afternoon, including the walk there and back through a tangle of mostly narrow streets, with sudden shifts from silence to deafening noise, from gloom to a gray radiance, from showers to sunshine (the ocean is not far away). On the way they cross a long bridge, over a deep chasm lined with hundreds of railroad tracks, leading from a nearby terminal into an enormous airy valley between two steep banks of houses, with its whirlpools and vapor clouds and the roar of express trains, a foretaste of the Atlantic beyond. This walk was repeated almost every day; in time the child ceased to be a burden and became a part of the carrier's body, and in the course of these afternoons the mere name—Square des Batignolles—came to stand, in the adult's mind, for an eternal moment with the child.

One spring evening he glimpsed the child there—"up there" in his private image—in a sandpile. In the midst of other children of about the same pre-walking age, she is playing by herself. Twilight mood, caused in part by the cover of foliage over the children; balmy, clear air, some of the faces and hands strikingly bright. He bends over the figure in the red dress. She recognizes him, and without smiling emanates light. She doesn't mind being there with the others, but she belongs to him and has long been waiting for him. Now, even more than at the time of her birth, the adult sees the enlightened, all-knowing countenance behind the baby face, and the calm, ageless eyes give him, now and for all time, a look of friendship; for two cents he would hide his face and weep.

Later that spring, in the same *square*, the child was sitting all by herself, astride a horse on one of the merry-go-rounds. It had just stopped raining, and the *square* is foaming white around the edge—like a reef. The merry-go-round starts with a jolt, and the child, distanced from the adult in a new way, looks up briefly, but then, carried away by the circular motion, forgets herself and has no eyes for anything else. Later the man, with this in mind, remembered a moment in his childhood when, though in the same room as his mother, he suddenly felt her to be heartbreakingly, outrageously far away from him. How can that woman over there be a different person from me here? The sight of the carousel with the circling, absent figure completes the picture: for the first time, the adult sees his child as a person in her own right, independent of the parent standing "over there"—someone who should be encouraged in her freedom! Indeed, the space separating the two seems to glow in triumph; the man and the little equestrian figure become in his eyes an exemplary group behind which the artificial waterfall on the *square* trumpets mightily. Wishing becomes possible; concomitantly, an awareness of the passage of time, painful, but not in the same way as his former inability to think of separateness.

In the autumn, when the child was able to walk, they often rode out to the edge of the city together. She sat motionless on the Métro, her dark eyes flashing momentarily as the train pulled into a station. On a warm day in

October, the adult lay reading in the grass of the sparsely wooded Bois; in the corner of his eye the child is a patch of nearby color, which at one point disappears from his field of vision and does not come back. When he looks up, he sees her walking among the trees far away. He runs after her but does not call, and keeps his distance from her. She walks straight ahead, even when there is no path. Walkers with dogs pass between them; one of the dogs jostles the child and knocks her down. Without so much as a look at the dog, she stands right up again and continues in the same direction. Beside a rivulet—its barely flowing water is black with blown leaves—two turkeys are copulating. When it's over, the male staggers and falls to the ground. The child keeps going, neither faster nor slower; she doesn't look around, doesn't even turn her head, and doesn't seem to get tired, as she ordinarily does after a very few steps. Still at the same distance, the two of them cross a patch of meadow, where a breeze can be felt from the nearby river. Much later, the child told the adult that "meadows" made her think of "Paradise." There's a lot of rotten wood under the fallen leaves; the child keeps stumbling but does not change direction. The park is full of people, but they all seem to be going the other way; from the stands of the nearby racetrack, shouts of encouragement as the horses turn into the home stretch. It seems to the adult that they have both become giants, with heads and shoulders at treetop level, yet invisible to passersby. They are the fabulous beings whom he has always regarded as the real powers, in the thick of human realities yet above them. Arrived at the river, the child stops and folds her hands behind her back. Not far away, on the grassy embankment, another adult is sitting with another child, their doubles or stand-ins, so to speak. Both are eating ice cream; the river flows past the gleaming globes of ice cream and the shimmering lines of their throats. Half underwater, a row of wooden cabins left over from a former bathing establishment. Across the river, to the west, a densely built-up chain of hills; halfway up the slope, orange-white-and-violet suburban trains dart past incessantly. The sunset sky is silvery; single leaves and then a whole branch go whirling into empty space. In miraculous accord the wind blows the bushes on the shore below and the hair in the foreground. The eyewitness implores a blessing on this image, yet keeps cool. He knows that every mystical moment carries within it a universal law, which it is incumbent on him to formulate and which will be valid only when given its appropriate form. He also knows that to think out the sequence of forms implicit in such a moment is the most difficult of human tasks. Then he called out to the child, who turned around to him without surprise, as to her self-evident bodyguard.

Throughout this period, relations between him and his wife were functional at best, and often they thought of each other as "that man" and "that woman." Formerly, when he took a distanced view of her professional activity, or while they were together traveling, or eating at a fashionable restaurant, he had sensed the luster of untouchability which alone can make a woman the guiding light a man longs for; which alone had enabled him to regard her as "his wife"; and for which he consequently honored her with grateful enthusiasm, as only a chosen one can. Now that the baby was there, they met almost exclusively in the cramped quarters of the household; here he came to look upon her with indifference and in time with distaste—just as no doubt she, who saw little more than before of "her hero" at his unique work, ceased to regard him as someone special; even at a distance, on the phone, never a note of recognition, let alone of expectancy, as though the other had ceased to be anything more than "that person who keeps calling up." Thoughtlessly, the man devalued the friendly, intimate, secret little gestures and exclamations, which had become habitual in his dealings with his wife, by transferring them to the child. It was almost as if in the child he had for the first time found what was right for him, as though a wife had become superfluous to him altogether. He even had the impression that he had "forced" the child on his wife—and that this was his "good fortune." (Many of the "young mothers" he saw struck him as sanctimonious; often as potential cutthroats.)

Even so, he could not conceive of being alone with the helpless little creature. In his wife's absence, he only stepped into the breach, so to speak; an incompetent nanny, he counted the days until she returned to her duties. But he worried about her as he had always done; he took his role of protector seriously; without him, he felt, she would go to the dogs.

As for his work in that first year, he postponed the great project he had in mind, though without losing sight of it for a single day. For the present, he was content with the little things that were not beyond his reach; they, too, bore his mark.

3

The idea made its way that the child should grow up outside the city's bustle, and not in an apartment, but in a house, in the open air. Early the following year, this culminated in a return to base—they were not unhappy about it, because it was also a return to a country where their own language was spoken. Later, in the spring, a plot of land was found. It was situated in a belt of woodland, with a view of a broad fluvial plain which day and night, on the ground and in the air, shimmers with the light of the metropolis nearby. The woman handled most of the business; the man didn't see the place until late summer, when the framework of the house was already complete. He contemplated it with a feeling of uncertainty; a flush of pleasure at his future independence was tempered by the thought that a house, especially a brand-new one, in a hitherto unspoiled bit of nature, was no longer the right thing.

The house would not be ready for some time, and in the meantime they stayed with friends, a couple with a large apartment in town. For the first time they lived at close quarters with others, and in the community resulting from the daily pursuit of common, previously recognized interests, the irritable, defiantly solitary man felt that he had at last discovered a natural mode of life. Accustomed to having no one to sympathize with the needs of his work, fully expecting to withdraw into his inner realm at the first sign of such disregard, he encountered, for once, not only respect for the results of his effort, but constant consideration for the effort itself. The group, whose members he could now rely on interchangeably, also helped him, not only to subordinate the state of the world to his work as he had done before, but, in addition, to clarify his demands on the world. And thanks primarily to the always present child, these demands became images—without which, of course, nothing could be clarified. No longer belonging to anyone in particular, she moved on those beautiful autumn days from one to another with a saving naturalness; she was the regulatory principle that seemed to foster unity among the various rooms. The calm severity of her features—most likely it's a jolt in the mind of the viewer, who takes her as a model. In the evening, a long oval table; on the square outside the window, the screeching of the streetcars and the luminous sign of a bar named after the bend in the tracks.

But the builders took longer than expected, and the necessary extension of the apartment-sharing arrangement brought about a change for the worse: the friends became landlords, the nomads became unwelcome guests, and all looked forward to the day when they would move out.

These friends were a couple who had deliberately remained childless. Each had adopted the other instead of a child. The consequence was that, once the "visiting" period had elapsed, the real child threatened the field of taste, smell, and touch that had grown up between them over the years and taken on vital importance. They were no longer inseparable as they had been, they became unsure of each other. More than a troublemaker, the child was a threat to their way of life. The adult had long seen his child at the receiving end of bored, exasperated, inconvenienced, out-of-sorts looks—which he himself may have caused; but never had he seen such merciless eyes in frozen faces, such unforgiving frowns as in that childless couple. These were looks of impotent rage, brought on by the consciousness that despite their perfect goodwill they were without rights as opposed to the little creature's outrageously overwhelming right. Of course they revealed nothing of the kind to the child—at most, they spoke more and more softly and coldly to her—but they showed it in the increasing criticism of the parents' pedagogical methods. (For this, there were frequent opportunities.) And their reproaches—or silent disapproval—struck the man not only as stupidly banal but also as coldhearted, perverse, and presumptuous.

He was later to come into contact with far worse prophets of childlessness, singly and in pairs. For the most part they were sharp-sighted, and thanks to their own terrifying freedom from guilt, they were able to say in technical language what was wrong with the child-parent relationship; some of them actually made a profession of their insight. In love with their own childhood and its continuance, they proved on closer acquaintance to be grownup monsters. After every encounter with them, it took the man a long time to purge his mind and soul of their analytical certainties, which cut into him like cankers. He cursed those mean, self-righteous prophets as the scum of *modern times*, and swore to hate them and combat them forever. The ancient dramatist supplied him with the appropriate curse for them: "Children are the soul of all men. He who has not learned this suffers less, but his well-being is of the wrong kind." (Something else again, it goes without saying, is the good-hearted, lovable sorrow and sympathy of other childless people.)

And so, despite the distaste inspired by the nondescript new house and the almost identical new houses around it, the little family felt it was returning to peace and order when at last, in the late fall, it moved into a home of its own.

Yet, on the whole, the time spent with friends exemplified a life in an airier, more wholesome, less spirit-killing environment than that of a small family. It made possible the daring flights of solitude which alone give the mind the daily world-exploring freedom it needs and spared it the ensuing collapse into forsakenness and unreality, in which there are neither tangible objects nor discourse. In such surroundings, moreover, one worries less about the child; no longer is it the oppressively close one-and-all; here it lives at the right distance, "one among others." And the child itself is freed from its confinement to its parents, those all-powerful duty figures who seem to block its freedom of movement; in the larger grouping, all become smaller and, whoever they may be, however awkward and self-absorbed, they become for the moment partners in a game. On the whole, the prevailing mood in those months was one of perfect naturalness, a balance between concentrated work in the daytime and relaxation in the evening, between introversion with its free, form-creating thought and formless extroversion; in short, a succession of days and evenings such as the adult would never again be able to give the child, except perhaps during short visits to the seashore.

A dark day in November. If nothing else, a first little living-room light is burning in the barely heated new house. Even in retrospect, a moving-in feeling never materialized, for one thing because the house long remained unfinished, but chiefly because this house had not involved the great decision it might have in times gone by; it was a mere acquisition, comparable to a useful gadget picked up at a bargain sale. Besides, the man had had next to nothing to do with building it, whereas he had once upon a time worked so hard on a house for his parents that those days still lived on for him in countless images. Some days later he attended the neighborhood gathering at which local residents spoke to new residents of a plan to run an express highway through their community, of the chronic water shortage, and the lack of accessible schools, and sent them home with a few words of consolation. Be that as it may, the man trudges homeward through the winter night, full of mysterious confidence in the world, for never before had he gone home to "my house" or "our community." The same snow-fraught air in the hollow below the S-Bahn as two years before on his return from a house-hunting expedition, followed by actual snowflakes, delicate taps in the darkness, swirls at the bends of the community's streets, a whooshing up at the edge of the woods; aimlessly he makes a long detour, in the course of which, with the help of the snowy night, the entire locality, the flat-roofed cubes with the woods in the background, takes form for the first time; and now the streets with their new houses and empty lots lead to something free, mysterious, old as the hills.

Late that winter, a few months after they had moved in, the woman went away to resume her work; she had made a break of this kind years before; was she in earnest this time? Still, she had objective reasons for leaving, and there was no formal break; after a first prolonged absence, she returned periodically to be with the child, and not as a visitor; but the fact remained that to all intents and purposes the man was left alone with his daughter. Again he was of two minds: he thought his wife had done right, yet he condemned her. How could anyone leave a child, even on an impulse that was part of her being? Wasn't a child a natural, obvious, reasonable obligation, beyond all questioning? Wasn't any goal achieved by turning one's back on this manifest, wholly-binding reality dishonorable and worthless by definition? And yet he knew that he, with his particular kind of work, was privileged; he had no need to "go out" as most people did—a circumstance which in a way justified his partner's divergent behavior.

Luckily he had a piece of unfinished work that could be carried on from day to day during his first period alone with the child. Early in the afternoon after his wife's departure, during the child's nap time, the adult crept almost stealthily to his unfinished project. He experienced the first transitional passage as a triumph against the rigors of fate (that day's "Carry on!" was to serve as his secret watchword on many future occasions).

But soon after the completion of this work, which had time and again brought something of the outside world, of the open air, into the walled-in room, the house with the child came to stand for a worse seclusion and immobility than ever before. It was this that first made him feel forsaken; and the embodiment of his forsakenness was the child playing by herself—alone in the room with the adult, who does nothing but stand there stiffly. Misery and forlornness—a sense of tragedy—spring at him from the crown of her head, the curve of her shoulders, her bare feet, though as a matter of fact the child (as he soon realized) was hardly conscious of any difference; she was already used to having only one parent look after her and after a while she made it clear, once and for all: "As long as one of you is here."

In those weeks of bewilderment, no future was thinkable, but he had no desire to go back. He realized that what had happened was irrevocable. His days, alone with the child, passed differently; they were no longer a mere interval. True, he still counted them, but now with a new kind of reckoning in which he had no right to appeal to an outsider for help. Beyond a doubt, he alone was needed, he and no one else; it was impossible to go on just doing his bit, undisturbed in his self-immersion, as he had done "before the war" (once in his thoughts he actually phrased it that way). Yes, the source of his inner happening—the free flow of his daydreams—was broken for good: by the crisis, which previously, during the period of listless peace, he had often thought would be the beginning of an alert, wide-awake kind of life, the right kind. And pathetically insignificant as this crisis turned out to be, the idea held good: the adult did not *resign* himself to his situation, he accepted it willingly, or so he thought. Of this, his new time reckoning, no longer implying an end, was a small, proud indication; and many a time his new way of counting helped him to go on. "Count and live."

That was the idea—and in each of the separate phases it was practicable; nothing humanly impossible was asked of him; just that he had to give up certain habits. But in daily practice he often failed. Here for the first time it became apparent that he, who had scarcely an equal for thinking himself above ingrained habits, was as much a slave to them as anyone else—his whole existence, like everyone else's, was made up of habits; they alone gave his life a semblance of regularity. Cut off from his personal routines (which now at a distance struck him as beautiful), his daily life, regulated by a child's rhythm and consisting almost exclusively of child's sounds and child's belongings, struck him more and more as a brutal and senseless doom. Things were out of kilter, as evil and unreal as weapons, and the interstices were as airless as the compartments of an arsenal. This was the world into which he had been banished, and in his mind all was hostile confusion. It was a long while before he learned not only to tolerate the child's playthings but in addition—however heedlessly and even contemptuously everything seemed to be scattered—to find order in disorder, and to feel at home in it as the child did (a free moment and an attentive look sufficed to bring a harmonious pattern out of the most hideous jumble). At first, however, he was seized with a frenzy for making order, though all he actually did was to thrash about in a vacuum. At such times he felt a malignant stupidity coming over him, and because he hardly saw anyone else, he stupidly blamed the child for it.

Confined as he was to the house and seldom enjoying a moment's peace, he gradually lost his feeling for colors and forms, as well as the spacing and arrangement of objects, and saw himself, in the sinister, vision-blurring half light, surrounded by them as by tarnished mirrors. And in the midst of all that, the child moved about like one indistinct object among others. This was unreality, and unreality means: You are alone. There is no one else. The next step was an absence of thought, scarcely distinguishable from madness. He had lost all power over himself, and fear deprived him of his will. Then came the day of guilt, the children's hour. The spring was far advanced. After a rainy night, the ground floor of the brand-new house was flooded. It had happened a few times before, but that morning the water was higher than ever; this time (after the usual letters to the builders) an honest-to-goodness flood. Still half asleep, he stared, with murder in his heart, at the brownish water. From upstairs he heard the child's repeated cries—something that stymied her—ending on a note of desperation. The adult, standing knee-deep in water, lost his head; rushing upstairs like a killer, he struck the child in the face with all his might, as he had never in all his life struck anyone. His horror was instantaneous. He carried the crying child—he himself suffering bitterly from his lack of tears—from room to room. Everywhere the gates of judgment stood open, bursts of heat struck him like blasts from muted trumpets. Though the child showed no ill effects other than a swollen cheek, he knew that he had hit her hard enough to kill her. At first he regarded himself as evil; he was not only a scoundrel, he was depraved, and no earthly punishment could atone for what he had done. One enduring real thing had given him his only happiness, and now he had destroyed it; he had betrayed the one thing he wanted to perpetuate and glorify. Eternally damned, he sat down with the child and spoke to her, more from the need to speak than really imbued with what he was saying, in the hitherto unutterable, unthinkable oldest forms of human speech. But the child nodded at his words, and then, as once before, there appeared in the quietly weeping face a clear, radiant pair of eyes, raised as it were above the mists of the environing world. Seldom has an unhappy mortal known brighter consolation (though the same person later declared herself to be "incapable of consoling"). So she understands the adult and takes pity on him; with this kindness the child, for the first time in her history, appears in the active role; and her action, like all her future actions on different occasions, is as casual as a meeting between forehead and forehead, and at the same time as perfectly laconic as the "Carry on" signal of an experienced referee (who is, in a very special sense, of this world).

Of course this mute, visual consolation was not enough; the adult's state of abjectness lasted until the incident had been explicitly, and not just once but time and time again, confessed to a third party (and even then it was only attenuated). That day stands out in the adult's memory as one of those exceptional days concerning which it can be said that the grass was green, the sun was shining, the rain falling, the clouds drifting, that dusk fell and the night was silent, all these being marks of a different sort, assuredly the right sort, of human life, at times surmised to be eternal. Then the wooded hill at the foot of which the community is situated emerges in the distance. From all sides the trees rise skyward in an even sweep, and the gentle, regular incline, which seems to lead onward to infinity, gives the hill a feeling of fertility. The bright rocky spots between the trees glitter in the distance like crests of sea foam and lie on the chest like liberating compresses. For a moment the foreign river meanders through the foreground, its radiance reaching out beyond all possible frontiers. Only in sorrow, over an omission or a commission (and then my eyes become magnetic and all-encompassing), does my life expand to epic proportions.

4

The child was now more than three years old. Thus far, she had played alone almost exclusively, turned inward in quiet contentment, unlike the gloomily self-absorbed adult. But in the course of time (and specifically of the seasons) both had made themselves at home in the community on the wooded slope, and the adult was sick of visitors who with their falsely sympathetic or ironically citified remarks about the house and its location regularly demolished what little spirit the place had. One, who expressed himself only in forced quips, with which indeed he made his living, spoke of the clip-clop community, the reference being to the clatter of high-heeled shoes in the silence of the night.

But more and more often children from the neighboring houses would come to visit, and through them a kind of neighborhood feeling arose. Being with others was something new to the child; it seemed to change her sensitiveness, in which the adult had so delighted, into a spoil-sport prissiness. The most trifling setback would throw her into such a rage that the other children would stand there gaping, and this in turn would transform her dismay into utter misery, so adding to the glee of the strangers around her, who would be as likely as not to ring the doorbell again the next day, possibly in the expectation of another such scene (but also perhaps because in the course of time all the rooms in the new house—the architect had surely intended nothing of the kind—had merged into one partitionless children's room).

At the same time a reversal occurred. No longer was the adult "alone with the child." Although her encounters with children of her age had almost always ended with a sense of injury and defeat, she soon began to look forward to these visits, not so much with pleasure as with excitement. For a while at least, she lost her ability to immerse herself, with splendid equanimity, in every trifle. The adult was no longer what she wanted; and often, when at last the voice of a neighbor child approached the house, the sound was welcome to the two of them (even if this particular child had been the cause of the past day's gloom).

Again he was of two minds. Would it be best to remain alone—the child playing, the adult working and to the best of his ability present, both prepared to speak and listen, yet "child" and "adult" as they had always been, without precocity on the one side or condescension on the other—or were "children" not a race apart, in their element only among themselves, and there alone, regardless of all the injury and injustice, capable of moving with self-awareness and making something of themselves? So weren't other children their true family and weren't adults entitled, at the most, to take care of them? Wasn't it plain in any case that even after the most unpleasant incident, the worst humiliation, the child would welcome another child as a bringer of good tidings?

The dilemma was solved when the man at last hit on an idea, implying a proposal to others (and here he was struck by the fact that in the course of the years he of all people, he who tended to regard himself as a loner, unable and unwilling to live in society, had repeatedly, quite on his own initiative, promoted social groups, though small ones; but that on each occasion a profound illumination or "synthesis" had been necessary, without which, he held, there could be no true community).

The material foundation of the idea, on the strength of which a proposal to others became possible, was, as it had always been, a specific place, a location. At first, conversation with the neighbors had been confined almost exclusively to the new community and the children. The complaints about the distance from all public conveniences and the desire, not for a kindergarten or its modern equivalent, but rather for a modest little meeting place, accessible without a car and open at definite hours—undoubtedly a necessity for those children who could not yet make a playground of the surrounding country and were consequently confined to their own house or the one next door. This desire became practicable (and its fulfillment a matter of course) when a locale was thought of: a large, hitherto unused room in the man's house, with a southern exposure and "free access" to a large "front yard." (Backed up by the image of running children, these terms meant something, for once.) The availability of the locale even made enthusiasm possible; this at last was the right thing to do. Dispelled were the suspicions usual among people who are strangers to one another. By early summer the room was suitably remodeled, and the following autumn a kind of club was opened informally with a few children.

In the ensuing period the adult spent a few half days as a kind of counselor, saw his own child with an unaccustomed number of others, and began—no other word would be appropriate—to doubt her; not as an individual, but as a superior authority. His dominant feeling for her, even outweighing affection, had always been an unconditional, enthusiastic confidence. Without ever forming an opinion of "children" in general, he believed in this particular child. He was convinced that she embodied an important law, which he himself had either forgotten or never known. In the very first moment of her life, he had seen her as his personal teacher. What he had faith in was not any particular utterance "from the mouth of a babe," but her mere existence as a human being who was what she was. The fact of her existence was to the adult the measure of truth, of a life as it should be. In this light, he was able to respect her dispassionately, and at times allow himself to utter certain words which he had hitherto rejected as pathos, shut his ears to at the movies, closed his eyes to as obsolete in old books, and which now turned out to be more real than anything else in the world. Who were the fools who had dared to claim that these "high-sounding" words were of purely "historical" interest, and that time had divested them of their meaning? Weren't they, in their blindness, or perhaps only lukewarmness and faintheartedness, confusing words with whole sentences? How did these modern people live? And with whom? And what had they forgotten, once and for all, that they should listen only to pusillanimous yet loudmouthed and, on the whole, anything but open-minded language? Why did all the terms current in public speeches, in the daily papers and on television, but also in new books and personal relations, have the crushing, stinkingly banal, soul-murdering, godless, nerve-shattering, harebrained quality of *dogs' names*? Why on all sides did one hear only the drone's language of a sheet-metal age? In any case, it was thanks to the child that the much despised great words became more intelligible to the adult with each passing day; these words didn't make for hubris but carried you to higher and higher levels; and anyone was welcome to them, the only prerequisites being "goodwill" and insight into "strict necessity."

Doubt came when he saw the child not alone or with random individuals but in her regular group. There, in the midst of a majority, she ceased to be a haven of peace, and was gradually, from day to day, metamorphosed into an earthworm, writhing with fear—more wretched than all the rest. No longer was she prissy, no longer ill-tempered or even listless (for that the adult would at least have found an explanation); she was simply beside herself with misery. In the group, the child who by herself had been so wonderfully slow-moving, humorous, and intelligent was at best excitable and obtuse; most of the time she displayed blind panic, accompanied by an acute, groundless, immediately perceptible anguish. No sooner in the crowd, she struggles, like one forcibly held underwater, to escape, looks in her misery for a secluded room, but is usually unable to find so much as a quiet corner. Thus far, her story has presented an even flow; only now is its irrevocable, diabolical inevitability revealed. And the adult's doubt, like his previous faith, pertains not so much to her special characteristics as to her whole existence: if she, as she is (that is, *her whole being*), is forced to become something different, she obviously ceases to be anything at all (but only suffers suffers suffers). But was she made for this apparently necessary tragedy of destruction? Here the adult is preoccupied with emotional, pointless questions that have probably been talked to death; yet they are made understandable by the despairing glances from the midst of the mob, which go straight to his heart and express something more urgent than mere doubt. Of course the parents connected with the group knew the reasons for the child's behavior (and hinted as much with kindly solicitude), but all he heard in their explanations was more dogs' names: seeing no cause, he was nevertheless convinced that he knew better.

Besides, it was plain that some of the children, even the smallest, were not right for one another. There may have been no "wicked" ones, but certainly all were not "innocent" (at the most, there were some who had started at an early age to wash their hands in innocence). All knew what was wrong and did wrong, not only in passion but also with premeditation, yet even then without *consciousness* of wrongdoing—with the result that their actions were often more sinister than those of the most sordid scoundrels, and just as revolting. It couldn't be denied that among the children—regardless of sex—there were some who from the start were quite at their ease playing the executioner in word and deed, with the adults looking on; they performed their act of destruction with cool expertness and when it was done walked calmly away as from an official function. And it was equally unquestionable that none of the children liked being scolded, made fun of, or beaten—in other words, victimized.

It was then the prevailing opinion that adults should not interfere in children's squabbles. Nevertheless, it was hard on the adult, seeing his child getting the short end of it day after day. For she alone never defended herself; even when punched in the face, her only response was to flail about in the void; and the sounds that came out of her mouth were not battle cries but helpless whimperings. When insulted or accused, she never replied in kind and never ran away, but stood spellbound on the spot, physically bent beneath the hostile harangue, which in the end boiled down to a repetition of one especially wounding word or phrase. In her rebuttal she did no more than tonelessly deny everything, thus by her voice and posture identifying herself as the accused. Impossible, at the sight of this pale, trembling thing, to refrain from stepping in. And so, as often as not, the adult stepped in, took sides—and found fault with his sniveling, solipsistic, asocial child.

But little by little, as time went on, the children merged into a free, easygoing, and even amiable little band. Or perhaps the adult had only learned to look at them with new eyes. One spring day he climbed a hill with them and, observing himself, saw perfect joy, simply because he was moving among so many different children. His enthusiasm gave him for the first time a voice to which they listened. It was as though he had leapt into their midst; here he no longer saw "ruffians" and "victims," as he had when looking at them from outside. No doubt about it. It was only when he began to take pleasure in their company that his forlorn standing-around and frantic running-around gave way to a natural buoyancy and ultimately to a proud, poised, and no longer childlike participation in their common adventure. A lasting image must as a rule be grounded, as it were, in the feel of a certain terrain, its upward or downward slope, roughness or smoothness. In this case we have a steep slope, which all the children are climbing vigorously; though they are strung out over quite a distance and they are constantly changing places, each one knows as a rule where the others are, and none will get lost. Never before has the adult been conscious of a gentler, happier power over others.

His newly won lightheartedness rubbed off on his own child; once more she was able to be what-she-was; among others her movements were distinctly more spontaneous and self-assured than in her solitary days. The adult realized that all he had to do was "leave her (as well as the others) be" but that the ideal ordering energy, the drive that held them all together, would operate only if he remained for her (and the others too) the "ever-present one"—with whom they could journey safely as in the hold of a ship of peace. True, he was not always equal to this twofold power. That would have been high art. But little by little he assimilated the idea of the good teacher.

Just then, however, just as he was taking comfort, he was forced to recognize that the child really was different from most of those in the group. She had ceased to be a loner, but she still got in the way, though not very noticeably, and when playing games showed the excess of zeal and slight muddlement that are sometimes found in obese children. But what particularly sets her apart from the other children is her manner of speaking (though it is quite free from specifically grownup locutions); or perhaps it is only that she spoke more deliberately, choosing her words with greater care: in any case, this habit of speech often made her lag behind or made what she was saying go unheard. True, the glance she casts at the adult from out of the turmoil is no longer a forlorn, imploring stare; it twinkles with good-natured irony. She is content to be with these people—but they are not her people. And here it passes through the adult's mind: Your people exist. They are somewhere else. A different people with a different history. We are not the only ones. At this very moment, we are moving through time with this other people. You will never be alone. And at the same time the adult once again caught sight of the drama to come and actually looked forward to it. For though he saw many parents who armed their children for the struggle, and though he understood this perfectly, he felt that the right way was to do nothing of the kind.

5

There was something outrageous about moving back to the beloved foreign city with the child, who by then was about five and had grown accustomed to the community on the edge of the woods; but he didn't hesitate long, for he thought of it as a natural and even necessary thing to do, requiring no justification. He felt that the image spoke for itself: a man taking his own and setting out for an unfamiliar world. Shouldn't everyone attempt something of the kind, time and time again? Wasn't it in foreign surroundings that a man's own becomes his determining certainty? Besides, in going back to the foreign city, he was simply resuming the regular life he had led there; throughout the interim, he had thought of the distant metropolis as his permanent base; it was the only place that gave him a feeling of "reality" for any length of time, a lasting tie between outside and inside, body and soul. And with regard to his charge, he had always thought: What's good for me is good for her (and conversely).

In the foreign country the child's history, without unusual events, became a small paradigm of the history of nations, and of ethnology as well; and the child herself, by none of her own doing, became the heroine of frightening, sublime, ridiculous, and on the whole plausible everyday-eternal happenings.

On a day in December they arrive in the somber apartment, brightened by the sparkling water that flows with brooklike gurgling in the gutter outside and by the vault, to be found nowhere else in the world, of the sky over the fringe of the metropolis, where the staggered traffic lights reach out into the void, incessantly jumping about, changing color, and pointing the way to a vast and sweetly mysterious western gate. Here the large grass plots around the house in the community, which brought nature constantly close, are replaced by narrow French windows with small diamond-shaped panes in which the outside world seems reduced to the right scale; and the silence of the house is replaced by the sound of steps from the floor above and the voices next door, which at first are welcome as something long missed. The many alien objects in the apartment borrow an air of familiarity from the few things that have been brought along—books and stuffed animals suffice; and the long hallway leading to the surprisingly light back rooms has the feel of a suite in a luxurious hotel.

The child had her first schoolday toward the end of winter, in midterm. This had not been planned by the adult, it just happened. The school also happened to be a special sort of school—intended, that is, only for children of the one "people" deserving of the name, the people of which, long before its dispersion to the four corners of the earth, it was said that, even "without prophets," "without sacrifices," "without idols"—and even "without names"—it would still be a "people"; and whom, in the words of a later biblical scholar, those wishing to know "the tradition," the "oldest and strictest law in the world" would be obliged to consult. It was the only actual "people" to which the adult had ever wished to belong.

The schoolhouse resembled many city schoolhouses, with a small, dusty yard, cramped, ill-lit rooms, and the rumbling of the Métro from deep underground. But taking the child there gave the adult a feeling that he was going the right way, a vast and for once absolutely suprapersonal feeling of happiness. His child, by birth and language a descendant of murderers who seemed condemned to flounder for all time, without aim or joy, metaphysically dead, would learn the binding tradition, would go her way with others of her kind, and embody that steadfast, living earnestness which he, who had been rendered incapable of tradition, knew to be necessary but forfeited day after day to frivolous caprice. Though the child was accepted only provisionally, for one semester, he hoped she would stay there for good, and not only in the school. Just as she was, despite the color of her hair and eyes, wasn't that where she belonged? And these strange holiday celebrations, in which the child, a participant and not just an onlooker, joined the others in the symbolic gestures recapitulating their exemplary history—didn't such celebrations at last supply a possible meaning for words such as "community" or "initiation"? And when for the first time the adult saw the child transcribing the strange characters of the ancient language, did he not experience the emotion of one witnessing a historical moment (and was he not at the same time determined, as the ancient historian had been, to understand it clearly)?

The child, too, was pleased with the school. She didn't even have to get used to it; with the first step across the threshold, into the little vestibule with its layers of different-colored coats hanging on hooks, she had forgotten her fear, as one sometimes forgets a burden; thanks no doubt to the teacher, by whom, through the usual hubbub, she immediately and for all time felt *seen*. This old woman had mastered the art of the inquiring yet overwhelmingly hospitable glance (though her interlocutor never felt observed, let alone scrutinized). And it was she—herself of German descent, she spoke German—who taught the child the language of the land in no time. It was not yet summer when the adult heard the child engaged in fluent conversation with the other children. How charming she seemed when speaking the foreign language. Whenever she slipped into it, she seemed to summon it up by magic, but never employed the unfortunate turns of phrase used by many of the native children. Listening to her, the adult remembered how he himself as a child had longed to speak a foreign language and had occasionally mistaken a certain play gibberish for one. He saw that his child was now in many respects ahead of him, and for that he was thankful to be living in the present time.

It seemed to the adult that the child's life and his own were on the right track. And so he argued with the fervor of one imbued with the exemplary fitness of things as they were, when toward the end of the school year the principal suggested that the child should be transferred to a different school. In the autumn, she said, religious instruction would begin, and since the child came of a basically different tradition, no good could come of it. Citing his experience of many years, the adult tried to persuade the woman that no tradition, however longed for, could ever be meaningful to someone like him, and that he could certainly transmit no trace of any tradition to his child. But the elderly teacher felt that she knew better and merely shook her head. When he left the schoolhouse with the child on the last day, it seemed to him that she had been banished without guilt, and that he, the scion of an unpeople, an unworthy man-of-no-people, bore the responsibility.

The same year witnessed a conflict between man and child that was something more than momentary irritation. In the past year he had adjusted his work schedule entirely to the child's needs. During the day he could be little more than her "provider," and in time he came to think of this as of a splendid role and worthy occupation (serving could be a pleasure), even when it proved almost impossible to switch to another activity in the evenings and he often sat silent for hours, not knowing how to go on, occasionally seized with a desperate longing for such accessories of leisure as wine, books, or a television set, until suddenly, amid a sea of silence, an idea might come to him and transform the table he was sitting at into a writing desk. But what emerged was transitional bits and pieces, and little by little he conceived a desire for the larger project he had long carried in the back of his mind. Often it appeared to him as a dream of paradise, the realization of which must, as hitherto, determine his continued existence.

The time seemed to have come—thanks to school, which in that country took up almost the entire day. But the eight hours of freedom were not enough; it turned out that his work "trip," if it were to carry exemplary force and proceed in the right sequence, would have to go on day and night (at least in his head), and though the child never particularly disturbed him, she interrupted his work dream—or rather prevented it from getting started. The present arrangement might leave room for a coherent act of minor insights, but he was not often able to convert experience into invention as one must if a piece of work is to be glorious and a joy to others. And this absence of form, he thought, was the fault of the child, who by her mere presence paralyzed his imagination and diverted him from his destiny.

There was no violence between them, only unfriendliness; on the adult's part, against his own better judgment, verging on hostility. He was unable to give himself wholly either to his work or to the child—and the child, sensing the change in him, withdrew of her own accord, not in an offended sulk, but proudly; on one occasion, she said of her father: "I don't want to see him anymore. Let him go away." This laconic threat of a rupture terrified the adult and brought him to his senses. He postponed his long journey and became suspicious of all those who, tied down as he was, had ever forsaken the day-to-day rut in the name of a lifelong dream. Their deeds lost their radiance; he no longer believed in them. (But still he dreamed.)

So once again he confined himself to his short-term projects, and in the end he was content with that. Often he did no work at all, wandered about the town in all directions, from its highest point to its lowest, and relished the freedom his idleness gave him. At this point his spells of activity coincided with the child's absences (in the country with her so-called green class, or during the summer months with her mother). But then there was something uneasy and secretive about the fanaticism with which he then stuck to his project day after day, as though what was a vision to the adolescent had become almost a vice to the adult. Even in his moments of Magical Light, the emptiness of the house, where he no longer had anyone to turn to, was overpowering, seeping into him like a poison gas, until he became rigid and empty. And then he knew: it was the child who gave the passing hours their consecration. Without the child he was godforsaken, and his activity seemed excessive and meaningless (though once he wondered how it would be to lead a life of debauchery, with the most beautiful woman in the world and *without* the child). Coming home one night, he stood leaning on something in the shrill silence of the apartment, and it occurred to him that some people must drop dead from sheer loneliness.

It was at that time that visitors began to tell the man that his way of living and working was taking him further and further from reality and the present. He had once taken such criticism seriously. But after all these years with the child, he felt that no one had a right to lecture him about reality. For gradually, through the insoluble conflict between his work and the child, he had come to the conclusion that with the child, free at last from the fraudulent life of "modern times," he was continuing a kind of transtemporal Middle Ages, which had perhaps never existed, but which to him, when beside the child's sickbed, when bidding her goodbye, or just hearing her bouncy step, struck him as the only true, authentic epoch, behind and beyond the so-called modern era.

The reality-mongers, he felt, were the tyrants of a new day; with their mania for measuring degrees of reality, they reminded him of those sea captains in the oldest accounts of naval battles who, once the fighting had stopped, would total up the corpses and the wreckage washed ashore and diagnose victory or defeat accordingly. They, too, belonged to human eternity—but to the bad kind. If you listened awhile to these born public prosecutors, it soon turned out that as a rule, with their counting of worlds—the "third" and "fourth" were the most "relevant"—they were trying to drown out a secret guilt if not an unforgivable betrayal: they had all done much evil. These reality-mongers—in all likelihood the world had always swarmed with them—struck the adult as Empty Existences, remote from Creation; though long dead, they kept going with a vigor equaled only by their wickedness, left nothing behind them that anyone could hold on to, and were good for nothing but war. It was useless to argue with them, because they were convinced that each new daily catastrophe confirmed their beliefs. If you had an idea, you couldn't talk to them or even approach them: they were strangers, and I don't talk to strangers —away with you, I am the voice, not you! And so he decided to close his door irrevocably to these depressing intruders, and in general not to "let their ships bar the seas to him" any longer. Only then did he hear the murmur of a reality again. O murmur, stay with us!

In the summer of the same year, the child returned with her parents to the country they came from, where she was to spend her vacation with her mother. For her return to her father in the autumn a new school had been found, not far from the old one. Their motor trip took them from the Metropolitan Basin, hardly above sea level, through a vast terraced landscape rising in an even rhythm to the low mountain range, from the crest of which one can look down across the frontier river to the next large country; those hilltops were much disputed in a world war and their almost total bareness (which stems from another cause) provides a more enduring reminder than the many commemorative monuments of the battles fought there.

On the afternoon of the trip, the three of them are sitting on one of these hillside slopes, looking westward. From here the structure of the terraced country, extending as far as the Metropolitan Basin, almost a day's journey distant, can be seen clearly. A quarrel starts up between man and woman. It is pretty much like some of their earlier quarrels and probably—as the man can't help thinking—makes use of the exact same terms as are passing back and forth between disunited mates all over the world at this same moment. (If thus far he had made no move toward a final separation, it was only because a third party in a position of authority, however experienced and knowledgeable, could not possibly have been expected to know anything about the woman, the child, and himself, and any court decision would have struck him as presumptuous and outrageous.) But it's serious all the same; and despite his better judgment, despite the peace that pervades the country all about, he lets himself be engulfed in a mechanical exchange of insults.

When at last he looks up, he sees that the child has sat down at some distance from both parents. Her face looks pale and severe in the distance. Far across the slope, blueberries sparkle in the sun. At the foot of the hill, a marshy pond. The light of this day is glistening bright, interspersed with great cloud shadows, and the three figures sit there like white tombstones.

Years later, in another summer, the man would approach the same mountain ridge, this time from the eastern plain over a road that often led through vineyards; and not in a car but on foot. And toward evening, when darkness had settled on the ridge, the slowly moving wayfarer suddenly saw himself sitting with the two absent ones in the distant inky blackness, just as in old legends kings sit enthroned on mountains. But he saw them not as kings, nor yet as a "family," but as an abstract triad, cloaked in an impenetrable substance. This was the only mystical moment in which the man had ever seen himself in the plural, and only such moments engender myths: the eternal story. The illumination vanishes, but a certain exaltation remains. Still, the wayfarer makes his way across the high plateau toward the blue-veiled mountain chain, still busy with the thought that can never be carried to a conclusion: I am working on the secret of the world. And this spot, like the square long ago, has a name of its own that is lastingly associated with the child: *Le Grand Ballon.*

6

But it was again through the child that in the following winter, a few months after their return to the city and the change of schools, the adult was brutally made aware of the hasty, impatient, and above all unrealistic nature of the striving for reconciliation that had guided him all his life—though he remained convinced that this was the rational attitude.

One day he received a letter with no return address.

In rather ornate and recondite terms (which, when the adult consulted the dictionary, proved to mean just what they were supposed to), this letter, in the name of "the one people," threatened the child, as a descendant of that people's worst persecutors, with death.

In the general neighborhood of the "people's" school, the man had made the acquaintance of a few adults connected with it, whom he continued to see later on, and whom he came to know much more intimately than any strangers he had ever met before. Thus it didn't take him long to find out who had written about "dissecting, dismembering," etc., inasmuch as "the millions of victims have not been raised from the dead," and at the end of the threatening letter given himself an Old Testament name. Detective-like, he ferreted out the man's address, put a knife into his pocket, and started out, feeling ungainly but at the same time aware of being at the center of a historic event. In the cab he visualized the exact sequence of quick movements ending with the knife thrust to the heart; he saw himself before the act, standing magnificent in an attitude of sternest judgment (for which the long ride to the opposite bank of the river was perfectly appropriate); but no sooner has he crossed the letter writer's threshold than the grotesqueness of the situation crowds out all other thoughts. He doesn't kill. Not this time. Weakness in the wrist. He does actually, in a manner of speaking, drive the other into a back room—where they just stand there with smug grins on their faces; both feeling rather flattered—the one, because his cleverness in locating the letter writer is admired; the other, because he is taken seriously. Together they leave the cold apartment and repair to the large cemetery nearby, where they trudge back and forth, talking of everything under the sun, at the end of which they know they will never be enemies, or allies either, for that matter.

It was only on his way home alone in the darkness that the man began to understand what had happened. In a quiet street near his apartment he glimpsed, high up in the night sky, a single attic window with a peaceful reddish-yellow light in it. He stood still. Now at last he is seized with real indignation—or rather bitterness; and now he curses those non-beings who need history for their lives; he curses history itself and personally disavows it; here for the first time he gains a vision of himself alone with the child in the night of the century and in the empty crypt of the continent—and yet all this provides energy for a new kind of freedom to come. But from that day on, his dominant feeling with regard to the child's history is one of bitterness. This was the feeling closest to reality—along with grief and joy.

During the first year at the new school the child was often unhappy. Yet one could not have conceived of a finer building or location. The building was small and full of twists and turns, yet as bright as a ship or a house on an island, and seemed to occupy a domain of its own, at sufficient distance from a large housing development. The garden surrounding it was irregularly shaped, offering plenty of hiding places for the not very numerous pupils. There were patches of tall grass or sand here and there, and chickens and other domestic animals in wire cages. Another part of it, fenced about as in an old manorial park, contained exotic shrubs and a miniature stone pool with bright-colored fish in it, and a small statue, overgrown with the same sort of foliage as the housefront.

Strangest of all, the road leading to the school—which branched off a busy thoroughfare heading out of the city, passed a few shop fronts and two or three imposing portals characteristic of the neighborhood, then narrowed abruptly and began to climb just a little—was unsurfaced from that point on, transforming itself into a dirt path, clay-yellow, eroded by the rain, and on both sides flanked by low walls like a sunken lane; here light and sounds are different from what they were a moment ago in the metropolis. And yet there is nothing rural about this Elysian meadow.

Nevertheless, the child had at first to be literally pushed and pulled through the garden gate into the schoolyard. If the adult didn't escape down the path immediately after disentangling himself from her grip, she would try to fight her way back through the crush in the narrow doorway.

The children who went to this school were not children of "the one people" but children of the city, of the neighborhood, of a wide variety of parents. During the first few months the adult, too, thought the school, compared to that of the year before, rather deadening. One reason for this—though the school had only a kind of transitional status, its function being to prepare children for the state secondary schools—was the blind learning of names without objects, which seemed to have the same effect on the child as ominous, though utterly unintelligible, official regulations. Later in the day the adult would see her at home, as she reeled off the lengths of rivers or the heights of mountains required for the next day's lesson, and time and again he would say to himself: Let it never be forgotten, let it be remembered till the end of time, with what wide-open, terror-stricken eyes the children of the present day recite the so-called knowledge of mankind.

Not until late spring did the child feel more at home in the school. With nothing particular in mind, only because he himself felt like it, the adult took her for walks around the neighborhood on warm evenings, and regularly they would turn off into the dirt path. Now the child sees her school deserted in the dusk. Sometimes the grumpy old woman who is the principal is watering plants out in front, raking the sand for the next day, and feeding the animals. The timbering in the walls is visible through the ivy. Far in the distance, the horns of calamitous motor vehicles. A rustling in the dark bushes. The sleeping chickens. The shimmering of the stone paths. "Could we stay here a little longer?"

On the last days of the school year, it gave the child pleasure to pass through the gate in the morning when no one else was there, stroll around in the garden, and exhibit herself to the next arrivals as "the first." In the following year, there were times when the child was reluctant to go home with the adult in the afternoon and would have preferred to stay outside the schoolhouse playing with the others. There, in what had become for her a particular place, she now found herself in good or at least satisfactory company, forgot her solitary brooding, but preserved her sensibility. In the winter, when she went to the mountains with her class, she hardly suffered at all from homesickness (which had dealt her progenitor well-nigh incurable wounds). On her first night away from home she had been one of the last in the dormitory to start crying, and even then it had only been "to keep the others company." It didn't trouble her that the teachers at school were sometimes unreasonably strict;

sometimes, in fact, she welcomed this as special attention. When faced with injustice, she expressed surprise (which, come to think of it, is a rather effective form of revolt); and as time went on, the lessons lost their earthbound heaviness and even became a sort of game, contrasting with the rest of the day; opening a copybook could—for the adult as well when "hearing her lessons"—offer a clear bright vista.

At the commencement exercises the following summer—after the second year at the little school—the adult detects a physical change in the child. He has got into the habit of regarding her as awkward and helpless. But now she is taking part in a kind of round dance in the garden; from the very first step she is self-assurance personified; and in this dance she isn't just one among others; no, as soon becomes evident, she is leading the round, without the slightest glimmer of the embarrassment the onlooker had feared. It is she who signals "faster" or "slower" or "change direction." And in the onlooker's afterimage, her air of quiet triumph makes the entire garden group amid the clouds of schoolyard dust burst into flaming color.

No doubt the transfiguration was largely a product of leave-taking, for on the same day the little school ceased to exist and its pupils went off in different directions. The following fall they dispersed to many different state schools.

7

They moved to a suburban house on a hill across the river. The new, state school was outside the city limits, not far from a main railroad line to the sea. The adult felt that the change would be bearable for the child; indeed, he was optimistic because the building and its location were similar in many respects to those of the beloved "little school." Here, too, the ivy-covered façade and the dark timbering of the walls suggested a country inn or manor rather than a school. And, likewise, the interior, the layout of the classrooms, the windows looking out on the garden, whose trees with their aerial roots, bushes, and underbrush offered the same sort of hiding places as the old garden (except that everything was a little bigger). One of the paths was even unsurfaced like the path leading to the other school, and also sloped gently—couldn't that be expected to make the child feel at home?

But the child froze at the sight of the new school, and time did not dispel her revulsion; indeed, it increased from day to day. Here the evening-walk formula was ineffectual—yes, the school grounds were a place of peace, but in the morning the placeless misery was back again. (Anticipatory strings of anguish spittle on her breakfast roll.) At first, school friends came to the house, but unmistakably avoided her the next day in class. And the child—who was not yet eight—knew the reason why. "They hate me because I'm German."

But that wasn't the worst—the hostility that could be expressed in words wasn't so bad; what hurt her most was being ignored, being shoved aside, looking in vain for a place—the most dreaded part of the day became the "recess." When the adult called for her in the late afternoon, she almost always, even if she was in some remote corner, saw him coming.

Grownups have their ways of hiding despair; in a child it is always noticeable; and the sight of a child who has given up hope was unbearable. He felt, with something approaching urgency, that his charge must be taken out of school; and once in those months when, to his own surprise, he said aloud that they could perfectly well manage by themselves, without other people, an almost uncanny cry, or sigh, of agreement came from the child's innermost soul.

He reflected: hadn't he learned something from the image of the child dancing around with other children?

No, the child did not belong to him alone. She needed a larger community; she was not only capable of "social life" but made for it. That was the right way, the right community existed, there could be no question of turning back.

A strange repetition of that dance brought certainty. A teacher from the "little school" had died, and one November evening the adult took the child from the suburb back to the old city neighborhood to attend the funeral service. Nearly all the former pupils had come to the church with their parents, and even during Mass the children, most of whom had not seen one another since the commencement exercises, kept turning to exchange looks. In the somber, vaulted church, not only the children's clothes seemed strangely brighter than those of the grownups, but their faces as well, and everything about them; or was that only because the grownups sat so still? Afterwards, when the mourners gather outside the church, children's voices are just about the only sound to be heard. The children scream, laugh aloud, grab hold of one another, run shouting among the soft-spoken mourners, who make no attempt to stop the dance, but are perhaps more deeply moved by the wild merriment all about them than they were by the funeral service. It's an unusually bright evening, with a shining yellow full moon overhead and the demonic dancing of the children down below. Parting comes hard, a disentangling of intertwined arms and legs, which had briefly belonged to a single body. It's late by the time the child is sitting in the suburban bus, almost alone with the adult. She is exhausted yet wide awake, and undoubtedly in seventh heaven. Most of all, she's surprised: suddenly seeing all those old friends, being greeted by them with such joy, and in dancing completely forgetting the teacher's death. The light inside the empty night bus is very white. They cross the bridge. The river is at high water and looks unusually wide and dark, with here and there a glimmer of moonlight and the top of a submerged bush. To the adult, the child's face, glowing with life and enthusiasm as she sits there reliving the hour spent with the other children, is a picture of tragic beauty.

The dead teacher had been especially fond of the child, and after the funeral it dawned on the adult that what repelled the child about the new school was not its "state" character—as he had overhastily concluded on the strength of his own past experience—but her class teacher, who was not right for her (for her alone?). It came to him that there is a kind of passionless, lifeless friendliness (without life-giving will to exert power or influence) which, coming from a teacher, can have the effect of hostility and unkindness. In this he may have recognized his own self-absorbed absence and realized what an inhuman effect it could have. (To make matters worse, some teachers live their whole lives without the vaguest notion of what a child is. They talk to a child—voicelessly; look at it, unseeing; and all their calm and patience with children in general is nothing but indifference.)

After the first term, the child gave up her resistance to the new school and from then on hardly spoke of daily happenings. She even seemed to accept her lot. But sometimes, when she looked up at him, the adult detected an air of resignation such as he had hitherto seen only in the eyes of one, much older person—a look suggesting the saddest, most extreme constraint.

In a peaceful hour, when he was once again able to question her, the child told him she didn't like herself anymore. The others weren't so bad, she said; but "there's just something **wrong** with me."

The next day the man went to see the class teacher, as he had done a few times before; he tried his best to keep calm but was unable to avoid such words as "loneliness," "despair," "exclusion," which in the foreign language may have sounded even more stereotyped than in his own. All at once, he noticed that the lady facing him did not—in the fullest sense—understand. A strange expression, which the petitioner would never forget, crept into the teacher's face—there was amusement in it, and, intermittently, outright contempt—the look of a person living in an airtight world, where such a thing as "forsakenness" was inconceivable.

In that moment, his mind was made up; midterm or not, the child would leave the school that very day. (An unconcealed grin on the face of the teacher, who, however, hands out leaflets for a faraway cause.) But on the other hand she would not spend a single day at home with the adult. From this interview he goes straight to another school, which is also near the railroad tracks, but on the other side. The one thing he knows about it is that it bears the name of a saint, who has his statue in the paved yard.

This school partakes of a religious tradition which in his childhood immersed him in deadly chill, belief in ghosts, and hatred of the intellect, but on his way there this does not trouble him; what he sees in it now is glorious color, fervor, neighborliness, childlike innocence, joy of life, and mystical unity, a view justified by the millennial history of the church (or at least by its basic writings). Living alone with him, the child had absorbed little of any tradition (except for a few Bible passages, in which only the events counted and no reference was made to the underlying meaning). A few times they had gone to Mass together—on one occasion the child had even remarked that the people had been "so good" to her—but as a rule they had been bored stiff at the very first sound and deeply offended by the mechanical, unfeeling demeanor of the false present-day priests and the equally evil, heartless, mindless voices of the false present-day faithful.

Nevertheless, on his way along the railroad tracks, the man is convinced that the school at the sign of the saint will now be the right place for the child; and he knows in advance that they will have to accept the child, that if there's no room for her, they will make room.

It's a bright cold morning in March. Behind a lone, broad-branching cedar, a smoky, tumultuous sky. Down in the chasm, the whistling, whirring, roaring of express trains; and cityward, the river, with its seemingly frozen meanders glinting through the jumble of buildings, lies like a sleeping giant. The adult quickens his step, as did the man approaching a decision according to the historian; rings at the wrong door, is taken to the right one, and there, sure enough—with his more stuttered than spoken appeal—he is successful. The very next morning, the misery school on the other side of the tracks is abandoned forever, and the child, convinced by the adult's enthusiasm that she will be happy, slips willingly, even gratefully, into the new surroundings. It was only a change of schools, but for once it seemed a matter of life and death.

The child finished out the year at the denominational school and stayed on for the following year (when it would have been time in any case to transfer to a so-called secondary school). It was not the school of schools—that lay behind her, it had gone out of existence (and the dirt walk had been surfaced). But the simplicity did the child good. The children came of different kinds of families but were all from the immediate neighborhood, and in this the suburb, which at first had seemed to merge undifferentiated with the surrounding communities, showed its individual, still rural character. And there was something "common" about this school which, as it turned out, did the child a world of good. She surprised the adult by showing that it suited her to be common now and then. At first the adult wanted to make her stop saying certain supposedly silly things, which, to make matters worse, she seemed to spout under remote control, but then he saw that the most idiotic jokes and turns of phrase helped the child in the group games of which she had so long been deprived. And another thing he liked was that there was never the slightest indication of piety; was a pious child even conceivable?

All in all, the child's life in that period, in contrast to the preceding years, was shaped not so much by her hours in school as by the time spent at home, during most of which the adult was her only company. Often, each was alone on a different floor. Someone who visited now and then remarked later that they had struck him at first as "rather sad figures," and that it took him some time to notice that they were not unhappy at all but actually quite cheerful and pleased with themselves. And the adult, too, reflected at a later day that he had never felt so close to perfect bliss as at that time.

But the great conflict of all those years in the foreign country became more and more pervasive, and the harmonious aspects of their life together did not enable him to think it away. Slowly, almost imperceptibly, the adult began to feel at home in the foreign language; the child, however, who had quickly learned to handle it better than many native children, disliked speaking this second language. It became clear that so-called bilinguality was not an unmixed blessing, that in the long run it could lead to a painful split. At home with the adult, the child never used the foreign language (or at the most in jest); all day long in school, however, she heard not a single word of her home language. When the adult saw her with native children out of school, he hardly knew his child. In speaking the foreign language, she put on a different voice, different gestures and facial expressions. The foreign manner of speaking brought with it a whole set of foreign, marionette-like movements, in which he discovered not just fear but panic (a phenomenon that may have been so prevalent as to seem hardly worth mentioning). In any event, a release of tension was always evident when the child came home to her first language. Once again she found her tongue, her body relaxed, she looked quietly around her. She herself told the adult how she had to "get ready inside" for the second language, and in particular adjust her voice.

During the school year the conflict was often forgotten; but it turned to disaster at the end of vacation, which the child always spent in her own country. The misery of the return to the wilderness of foreign signs and sounds was unparalleled; and of all foreign parts, there was none more glacial than this foreign-language suburb.

Her first days back made it plain to the adult that she would have to be taken to a place where her native language was spoken, and as soon as possible (though this step was regularly postponed, because by the following morning the misery was usually dispelled by the house, the nooks and crannies in the garden, the usual sights and itineraries). And wasn't it reason enough to return home that in five years in the foreign country she had not made friends with a single native child, but only with other foreign children, mostly from other continents and of different races?

No more shilly-shallying, the child would return to the place of her first language. The decision had become possible because the adult now saw the need for a change in his own life as well. Because of the child (who really did not leave him time for a project of any length), he had gradually forgotten his old ambition and sunk into a more and more pleasurable idleness. If he had a clear conscience, it was not only thanks to the child but also to the foreign surroundings, in which no one asked him about his occupation. Here, in a manner of speaking, he was a "licensed foreigner," which fell in with his existential ideal. There was no compelling need to work, since sufficient money remained from earlier exertions. On long walks through the many overlapping suburbs, a marvelous landscape spread out before him; years later he could have sketched a perfect map of those suburbs. Wasn't this the life? How would it be to undertake no new work but just remain sequestered with the child (looking after her to the best of his ability) in the clearing named "abroad"; sequestered in a foreign suburban house near the foreign school; hidden in the ups and downs of the admirably deserted suburban streets, from the high points of which the metropolis below could be seen to glitter in forever-new moments of eternity?

Yet this very pleasure in doing nothing led to such imperious visions of a larger, more peaceful, more generous plan of existence, the only good one, that he came to long, more and more urgently, to do something persevering, something continuous, that could be handed down. "If not for my love of form, I would have become a mystic." The idler, often unnerved by solitude, had taken these words, spoken by a kindred spirit of the last century, as a guiding maxim. Yes, he, too, was becoming an ecstatic or visionary, contenting himself with pure contemplation; he must become master of his insights, and for that he would have to get back to work.

He therefore decided to part with the child for a year. She would stay with her mother, who had never become an "outsider," and would go to school in her own country—her birthplace, as it happened. The separation was no great blow to the child; what she needed now was her own language and friends (for the first time she had friends living in the same house). And the adult, who had once despised those who gave up their normal everyday life for the sake of "work," went away convinced that he had every right to do what he was doing; after six years almost uninterruptedly alone with the child, he was entitled to commit himself to the fullest, and that seemed possible only if there was nothing to distract him. (Besides, he felt sure the absence of her "constant companion" would be good for the child.)

The day of parting comes at the end of summer, in a third country where they have spent their last weeks together. The child leaves first, heading in the new direction with her mother. The man stands on the airport balcony and sees the plane taking off. High in the sky, already very small, it loops northward. In the end, it is only a flashing light in an opening between clouds. At my feet flagstones, still wet after a shower.

8

Ordinarily the adult had looked upon children in general as an alien race; sometimes as a relentlessly cruel enemy tribe "that takes no prisoners"—barbarous to the point of cannibalism; if not exactly hostile to humans, at least disloyal and useless; and in the long run stultifying and dispiriting to one who had no other company but such utterly asocial hordes and mobs. From this recurrent estimation he did not exclude his own offspring. But in that year of absence and work, which he spent almost entirely traveling on different continents, children, with little effort on their part, became his great helpers. They are the "strangers" who "greet" him; they prevent his gaze from going too far and losing itself. In a moment of crisis—one such crisis engendered the next—a child rang his doorbell, having stopped at the wrong floor, and the sight of this child was a disturbance just when needed; it inspired him—like caravan music—to carry on. In the late fall, while sitting on a bench in a hilly park, he watched a group of schoolchildren playing ball in a gully. One child remained apart from the game; he worked his way out of the group in larger and larger spirals, all the while looking around for someone. When the ball rolls toward him, he calmly moves out of the way; he stands for a while, swaying from side to side, then sits down on a bench, slides forward and backward, soundlessly opens his mouth, closes it, opens it again. He seems not only forlorn but also gentle and self-assured. His coat, which is too long for him, is buttoned up to his chin; a smoke-like vapor rises from the mud in the gully; a dancing of light on the children's hair. Late that winter, a bus ride through a mountain valley; the only other passengers are strangely quiet children on their way home from school; they alight singly or in small groups and vanish down the highway or on side roads; early twilight, snow flurries, frozen waterfalls; once, through the open door of the bus, an exchange of song between two birds in the cold outside, heartbreakingly sad, yet so beautiful that the listener wishes he could remember it forever and write music. The following spring, on a train trip through a dismal wet valley, he sees a child hop-skip-jumping along beside the tracks and says to the child in his thoughts: God bless you, hop-skip-jumping stranger! And then another bus ride—once again accompanied almost exclusively by children, in the dusk and then darkness—and the involuntary words: "Can the children be saved?"

For in the course of time the traveler seems to have discovered that children without exception are deprived of something and also expect something. The babies he saw on planes, in waiting rooms, or elsewhere were not just cranky or restless; they screamed from the depth of their souls. In the most peaceful countrysides, children bellowed for a member of their family. But apparently they also needed the random stranger who crossed their path: on crowded boulevards, in supermarkets and subway stations, time and time again the adult found his only certainty in those wide-open, almost unblinking eyes at a level with a grownup's waist, which took in every individual in the largest crowd, on the lookout for a responsive glance. The passerby could count on their helpful notice.

Then he realized that the modern times he had so often cursed and rejected did not exist, and that the "end of time" was also a figment of the brain. The same possibilities were reborn with every new consciousness, and the eyes of children in a crowd—just look at them!—transmitted the eternal spirit. Woe unto you who fail to see those eyes.

One day he is in a museum looking at a painting of the Massacre of the Innocents: an infant in the snow raises its arms to its mother in headscarf and apron; one of her legs is twisted back; already the soldier, crooked index finger, is reaching out for the child, and as though all this were happening now, the beholder thinks, literally: This must not be! And resolves for his part to embark on a different tradition.

One Sunday afternoon in early summer, on his deliberately circuitous return journey, he is on a steamer, crossing a large lake—already in his own language zone. The much invoked community (which he, too, had dreamed of) had long—of that he was now certain—ceased to exist; those who had fostered the beauty of the country were long dead; and most of the living population glowered and sulked because there was no war. From all the walnuts on the trees—such was his curse—let sharp knives fall on these unfruitful people down in the shade and wipe them out! But on that particular day a man in a black suit and an open white shirt sat across from him on deck; beside him a child, dressed in pretty much the same way. It's unusual for the two to be together like this. The man is employed on some large construction project and seldom sees his child; they're from a region where there are neither lakes nor ships. But they are not tourists from a far country; they are natives on an excursion. This may be the first time they have gone anywhere together, and in any case it is only for this Sunday afternoon. They don't seem especially joyful; they sit still and very straight, attentive and wide awake. The air is clear, the shore seems hardly a stone's throw away, chains of hills cloaked in conifer brown. Man and child sit with their hands on their knees. From time to time the child asks a question; not a childlike voice; the man answers in monosyllables, but with thoroughness; not a trace of the sugary tone (masking indifference) with which adults so often speak to children; some going so far as to affect a sort of baby talk. The trip takes all afternoon, zigzagging back and forth across the lake from landing to landing. The unknown man's face is more and more shaded; the child is as grave as ever. They are still sitting at the same distance from each other, forming a dark group of their own—the only one on the boat. They emanate sorrow, but also dignity and nobility; for the first time the observer sees their blackness as a color and recognizes it to be the color of a people; he has never seen two human beings closer to heaven—heaven, that is, no longer seems so very far away from them. Behind the chain of hills, a wall of thunderclouds; and the treetops on the crest show a bright border, not a mere glow, but something substantial, out of which ocean waves raised by the wind squalls roll one after another to the horizon, heralding the *target age,* the age of humanity, eternity. In the dusk, the two will leave the ship and walk through the town to the bus station. Folding doors will open and clouds of dust will blow across the deserted field. With the first raindrops, balls of dust will form. All night long the bus will stand empty, out in the country somewhere, in a village named Galicia, ready for the return trip to the city in the gray of dawn. (The third place name in the story of the child.)

Foggy day of arrival in the late fall; only the returnee is real. Without him, the child has become more robust. Now she is able to defend herself and can't see why in the past she "never put up a fight." But she remains as vulnerable as ever, with a tendency to stand aside, as if she didn't belong.

The many changes of place haven't impaired her orientation; she even knows the direction of the North Pole and the South Pole from the house where she lives. She has taken on very little of the local accent; but a few grownup expressions have turned up in her speech (along with some far more acceptable comic-book locutions), and the adult is inclined to ask her: "Are you still a child or have you become a German?" Her playmate, however, is not a local child but hails from a good old foreign country, and the kinship between them is such that one can phone the other "on account of a cloud." (To most of the other children, trees and the stuff that goes on in the sky are "nothing at all.")

She listens to the same songs, popular and folk, which gave the man his first notions of charm and freedom. Worrisome perhaps how often, when alone, she spends her time moving absently from TV to cassette player and back. But the adult commands himself to be trusting; here again he recognizes the order behind the confusion and is able, sometimes at least, to refrain from interfering.

At times he surprises in himself a novel impulse "to educate"—though the only thing he could teach her springs from the innermost language of the "I am the strongest of all" (and he refuses "to tolerate a badge with any slogan whatsoever on your school bag!"). But to be heard by the child, one would have to be much more succinct. And so the child remains the teacher, for she teaches him to have more time for the colors of the world outside, to see forms more accurately; and therefore (not only as a matter of atmospherics but in a deeper sense) to read the changes of the seasons in an uncurled fern, in the leatheriness of a leaf, or the new rings on a snail shell.

From her, too, he learns the truth about the essence of beauty: "Beauty is so hard to see." At times (like many other children, no doubt) she really had magical powers—the man has learned that from the year of absence. Her modesty conceals demonic capabilities and skills, and one day, as she is exercising them, the adult for the first time smells something resembling sweat on the child's body—the sweet, fruitful sweat of creativeness. One afternoon he sees her going about the city alone, seen by no one but taking it all in like the caliph in the legend. And then he sees other comparable vagrants, savoring the joys of invisibility, the secret sovereigns of all markets, streets, and back alleys.

At the same time, of course, actions (and, far more often, omissions) bring home to him the need for regularity in her upbringing. No malice or wickedness, something more like negligence or indifference to others, which is infuriating as only lawlessness can be. The adult once heard a man address the following diatribe to his own son: "Disgrace to your parents! Lickspittle! Unfeeling simpleton! Slave to your passions! Monster of ingratitude! Golden Calf to yourself! Great salt pillar of ruthlessness! Source of all my bitterness! Monument of selfishness! Heartless tyrant! Prodigy of sloth! Temple of laziness! Seat of every vice! Epitome of aimlessness! Wolf in sheep's clothing! Preventer of greatness and goodness! My closest kin and worst enemy! Cause and content of my nightmares! Incurable wound in my bosom! Model of smugness, incapacity for sympathy, captiousness and philistinism! It's all over between us! I never want to hear of you again! Never again shall your name be uttered in this house! Begone!" And the boy addressed with such biblical clarity understood; he went pale and hadn't a word to say for himself. The witness thought he would take this litany as an example. But whenever he attempted anything of the kind, he failed to summon up the passion that had given his prototype the voice of a thunder god. The next time he emits soundless shouts, he notices in mid-harangue that his victim has been waiting the whole time for a glance, that she is not standing in front of him or opposite, but *below* him.

The following spring, the child turned ten. She enjoyed her birthday and accepted congratulations with self-possession. After that, she spent whole days without grownups and managed by herself or with other children.

In a forest (after another move, but still in a country where her native language was spoken—some people seem to require such a home), which she now passes through on her way to school, almost all the birdhouses have swastikas daubed on them. No one seems to notice them; but when the adult mentions the swastikas to the child, she knows all the bad places. During the following winter, when the leaves that half concealed the birdhouses have fallen, the sight becomes intolerable. The adult suggests that they go together and paint out the malignant symbols; at first he himself finds the idea rather extravagant; but to his surprise the child is all in favor, and they spend a whole morning among the trees with paint and brush.

A trifling action; shouts of approval; darkly flashing avenger eyes.

The spring after that, on a windy Sunday—unusually mild for that latitude—the child is standing in a sandy front yard. The grounds, on a slight incline, are bordered by a row of bushes. Deep black gaps open in the bushes, in rhythm with the hair flying in the foreground, very much like the time almost ten years earlier when the child wandered off alone to the bank of the foreign river (except that her hair has grown longer and is interspersed with darker strands). Now she is moving through those gaps, while everything blows wildly about her, moving as though to the end of the world. Never should such moments pass or be forgotten; they demand more time and space in which to pulsate; a melody; SONG.

On a rainy morning the following autumn, the adult is taking the child part of the way to school. Over the years her school bag has become so heavy that its bearer has been nicknamed the "school slave." Other schoolchildren come along, and the child continues on with them. The wet, dark road leads to a cluster of new houses. In front of them the steady swinging of the plane-tree crowns. The bright parts of the picture are the balcony railings and the flashing window squares at the end of the street, and in the foreground the metal clasps and nameplates of the bags on the backs of the walking children. Now the two combine to form a single, one and only, flaming, eye-catching inscription that remains to be deciphered. Now, and often later, the eyewitness ponders the words of the poet, which should apply to every story about a child, and not only written ones: "Cantilena: perpetuating the plenitude of love and of all passionate happiness."

Ὄρσο, τέκνον,
δεῦρο πάγκοινον ἐς χώραν
ἴμεν φάμας ὄπισθεν

About the Author

Peter Handke was born in Griffen, Austria, in 1942. After graduating from a Catholic seminary in 1959 he studied law at the University of Graz. Handke first attracted public notice in 1966 when he delivered an unprecedented attack on contemporary German writing at a seminar at Princeton University. That same year saw the publication of his first novel, *The Hornets*, and his first stage success, *Offending the Audience*. His other works include *Across* (1986), *The Weight of the World* (1984), *The Left-Handed Woman* (1978), *A Moment of True Feeling* (1977), *Short Letter, Long Farewell* (1974), *A Sorrow Beyond Dreams* (1974), and *The Goalie's Anxiety at the Penalty Kick* (1972)—all of which are forthcoming from Collier Fiction. He is widely regarded as the most important postmodern writer since Beckett.